I0689675

ChangelingPress.com

Prophet/Cowboy Up Duet
A Dixie Reapers Bad Boys Romance
Harley Wylde

Prophet/Cowboy Up Duet
A Dixie Reapers Bad Boys Romance
Harley Wylde

ISBN: 978-1-60521-797-0

Publisher:
Changeling Press LLC
315 N. Centre St.
Martinsburg, WV 25404
ChangelingPress.com

Printed in the U.S.A.

Editor: Crystal Esau
Cover Artist: Bryan Keller

The individual stories in this anthology have been previously released in E-Book format.

Table of Contents

Prophet (Dixie Reapers MC 20)..4
    Prologue..5
    Chapter One...11
    Chapter Two 21
    Chapter Three...31
    Chapter Four 41
    Chapter Five...53
    Chapter Six...64
    Chapter Seven..73
    Chapter Eight..83
    Chapter Nine..89
    Chapter Ten..98
    Chapter Eleven...107
    Chapter Twelve...115
    Chapter Thirteen..125
    Chapter Fourteen 134
    Epilogue...145
Cowboy Up (A Bad Boy Romance 6) 151
    Chapter One...152
    Chapter Two 166
    Chapter Three...174
    Chapter Four 184
    Chapter Five...197
    Chapter Six...207
    Chapter Seven..218
    Chapter Eight..229
    Chapter Nine..244
    Chapter Ten..255
    Chapter Eleven...264
    Chapter Twelve...274
    Chapter Thirteen..284
    Epilogue...295
Harley Wylde..305
Bad Boys Multiverse 306
Changeling Press LLC..307

Prophet (Dixie Reapers MC 20)
A Dixie Reapers Bad Boys Romance
Harley Wylde

They took what was mine. Now I'm going to slaughter them all and get my woman back.

Ares -- My life hasn't always been kittens and rainbows. I spent years as a captive, so when someone breaks into the compound and threatens my little siblings, I go with the kidnappers instead. I've survived being enslaved before, but the little ones wouldn't make it. I can only hope the club will find me in time.

Prophet -- I've been patiently waiting for Ares to not only be old enough for me to date her, but also for her to be ready. But I waited too f**king long, and now she's been taken. The bastard who has her is going to pay, and once she's back in my arms, I'm never letting her go again.

Prologue

Ares

Fear settled over the Dixie Reapers compound, seeping through the walls and into each and every home. The women and children were either on lockdown or high alert if they left the safety of gates. Joker's wife might be a sweetheart, but her family were monsters of the worst sort. With the threat of human traffickers hanging over our heads, the tension around the club had been off-the-charts.

I knew Dad worried about me the most. The club President might not be my birth father, but some bonds were even stronger than sharing the same DNA. He'd saved me from traffickers before, then he'd adopted me. Now I had an amazing stepmother and three adorable little siblings -- Junie, Judd, and Marnie. But with the Lathems lurking in the shadows, I knew Dad felt torn between his duty to the club and watching over his eldest child.

The sun shone in my eyes as I stepped out of the house. Foster and Owen were in the driveway, both leaning against their bikes. What the hell did they want? Both were sons of patched members and had grown up here. Unfortunately, Foster didn't seem to take after either of his parents and had a tendency to cause trouble -- especially if women were involved. How the hell he'd been approved as a Prospect was beyond me.

"Hey, Ares." His voice held a cocky undertone that always set my teeth on edge. He pushed off from his bike and sauntered closer. If ever there was a human who had the swagger of a rooster, it would be Foster. It made me want to knock him on his ass. "Do you have a minute?"

"Spit it out." I stopped, crossing my arms.

"Thing is --" Foster began, but Owen cut him off, his words tumbling out in a rush.

"Some of our friends wanted to party. Guys we knew in high school. Foster ran his mouth like always."

Foster shrugged. "They wanted us to bring some girls, and I know two of them have a crush on you. I told them you'd be there. I thought…"

I held up a hand, stopping him. "Thought? Thinking isn't your strong suit. In fact, I'm not sure you ever think."

I saw anger flare in his eyes for a moment, then he sighed and pinched the back of his neck with one of his massive hands. "Sorry, Ares."

"Fix it," I demanded. "Now. Make sure those shitheads know I won't be there. Make it clear I'm not interested in them and never will be. I know you struggle with the word no, but it's past time you learned what it means, Foster. This shit is getting ridiculous. Not to mention, why the hell would I go to a party with you right now? With everything going on, the last place I need to be is outside the compound at a party."

"Sure, sure, we'll handle it," Owen said quickly. I didn't know why he hadn't dropped Foster by now. I knew they'd grown up together and were close. Wasn't he tired of constantly being dragged into messes by his friend?

"Damn right you will," I shot back, locking eyes with each of them. "Because if my dad finds out, it'll be the least of your worries compared to what I'll do to you myself. But just saying, how do you think Savior will react when he finds out you offered up his daughter as entertainment?"

Owen paled. "It's not like that. They just wanted to hang with you. You know we'd never do something like that, Ares."

"No, I know *you* wouldn't, but your buddy is another matter. He seems to have a bit of trouble distinguishing between right and wrong sometimes. First, he had the pregnancy scare with his high school girlfriend. Then he latched onto Leigha like a damn tick to the point she ran off to the Reckless Kings to escape him. At what point are you going to stop going along with him and force him to grow the fuck up?"

Owen winced. He knew I was right. I saw the fury etched on Foster's face, but I didn't care. Enough was enough. We had so much going on around here. His bullshit was the last thing I needed to worry about.

They got on their bikes and took off, both heading for the front gates. I ran my hand over my face and wondered if I'd done the right thing. Should I have told Foster's dad? He was a bit old for me to tattle on him, but I couldn't think of another way to get that jackass under control. It wasn't that he was a bad guy. He seriously just didn't realize some of the things he did were wrong.

I eyed the fence line and wondered if the Lathems were watching even now. They'd wanted Cleo. Not only was she married, but she'd also hidden a heart condition from everyone. Her family no longer saw her as an option, which made the club think someone else was on their radar. Possibly someone here at the compound.

I'd already lived a life in slavery. My mind drifted to those years...

The cold concrete pressed against me as I huddled in a corner, making myself as small as possible. Squeezing my eyes shut, I tried to pretend I was somewhere safe. I willed myself to disappear from the hell I'd tumbled into.

Heavy footsteps approached, and I fought not to cry or whimper. A meaty hand gripped my arm and my eyes opened. I stared at the man, hoping I wouldn't throw up on him. I already knew what would happen if I did that.

"Look at this one," he said, a leer on his lips. "I bet she screams real nice."

My heart hammered in my chest, and I knew what would happen next. He yanked me from the containment cell and dragged me to one of the rooms down the hall. A dingy mattress atop a metal frame was the only thing in the space. As the door shut and the lock clicked into place, I felt my skin crawl and wondered if this would be the time they managed to break me.

I blinked and came back to the present, the fear still thrumming in my veins. When Savior hauled me out of that nightmare, I'd vowed to live my life to the fullest and never look back. Except there were times I couldn't help the thoughts creeping into my mind. Like now.

I was younger then. Small and scared. Hell, the thought of someone like that getting their hands on me again still terrified me. In the years I'd been with the Dixie Reapers, I'd become strong. Sometimes even defiant, much to my dad's horror. I didn't want to become a victim ever again, so the thought of human traffickers watching the club made me want to run far away.

I stopped beside my car, wondering if I really wanted to leave the compound. I'd told Dessa I'd go to the store and get the things she needed, but…

The roar of a Harley Davidson drew my attention to the road, and I saw Prophet pulling to a stop in front of the house. He watched me, and I knew what he saw… the lingering fear from my flashback.

Without a word, he turned off the engine and got off his bike. He came closer and laced our fingers together. Gently, he took my keys from me and popped the locks on my car, then led me to the passenger side and helped me in. I held his gaze as he buckled me, then shut the door.

"You don't have to do this," I said.

"Yeah, I do. Don't argue with me, Ares. Who knows when those people will make their move? I don't want you going anywhere alone. Hell, your dad already told all the women and kids to go places in groups of three or more and take either a Prospect or brother with them. And here you are, ready to race off on an errand all by yourself. What kind of example does that set for everyone else?"

I closed my eyes and leaned my head back. "I know. I'm sorry. My mind is a total mess right now."

He reached out, brushing a stray lock of hair from my face with a gentleness that belied his brute strength. The contact was brief, almost reverent, and wholly unexpected. My breath hitched, but I didn't pull away. Trust wasn't given easily, not in my world, but Prophet had earned every ounce of mine. He'd already saved my life once before.

"Where are we going?" he asked.

"Dessa needed some things from the grocery for Junie and Judd. I offered to get them." My stepmother got around just fine, but she couldn't walk. It was easier for me to run to the store than for her to lift herself into a vehicle, take her wheelchair apart, then do the reverse when she got to where she was going. So I always offered if I knew she really didn't want to go.

Until now, I hadn't realized how scared I was to leave the compound. The memories of my past were coming more frequently these days. Haunting me in my sleep, even while I was awake. I'd kept it to myself so far. Everyone had enough to worry about without me adding to the problem.

There were times I felt useless. I didn't know how to help my family… the club. It wasn't that they expected me to protect them, or myself really, but I wanted to be of some use to them. The Dixie Reapers had given me so much. For now, I'd help Dessa with the kids. It was all I could really do. But I'd wait for an opportunity, and when it came, I'd take it. I felt like I owed all of them, especially Savior.

Chapter One

Ares

Times had changed. The Dixie Reapers' clubhouse no longer boasted loud parties and naked women. Well, the naked women were gone, at any rate. Music pulsed from the speakers as everyone took a much-needed break. My dad had been in Church off and on since this mess started, and more often than not, the members hung out in the clubhouse discussing the issue at hand. Except right now, the doors were open to anyone.

I sat at the bar with a soda. Portia sat on one side of me and Venom's youngest, Dawson, was on my other side. Patched members lined the bar on either side of them.

"Pass me a beer, Ares," Bull shouted from farther down. I reached over the counter into the ice chest, then slid the longneck down the bar top. I caught a smirk from my father as he watched.

"Hey, Pres. Think your girl has a future as a bartender," Bull said. He chuckled and twisted the top off. "She's got good aim."

"Better than Foster's aim last week," I shot back, a playful jab at his son's appalling shooting during target practice. He snorted and took a swallow of his beer, while Foster shot me a glare.

This place was my home. Dad and the Dixie Reapers had been my salvation, pulling me from the abyss with hands as rough as the life they led. Even though I couldn't be a patched member, I was a Reaper's kid. My dad had given me permission to get the club colors inked on my shoulder blade. It was a super small one compared to the ones the guys here had. I'd seen quite a few with the colors covering their entire backs. In addition, I'd gotten a phoenix rising from the ashes inked on the outside of my right thigh -- a mirror of my own rebirth.

Foster might be mad at me right now, but I knew he'd get over it. In a lot of ways, he was like a brother to me. All of the kids here close to my age felt like family. Although, Foster, Owen, and Dawson were all older than me. Not that I could tell when it came to Foster.

Cowboy's son, Jackson, entered the clubhouse, his cowboy boots thudding against the wood floor as he came closer. He put his arms around me and hugged me from behind.

"You smell like horses and dirt."

"Mom always said it was the best scent in the world."

I couldn't help but laugh a little. Yeah, I could see his mother saying that. "Well, it's better than sweat, I guess. Preparing for your next rodeo?"

"I was planning to head out in the morning, but with everything going on…"

I tipped my head back to look up at him. "You should go. If you put your life on hold every time something bad happens around here, you'll never get to do the one thing you love most."

He kissed the top of my head. "Yeah, I know. You're awfully smart for someone so young."

"You're only six years older than me, Jackson. It's not like you're ancient."

"In rodeo years, I'm over a decade older than you."

I really did laugh that time. "Is that like dog years or something?"

"Close enough. Hand me a beer. I'm going to go with Akira. She's in the corner with her nose in a book again."

I reached over for another longneck and passed it to him. He patted my shoulder before wandering off. I watched him, noticing he hadn't lied. Akira, Wraith's daughter, really did have a book in front of her face. From the cover, no one would realize she was reading smut. If her parents had any idea of the types of books she bought, they'd both have a fit.

I sipped on my soda and just soaked up the atmosphere. My friends and family were all talking or laughing. Despite everything going on outside the club gates, they seemed at peace in this particular moment. Happy. I hoped things could stay like this. I didn't want anyone here to suffer the way I had.

"Never thought I'd see the day," Tank said, approaching with a smile on his face. "Ares Black, quiet as a church mouse."

I smirked, nudging him with my elbow. "Just soaking it all in. Some days, I don't remember how blessed I am, until we're all together like this. Family. Friendship. As long as we have those, we can weather any storm."

"Damn straight." He clapped a heavy hand on my shoulder. "We're always in your corner, Ares."

"Same here," I replied. It wasn't just words -- it was a promise. We were the Dixie Reapers, and we protected our own with the ferocity of a mother bear defending her cubs. I might not be a member of the club itself, but as the President's daughter, these people were still my family, and I'd die to keep them safe.

I glanced at my watch and stood. Joker wanted Cleo to feel welcome here, and while I wasn't quite ready to be friends with the woman, I also knew what it was like to be the outsider. I'd promised to head over and play a board game. Instead of driving, I decided to walk. The fresh air would be nice, and it would give me time to get my thoughts in order. It felt like utter chaos inside my head these days.

Ridley and Isabella were already there when I arrived. I fell into step behind them as they entered Joker's home. Ridley had a few board games tucked under her arm. At least they'd come prepared, because I doubted Joker had any. I'd already given them a few of the ones we had at home that I thought might be fun.

"Hey, Cleo," I said.

"Good to see you guys." Her voice sounded hollow, and it looked like she hadn't been sleeping well.

Isabella walked over to her first, giving her a hug. "How are you holding up?"

"Counting down the minutes," she said.

Ridley clapped her hands together, the sound sharp in the quiet room. "We're here to take your mind off things. Right, Ares?"

I nodded. "Yeah, we brought some board games. Thought we could all use a distraction."

"Thanks," she murmured.

We settled around her kitchen table. Before we'd even had a chance to set up the game, someone knocked on the door. Joker went to answer. Ridley started to set up one of the games, and Isabella and I helped. I noticed Cleo kept glancing toward the door.

He returned with an envelope and handed it to Cleo. "For you."

"Who's it from?" she asked. She ripped open the envelope and as she read the contents the paper inside, she paled a bit.

"Everything all right?" Isabella asked.

"Fine," she said. Did anyone else notice the tremor in her voice or the way her hands trembled? "Just a reminder about my appointment."

"Ah, can't forget that," Ridley said.

"Let's focus on the game," Cleo suggested.

I rolled the dice and gave a little shout of excitement, hoping to make things seem as normal as possible. "All right!"

Everyone took their turns rolling the dice and moving their tokens. When it went around to Cleo, she stared at the board, almost as if she wasn't fully present. I glanced at Ridley and Isabella, and realized they'd noticed it too. Cleo must have a lot on her mind between the issues with her family and her heart problem.

"Your move, Cleo," Ridley prompted.

"Right," she mumbled.

We played for quite a while, until the sky started to darken. I didn't know if this had distracted Cleo or not, but it had kept me from focusing on things for a while. I hadn't realized how much I'd needed this until now. I helped clean up the games, then we told Joker and Cleo goodbye.

Ridley offered me a ride, but I waved her off. The walk would do me some good. I paused at the clubhouse and stared at my car. It didn't make sense to leave it here overnight, but at the same time, I'd prefer to get home on my own two feet than by driving there. I decided to leave it and kept walking.

A sudden chill prickled my skin, a whisper of danger that tightened my muscles. A feeling of unease skittered down my spine, and I wondered if trouble was drawing closer than any of us realized.

When I got home, there was a wrongness I felt all the way to my core. I slowly approached the house, keeping an eye on my surroundings, just the way Dad had taught me. I twisted the knob on the front door and pushed it open.

"Mom? Are you here?" I called out. Nothing. Not so much as a whisper of sound. I eased farther into the house, wondering if I should call Dad. Dessa's car was outside, which meant she had to be here. She hadn't ridden with him to the clubhouse earlier, even though she'd been there with the kids.

"Junie, Judd, Marnie!" I shouted.

No one answered, and I couldn't find anyone at home. I went back outside, wondering if maybe they went to a neighbor's house. Before I'd made it to the end of the driveway, I felt the cold kiss of metal against my neck.

"Move and those little children will be the ones we take," said a cold voice near my ear. I knew this man had to have broken into the compound. If he wasn't one of Cleo's relatives, then he was working for them. I didn't know how I knew, but I did.

My breath hitched, the instinct to fight warring with the need to keep Junie, Marnie, and Judd safe. I didn't know where they were, or if this man had already hurt them. If I did what he said, maybe he'd leave them alone.

"Go with us quietly, or those little ones will be coming with us instead," he said.

"Take me," I choked out, my words barely above a whisper. "But let them live. Please don't hurt them."

I knew without a doubt my three siblings wouldn't survive the horrors I'd faced before. All of them were babies, not a single one older than seven years old.

"Smart girl." He shoved me forward. My world narrowed to the pounding of my heart and the conviction that I would do anything for my family. As we approached the fence, I saw where they'd cut their way into the compound. With everything going on, it was no wonder no one had noticed. Normally, security was incredibly tight here, especially with all the trouble over the years. But I doubted Wire was monitoring the cameras since he was busy trying to determine the Lathems' next move.

"This is going to sting," he said. I didn't get a chance to process what was happening before I felt a prick of a needle in my neck, and then my body became dead weight. I couldn't move, even though I was still awake. The world spun a bit, and I couldn't even open my mouth to scream.

The man hefted me over his shoulder and stepped through the cut fence line. It wasn't long before I'd been tossed into the back of a van.

I'm sorry, Dad, but this was the only way.

* * *

The metal of the cage was cold against my skin, a stark contrast to the adrenaline that burned through my veins. I'd been shoved into the small, confined space so violently that my breath hitched in my throat, the impact rattling my bones and leaving me momentarily winded. The acrid stench of fear and sweat hung heavy in the air as I forced myself onto shaky legs, my heart thumping wildly in my chest. At least I was able to move again.

The van ride hadn't been pleasant, and it had taken what felt like forever before I was able to move again. I didn't have any concept of time right now. Had a half hour passed since they'd put me in here? An hour? Longer?

"Quiet down," one of the men yelled, his eyes glinting with malice through the bars. They didn't see us as people. To them, we were just cargo, products for their sick trade. I glanced around, taking in the sight of other victims huddled in the corners of their own cages, their faces etched with despair. My gut twisted at the realization of what awaited us, old memories clawing their way to the surface. *Not again*.

"Please," a soft voice whimpered from a cage nearby. "I want to go home."

The plea sliced through me, a painful reminder of my own stolen innocence years ago. I suppressed the urge to reach out, to offer comfort. Instead, I remained still, my gaze fixed on the concrete floor. Survival meant keeping distance between myself and the others. I couldn't save them. I needed all the strength I could muster so I wouldn't break this time.

As silence fell over us, punctuated only by the occasional sob or shuffling feet, dread settled in my stomach like a lead weight. What would happen to Junie, Marnie, and Judd if I didn't make it back? What about Dad and Dessa? Would everyone blame themselves for what happened to me? I had no doubt the club would tear down heaven and hell to find me, but time wasn't on our side. The warehouse wasn't set up for long-term storage, which meant they were going to sell us fast, and then they'd be in the wind.

"Stay strong, Ares," I whispered to myself. My will to fight, to survive, was rooted deep within me. But even the fiercest warrior felt fear, and mine was a roaring inferno threatening to consume me.

The stale air made bile rise up my throat and I swallowed it down. I couldn't show even a hint of weakness. The darkness seemed to swallow everything around me. The glow of a computer screen illuminated the men holding us hostage. Were they selling us online? Or in person? Not that either option was good.

"Stream's going live in five," one of them said, a ghoulish excitement in his voice. "Bids are already piling up."

I shivered. Shit. They were auctioning us online, which meant they were on the dark web. I'd heard Wire and Lavender talk about it before. A hidden network filled with humanity's dregs. They'd trade lives like stocks. Girls like us were reduced to thumbnails on a screen, and depraved men and women would bid outrageous amounts to see who would be taking us home.

My heart hammered against my ribs, each beat a stark reminder of the stakes. I had to escape, to return to those who were waiting, praying for my safety. Even if they hadn't noticed I was missing yet, it wouldn't be long before they did. My phone had been tossed before they'd dumped me in the van, which meant Wire wouldn't be able to track me.

The men continued to set up their equipment, oblivious -- or indifferent -- to the terror they sowed. More screens flickered to life, revealing an online auction room, a digital Colosseum where twisted individuals raised their bids with the click of a mouse. I closed my eyes, trying to shut out the sight, but the sounds of their operation, the clicking of keyboards, and the muttered confirmations of received payments invaded my senses.

"Looks like this batch is gonna fetch a high price," another voice crooned, greed lacing every syllable.

I steeled myself, refusing to be broken by their words. I wouldn't be a passive victim. I would fight, endure, survive.

"The bitch from the motorcycle club will draw a lot of bidders. Already got a bunch checking out her listing," one of them said. "The interest on her is really damn high. We struck gold with that one!"

My stomach knotted, and I closed my eyes, hoping Wire would find me before it was too late.

Chapter Two

Prophet

Nights blended into a single, elongated nightmare. Sleep was a stranger, elusive and unwelcome, as I paced the length of the clubhouse floor. I kept glancing at Wire, where he worked diligently on his keyboard to try and find Ares. She'd been missing for more than twenty-four hours when Wire had found a record of her being sold. They'd auctioned her online before we had a chance to raid the warehouse. She'd slipped through our fingers so easily.

It felt like my heart had shattered at my feet. Why hadn't I made my move sooner? If I'd claimed her, she'd have been home with me. At first, I'd had to wait because she wasn't old enough. Even still, the Pres had given permission for me to spend time with her. Strictly platonic. We occasionally would hold hands, or hug, but nothing more than that. I'd take her to movies, or out shopping. Sometimes we'd just hang out around the compound.

The minute she turned eighteen, I should have made her mine. Instead, I'd wanted to wait and make sure it was what she wanted, and maybe come up with a romantic gesture. Look where that fucking got me! *Come back to me, Ares.*

What if it was too late when we finally tracked her down? What if the bastard who bought her broke her beyond repair, or killed her? I wasn't sure I'd survive if either of those things happened. I'd have to be strong for her, give her a shoulder to cry on, or whatever she needed.

Night after night, I stared into the darkness, wondering where she was and if she was doing okay.

As the days passed and we didn't seem to get any closer to finding her, it felt more and more hopeless. I'd never felt so weak in my entire life!

In my mind, I saw her abduction again and again. Where was I when it happened? Why hadn't I been with her? I had to wonder if they targeted her because she'd been alone. She'd gone to Joker's house for a game night, and then she'd vanished. Other than the footage Wire found of a man carrying her through a cut piece of fencing, we had nothing to go on.

Every tick of the clock weighed on my conscience. Was Ares watching the time pass? Had the bastard who bought her already ripped her apart? What horrors had she faced since she'd been taken?

"Hold on for me, Ares. As soon as I know where you are, I'm coming for you!" Didn't matter what time of night or day it was, or how far I had to go. I'd travel to the ends of the earth to bring her back.

Everyone had gathered in the clubhouse where Wire was doing his best to find Ares using his hacking skills. His fingers flew over the keys, and someone kept him stocked with drinks and snacks. The moment he took a break, all he'd do was stare at his laptop. I didn't know how the man remained upright, but I was grateful for everything he was doing for Ares.

"I found something," Wire shouted, his fingers moving even faster than before.

"What do we know?" Savior asked. "Where is my daughter?"

Bull leaned in over Wire's shoulder. With the big man in the way, no else could see a fucking thing.

"Georgia," Bull said. "Some bigwig with a taste for young girls bought her. Wire is trying to hack into his camera feeds right now. Place looks like it has every room wired."

Georgia was closer than I'd thought she'd be. Still not as nearby as I'd have liked.

"Damn it." Joker paced. I could tell he felt responsible for this mess.

"If there's a camera in whatever place they're holding her, I'll find it," Wire said, not even pausing in his typing.

The clubhouse thrummed with the pulse of urgency, every brother's attention riveted on the mission at hand. The weight of their collective focus was like a physical force.

"Come on, come on," Joker muttered. I knew this had to be hurting him. He no doubt felt responsible to some degree, since his wife's family had orchestrated Ares' abduction and sale.

Minutes dragged by, each one an eternity, stretching until they were thin and taut enough to snap. The sharp click of keys filled the room.

"Got something!" Wire shouted. All of us descended on him.

On the screen, pixels shifted, revealing the grainy image of a mansion, its walls a silent testament to the secrets they kept. Wire's hands flew over the controls, coaxing the feed to reveal its hidden truths. It looked like the bastard had several set up. Wire flicked through them one at a time.

"Come on, baby," Wire whispered, his voice a mixture of technician and sorcerer calling forth images from the digital ether.

"Anything?" Savior asked.

"Wait..." Wire's words trailed off as he shifted to another feed, giving us a glimpse of pure hell.

"Is that --" Bull began, but no one finished the sentence. We didn't need to.

Our silence was a shared language, spoken in the

glances we exchanged, the set of our shoulders, the tightening of our fists. The image on the screen held us captive. We'd finally found her. I only hoped she hadn't been completely broken.

Seeing her on the screen, and realizing what she'd been through, made it feel like my mind was going to break. I didn't know if she'd be able to come back from this. She'd survived it once, but twice?

"Get the location," Joker said. He eyed Savior, and I knew he had to be waiting for the Pres to lose his shit.

I glanced at Savior. That might be the woman I loved on the screen, but it was his daughter. His face had turned nearly purple as the rage built inside him. He stared at his daughter and the signs of the abuse she'd suffered.

With a loud roar, he picked up a chair and threw it across the room. The wood shattered on impact. He lifted another and smashed it as well. Flicker and Saint grabbed him.

"Easy, brother," Saint murmured, his hold tightening. They dragged him toward the door, away from the screen that continued to display a nightmare we'd all be reliving for a long time to come.

"Let me go!" Savior roared.

I knew exactly how he felt. I wanted to tear this place apart, beat every bastard who'd had a hand in Ares being sold, and then set the entire fucking world on fire and raze everything to the ground.

"Shh, we got you," Flicker coaxed, his tone soft, a counterpoint to the chaos. "We're going to get her back, Savior. Right now, we need you to cool down and think about this logically."

They took him outside before he could demolish the entire clubhouse. Not that any of us would blame him.

"Almost got it," Wire said, his fingers a blur. "Found the exact coordinates!"

"Prophet." Joker turned to me. I held his gaze, letting him see everything I was feeling in that moment. "We're bringing her home."

"Like hell *we* are." No. There would be no we in this. *I* would bring her home. Ares was mine, and I was going to be the one to rescue her from that hell, no matter the cost. I didn't care if I fucking died in the process. As long as she was no longer with that wretched man and could have a chance at living a normal life again, then I'd pay any cost.

I stared at the screen and watched Ares, her form small and broken as she huddled in the corner, knees hugged tightly to her chest. Her once vibrant eyes had lost their flame, replaced by a haunting emptiness that dug its claws into my soul. Blood smeared across her skin, and bruises had already formed on every visible part of her body. They hadn't even allowed her to keep her clothes in the dank cell where they'd dumped her after doing God knew what to her.

"Close it, Wire!" Joker barked.

"Trying!" Wire's fingers danced frantically across the keyboard, but it was too late. I'd already seen it all and realized what had been done to my precious girl. When I got my hands on the man who'd hurt her, I'd send him straight to hell.

"Prophet, man," Joker said, reaching out, but I shrugged off his hand.

Wire's fingers halted their frenetic dance across the keyboard, and he turned slowly, a slip of paper clutched in his grasp.

"The mansion's south of Atlanta. Only building within fifty miles. Heavily fortified."

"Let me see," Joker demanded, snatching the paper from him. "Prophet…"

Before he could say anything more, I took note of the address, then turned and walked away. I knew they'd send brothers after me, a guarantee that I wouldn't do something stupid as well as backup for getting Ares safely out of that place. I wasn't waiting on them. I got on my bike and, without even going home to pack, I left the compound and hit the road. I had a lot of miles to cover if I wanted to get Ares back tonight.

It didn't take long for Warden and Foster to catch up to me. I didn't know if they'd volunteered or were assigned the task of saving Ares. Since there were only two, I had a feeling we'd end up with help from other clubs. Since Ares was being held in Georgia, the Devil's Fury would likely be there. If the Reckless Kings sent someone, I wondered if Logan would join us. He'd decided to prospect for their club after his sister, Leigha, got claimed by Cyclops.

Other than stopping for gas, I didn't take any breaks on the way. I stopped for gas one last time before making the final haul to the location. I parked my bike after filling the tank, needing to get my mind off Ares and more on how I'd save her. Warden and Foster stopped beside me and got off their bikes.

"Got a text from Wire," Warden said. "He sent details about the place we need to break into, as well as who would be coming to help."

"So who are we expecting?" I asked, "And how fucking long before they get here?"

"Devil's Fury is sending Frost and Ripper. And the Devil's Boneyard sent Magnus and Gator. In fact, I'm betting they're already here somewhere," Warden said. "I've made sure Wire is tracking me through my phone, so he knows where we are every step of the way. I'm sure he's updating those coming to help us."

My phone chimed and I realized it was Magnus reaching out. *Look to your left.*

I glanced down the street and saw the two men waiting for us. We made our way over and I checked my phone when it vibrated. Wire had sent images of the place we'd be breaking into. Fence had to be more than seven feet. Looked like guards were patrolling inside. Heavily armed.

"There's cameras too," Magnus said, leaning over to look at my phone screen.

"Don't forget the fucking dogs," Gator muttered.

"I don't suppose any of the hackers offered assistance with the cameras?" I asked.

"Think they're working on it. For now, we need to figure out where the Devil's Fury are. There's no fucking way we beat them here," Magnus said.

"Anyone have the number for either Frost or Ripper?" I asked.

"Nope." Both men shook their heads. I glanced at Foster, and he held up a finger.

"Give me a sec. I'll reach out to Logan. I'm sure he knows how to reach them." I watched him send a text, and it wasn't long before we got a response. Foster showed me the numbers and I sent a text to both.

Where the fuck are you? I want Ares out of that place now!

Magnus snorted. "I'm sure that's going to go over well. Even if the hackers can take out the cameras or screw with the feed, we're going to need more firepower to get through all the damn guards. And no offense, but I'm not shooting any dogs. Doolittle would have my ass."

"No shit," Gator said. "Too bad he didn't volunteer for this little trip. I bet he could have charmed them or something. Man has a way with animals."

My phone dinged with a text. *We're getting supplies.*

What the fuck kind of supplies did they need? I leaned against the brick wall behind me and stared at the image on my phone again. I scrolled through the next three he sent me. I felt a little out of my depth, but there was no fucking way I'd back down. I'd get her out there no matter what.

"There's a café not too far from here. Why don't we walk over?" Magnus asked.

"So I'm supposed to what? Eat a fucking waffle or something while my woman is in there being tortured?" I asked, fury filling me.

"No." Magnus put his hand on my shoulder. "You're going to get some coffee while we wait on reinforcements. Then we're going to come up with a plan so we don't all get killed trying to get her out of there. I know you want to rip the place apart with your bare hands. I get it. But that's not going to help Ares."

"Fine. I'll give them a half hour. If those fuckers don't show up by then, I'll go in alone if I have to."

How the fuck could they ask me to wait? Did they not understand what she was suffering at the hands of that asshole? Knowing she was so close yet out of reach was driving me crazy. The sooner I had her in my arms, the better.

Hold on, Ares. I'll be there soon.

We found the café and got a table in a quiet corner. I had to admit the walk had been good for me. My muscles had started to stiffen up from riding for hours with so few breaks. No one batted an eye at a bunch of bikers coming inside the cafe, which made me wonder if there was a club in the area. Had anyone bothered to check? The last thing I needed was to piss off a bunch of bikers who might try to stop me from getting my woman back.

After we'd ordered, the Devil's Fury showed up, and they weren't alone. I saw five big bastards come in wearing cuts I wasn't familiar with -- Wild & Reckless MC. Were they local? Why hadn't I heard of them before?

Ripper sat and motioned to the Wild & Reckless men. "These are the locals. Stopped to get permission to be here and explained the situation. Although the place we're infiltrating isn't technically part of this town. It's got its own fucking zip code if you can believe that shit."

One of them held out his hand and I noticed his cut said he was the President. "Name's Highlander. We're a small club. Including Prospects, there's only seven of us right now, but we're all ex-military."

One of the men nudged him. "Almost all. Shaker, our Treasurer, is former FBI. As you can probably tell from Highlander's name and slight accent, he's originally from Scotland. The rest of us were born in the US. I'm Wings, the Road Captain."

"We left the Prospects back at the clubhouse," another man said. His cut said he was their Secretary. As I looked at each of them, I realized all of their officers had come today.

"Are you here to help or throw us out?" I asked.

"Oh, we're definitely here to help." Highlander gave me a smile that chilled me to the bone. "I won't tolerate the likes of that bastard lurking anywhere near my town. Fifty miles is too fucking close for comfort. Considering why you're here, I have to wonder if he might be responsible for some of the local girls going missing."

"Our club is relatively new," Wings said. "We've been riding together for a while but decided to make it official two years ago. Settled down in this place."

"Anyone have a plan in mind?" I asked.

"We may have something." Wings and Highlander shared a look. They settled in and disclosed what info they had on the man who held Ares captive. As the minutes passed, I felt both anxious over what she might be suffering, and relieved that it appeared I'd have her back soon.

But it seemed we needed to wait until dark to retrieve her... I only hoped she could hold on that long.

Chapter Three

Ares

Consciousness crept back to me like a thief, slow and unwelcome. I had no idea how much time had passed. Every time my owner entered the room, the pain became so bad I couldn't handle it. More than once, I'd passed out only to awaken alone and in the dark. Had it only been days since I'd been brought here? Weeks? I didn't even know where *here* was. I'd been drugged before my owner came to claim me and had no way of knowing if I even remained in Alabama.

The chill of the concrete floor seeped through my skin, a stark contrast to the heat of the pain throbbing in my head. No matter how hard I strained to see my surroundings, the darkness held on stubbornly, offering only shadows cast by a flickering light somewhere above me. I tried to lift my hands to my face, to wipe away the grogginess, but they wouldn't move. Panic clawed at my throat as I felt the bite of rope digging into my wrists.

"Damnit," I hissed under my breath, twisting my arms in an attempt to assess how much give I had. Not much. The familiar burn of abraded skin began to flare as I worked against my bindings, memories of a past I had fought so hard to overcome flashing in my mind. Until now, my owner hadn't tied me up like this. Was this a new way of torturing me?

"Think, Ares, think," I muttered to myself, forcing my breathing to slow, to keep the terror at bay. They'd gotten to me once when I was just a kid, but I wasn't that helpless child anymore. I'd already survived hell before, and the Dixie Reapers had made sure I knew how to protect myself. Maybe someone should have taught me how to escape ropes.

The rough hemp of the rope seemed to mock me, tightening its grip as I struggled. Each movement sent fresh waves of agony down my arms, but surrender wasn't in my blood. With each twist, with each pull, I poured all my fear and fury into the fight against my restraints. I appeared to be in my usual room. More of a cage really, even if it didn't have bars to contain me.

"Come on," I encouraged myself, the words barely a whisper, drowned out by the pounding in my skull. "You've survived worse."

I shifted, trying to find some leverage, any weakness in the knots that bound me. But the ropes were relentless, unyielding. My heart hammered in my chest. I needed to get out, to get back to my family. They'd be looking for me, Prophet especially. His face flashed in my mind's eye, stern yet caring, and I clung to the image like a lifeline. If anyone would come for me, I knew it would be him. All he needed was a direction, and he'd track me down. Of that, I had no doubt.

The entire club would turn the world upside down if they had to. I just had to hold on, to survive until then. Because this was not where my story ended. Not in some dimly lit room at the hands of monsters who thought they could use me however they pleased. Whatever it took, I had to stay alive.

The door creaked open with a groan that seemed to echo my dread. A tall, thin man slithered into the room. Dressed all in black, he blended with the shadows. He had a chilling presence -- his eyes, those cold chips of ice, found mine in the gloom and held them captive. The first few times someone had come in here, I'd been blindfolded. The others, it had been pitch-black and I hadn't been able to see more than shadows. Not that it had stopped the bastard from doing what he wanted.

"Ah, Ares," he cooed. A shiver raced down my spine. The tone of his voice alone was enough to tell me if there had ever been any humanity in this man, it was long gone. And his voice... I'd never forget it for as long as I lived. "You look... uncomfortable."

I squirmed under his gaze, the raw fear skittering through me. But I wasn't about to let him see me crack, not even as his lips curled into a satisfied smirk at my predicament. Sick bastard was loving this. I tried not to think of all the things he'd done to me already. Part of me wanted to curl up and hide, but I knew it wouldn't do any good.

"Bet you're feeling all tied up right about now," he taunted, pacing in front of me like a vulture ready to feast on carrion. I bit my tongue so I wouldn't make a smartass remark. I had a feeling doing so would be really bad for me right now. "But don't worry, my dear. You'll get used to it."

I fixed my eyes on a crack in the nearby wall. My jaw clenched so hard it ached, but the pain was good -- it reminded me I was still here, still fighting. I refused to give this man what he wanted. I wouldn't beg for my freedom or my life. Wouldn't yield to whatever sadistic plans he had for me. I'd fight. If I didn't, I'd never be able to look my family in the eye again.

"Looking away won't save you," he whispered, leaning close enough for me to feel his breath.

I forced myself to meet his gaze, to show him the fire he hadn't extinguished. "You don't scare me," I lied through gritted teeth, the words tasting like ash.

"Brave words for someone in your... predicament." His voice made my skin crawl.

As he stepped back, his shadow seemed to stretch across the room, imprinting itself onto the walls, the ceiling, the very air around me. I wondered if he'd designed this room so that very thing would happen, making the trapped person feel as if he surrounded them.

Despite my fear, I also felt determined. I would survive this. Because somewhere out there, Prophet and the Dixie Reapers were tearing the world apart to find me. For them, for myself, I would endure. I had to. There wasn't another option. I knew it would destroy my family and Prophet if I didn't live long enough for them to save me.

"Go ahead," I said, summoning every ounce of defiance I could muster. "Do your worst. You'll see. I won't break that easily. I haven't yet, have I?"

His cruel smile never wavered as he turned to leave, but I caught the flicker of annoyance in his eyes. It was small, almost imperceptible, but it was there -- a crack in his armor. And that was all I needed.

With each second that ticked by in his absence, the ember of resolve within me began to fade. I knew I needed to fight back, but I didn't know how much more I could endure. I had no idea how long I'd been gone. Had several days passed since I'd been kidnapped? Weeks? There was no telling how long I'd been unconscious. I knew from experience they could keep me knocked out for weeks if that's what they wanted.

The room dipped in and out of focus until the man returned, bringing with him a rolling cart full of items meant to torture me. They clattered ominously as he pushed the cart closer to me.

"Let's begin," he whispered. I could hear the delight in his voice, the pure glee that he'd make me scream. I knew I needed to hold out, but at the same time, if I never screamed, would he lose his patience and kill me? It wasn't like I was dealing with a sane man.

I braced myself, clenching my teeth so hard I feared they might crack. The cold touch of steel traced the exposed skin of my arm, leaving a trail of fire in its wake. My breath hitched, but I refused to voice the pain I felt.

I wouldn't give him the satisfaction.

Another slash, sharp and precise, bit into my flesh. My body jolted involuntarily, straining against the rough ropes. Pain splintered through me, branching out to every nerve ending. But beneath it all, simmering like molten lava, was the anger -- an inferno threatening to erupt. How dare he do this to me? How many others had there been? Was I the only captive here right now? Or did he have a stable of us like my previous Master?

"Beautiful," he murmured, studying the cuts that painted my skin like grotesque art.

I ground my teeth, swallowing the bile that rose in my throat. My thoughts spun, a maelstrom of fear and fury.

"Is this all you've got?" My voice trembled with the effort to remain defiant.

My Master paused, his head tilting in that unnerving way of his, as if considering a particularly interesting specimen under a microscope.

"Patience, Ares," he cooed. "We're only just getting started."

Fuck. Me. I was no longer confident I could last without giving him what he wanted. While I'd become stronger in some ways since being adopted by Savior, I'd grown weak in others. The old Ares would have retreated from the pain, disappearing into her own mind. The new version of me didn't remember how to do it.

The next onslaught came without warning. This time he'd grabbed a whip off the cart. Blows rained down, each one a brutal crescendo that left me reeling. Tears slipped down my cheeks, and I hated that I was giving him one of the things I knew he wanted, but I couldn't help it. What would Prophet think when he saw me like this? Stripped bare. Cut. Beaten. I doubted the man was going to stop here. No, he had more planned for me. I could see it in his eyes.

"Still holding on?" Master taunted, his breath hot against my ear. "You're more resilient than I gave you credit for."

His tongue flicked out to lick the shell of my ear and I fought hard not to throw up. I could see his hard cock outlined in his pants and knew he was getting off on this. If I were lucky, my pain would be enough to make him come. And if I wasn't… I didn't even want to think of what would happen to me.

"Stronger than you'll ever be," I managed to choke out, my voice barely above a whisper.

He laughed then, a sound devoid of any humanity, and continued his cruel work. I retreated within myself, building walls around my mind to shield it from the relentless assault. It had been so long I was out of practice. The walls would crack, and he'd reach me. Then I'd rebuild, stronger than the last time.

I heard the clink of his belt and knew what would happen next. I closed my eyes and forced myself to slip away. It was the only way I'd survive what he did next.

* * *

In the suffocating stillness of the dimly lit room, I lay sprawled on the cold floor, every breath a battle, every heartbeat a rebellion. Master had left, confident he'd broken me. He didn't know me -- not truly. He saw someone to own, to crush. He didn't know I'd been through this before, and I had a reason to survive this time.

He'd left me unbound, and for good reason. I didn't think I would be able to easily sit up, much less try to escape. My blood dripped onto the floor. Every part of me ached, and I fought back tears. I'd never voluntarily been with anyone before, and I'd been looking forward to Prophet claiming me in every way possible.

Now I felt dirty again. Unworthy of someone like Prophet. I knew he wouldn't turn away from me. He wasn't that type. If anything, he'd probably blame himself for what happened to me. I didn't know how he'd make this his fault, but he would. It was just the sort of man he was, and I loved him for it.

I'd been so frustrated with him for a while. Until the day he'd saved me. I'd opened myself up to exploring the possibility of a future relationship with him at that point. We'd grown closer, even though he was always respectful, mindful of the fact I hadn't been eighteen until recently.

I groaned and struggled to sit upright. Leaning against the wall, every breath felt like it might destroy me. I gingerly touched my ribs, wondering if he'd broken any. I winced and looked down, seeing the bruises covering my body.

Drawing my knees up to my chest, I wrapped my arms around them and dropped my head. How many more times would the Master come to visit me?

I lifted my head, resolve filling me. No matter how much it hurt, I had to push through. I managed to stand, swaying as dizziness threatened to claim me. The world tilted and spun, but I willed it to steady. I wouldn't succumb to weakness -- not now.

Cautious steps took me to the door, my limbs protesting with the echo of recent torment. Yet, as I reached for the handle, a new kind of fear gripped me. The unknown lay beyond. What if something worse was on the other side?

I thought of my dad. Dessa and the kids. I needed to survive. To escape. I turned the handle and stepped into the abyss, ready to face whatever hell awaited me in the quest for my freedom. Or so I thought.

The corridor stretched before me, an unending tunnel of dim light and deeper shadows. Each step was tentative, as I feared I'd give myself away and be discovered. My mouth went dry and I licked my lips. I needed to keep quiet and keep moving. No matter what I saw or heard, I couldn't stop.

My eyes flicked from one closed door to another, seeking signs of life -- or rather, the lack of it. I heard a few whimpers, and wondered if they belonged to women like me. Stolen from their families, sold by monsters.

A shiver ran down my spine as I sidestepped a patch of light. For all I knew, someone was watching me, waiting in the darkness. Maybe they were enjoying my attempt at an escape, laughing at my pathetic effort to free myself.

In the darkness, my fingers found the cool metal of a doorknob, hope surging momentarily before I turned it and met resistance. Locked. A stifled groan escaped my throat as I leaned against the unyielding wood, the weight of despair momentarily crushing. I should have known. Why else would he have left me untied and in an unlocked room? He'd known I wouldn't get far.

The urge to panic was like a living thing inside me, clawing at my resolve.

With every shallow breath, I fought to quell the terror threatening to overwhelm me. I pressed my ear against the door, straining to hear anything beyond the thudding of my own pulse. Silence. Perhaps it was a cruel trick of hope, but silence was an invitation I had to accept.

I stepped back, surveying the hallway for anything, anything that could aid in my escape. My gaze fell upon a heavy-looking vase perched on a pedestal. Without a second thought, I grasped it, the weight reassuring in my hands. If I couldn't unlock the door, maybe I could break through it somehow -- or at least cause enough noise to summon an opportunity out of the ensuing chaos. I didn't know how many women were held captive down here – or how many men they might send to check on any disturbance, but that was a gamble I was willing to take. I'd bash whoever came through over the head with the vase.

"Prophet," I whispered, "I'm still fighting. Please come get me." My legs gave out and I collapsed on the floor, leaning my head back against the wall to wait. Closing my eyes, I wondered how close the club was to finding me. Had Wire managed to locate me with his hacking skills? Was the club outside this place right now, just waiting to bust in and get me out of here?

Or was I lost? Would my captors find me and punish me?

My heart ached and tears slipped down my cheeks.

The door opened and I looked up, seeing my Master and another man. The stronger of the two lifted me over his shoulder and carried me back to my prison. The light in Master's eyes was enough warning to know this would be a long night full of pain and suffering. Closing my eyes again, I had to wonder if I really could survive until the club rescued me… or if this man was the one who would finally break me.

Chapter Four

Prophet

The air in the room was heavy, thick with the stench of oil and leather. I stood in the middle of the Wild & Reckless MC clubhouse, surrounded by my brothers-in-arms -- Foster and Warden -- as well as our allies from the Devil's Boneyard and the Devil's Fury. Our new friends, the Wild & Reckless MC, had been a great help to us, and I hoped the friendship would carry forward after this was over.

"We've got enough firepower to start a small war," Magnum said, his hands running over the cache of weapons that lay sprawled across the table.

Gator nodded, his eyes cold as ice. "And we'll bring hell to their doorstep. I can't stand sick fucks like that bastard."

I felt the weight of the guns in my hands, the grip familiar and strangely comforting. There were no heroes here, just men ready to descend into the abyss. The Wild & Reckless guys -- Highlander, Wings, and Poker -- stood at the edge, their expressions grim. Their other two brothers were in the background, ready if we needed them.

"Highlander has a plan," I said, my voice steady despite the turmoil inside me.

The room fell silent, all eyes on the tall Scotsman. Highlander was built like a tank, his presence commanding attention without a word. He laid out the map, his finger tracing the route we would take to infiltrate the asshole's stronghold.

"Precision," Highlander emphasized. "That's how we do it. No room for mistakes."

Wings stepped forward. "We'll cover your back and help with the cleanup."

Poker gave a curt nod. "You get in, you get out. We'll handle the rest."

I stared at the map and the layout of the mansion. Although, we had no way of knowing if it was entirely accurate. Shade had managed to find it and sent it over to Magnum. It was better than nothing. It was most likely they were holding Ares in the basement, but the place had so many rooms she could be anywhere on any floor.

"Let's do this," I said, ready to have Ares in my arms, safe and sound.

There was a chorus of agreement. I looked at each man, brothers forged in violence and necessity, and knew that no matter what, we'd stand together. Even though we weren't all part of the same club, today we shared the same mission.

We armed ourselves, each weapon a promise of vengeance, each bullet a whisper of justice. As I checked my own gear, I thought of Ares, and rage coursed through me, burning away any doubt.

We moved as one, a dark tide rolling toward an uncertain dawn. Fear clung to us, a constant companion, but it didn't rule us. Tonight, we were the hunters and not the hunted. We'd show that asshole what it meant to suffer.

The cold steel of the knife slid against my palm as I strapped it to my thigh, a silent promise of violence. My hands didn't shake. They couldn't afford to as I loaded my gun. Every bullet that snicked into place in the magazine was a promise of retribution. Poker handed me another 9mm, its weight familiar and oddly comforting in my palm.

"Watch your back," he said, his eyes dark with the same fury that fed my pulse.

"Always do," I replied, the words terse and low.

We stepped out of the clubhouse and got onto our bikes. I felt the engine roar to life beneath me. The throttle twisted under my grip, a surge of power coursing through the machine like adrenaline. I shot forward, the world blurring into streaks of color and light as I wove through traffic, heading out of town and toward the mansion. The wind lashed at me like a living thing, but I welcomed its icy caress -- it sharpened my senses, kept me tethered to the moment.

I could almost hear her voice over the rush of air, a siren's call urging me on, faster, ever faster. Ares needed me. That single thought cleaved through the haze of fear. I would tear apart anyone who stood between us, rend flesh from bone if I had to. There was no room for doubt, no space for hesitation. Only the mission, only her.

Each mile devoured by the wheels on my bike brought me closer to her. I would finally put an end to this nightmare and save the woman I loved.

Tonight, I'd go into that fucking house, and I'd do whatever it took to get Ares back where she belonged -- safe in my arms. I'd make sure the threat that cast its shadow over her was extinguished, forever silenced. I'd worry about what came next once I had her out of that place.

The rumble of my bike's engine died as I coasted to a halt, the mansion's imposing silhouette looming ahead. A chill prickled my skin -- not from the night air, but from the malice that seemed to seep from the estate's very walls. I let the silence settle over me, eyes scanning for any sign of movement.

Security was tight. Cameras perched like predatory birds. Guards prowled the perimeter with a military precision that spoke of the man's paranoia. This was it -- the fortress where Ares was trapped. A fortress I intended to breach.

"Stay sharp," I muttered under my breath, a silent mantra to keep focused. I slid off my motorcycle, crouching low in the shadows, my hands steady despite the inferno of fear threatening to consume me. Not for myself, but for Ares. If I failed, I knew she'd end up dying in this place.

A flicker of motion caught my eye -- Wings and Gator, positioned across the lawn, gave the signal. Distraction was key, and those two had promised to cause a big ruckus. I watched as they lobbed a couple of well-placed rocks, the guards shifting like agitated hounds toward the source of the noise. It seemed almost too easy.

Slinking forward, I moved like a ghost, my boots barely kissing the earth beneath them. The darkness was a friend, an ally that embraced me as one of its own. Each step took me deeper into enemy territory, every shadow a potential threat.

A guard rounded the corner, his flashlight cutting a swath through the night. My grip tightened on the knife strapped to my thigh. There was no room for mercy, not here, not tonight. As he edged closer, oblivious to his impending doom, I struck. The blade found its home, swift and silent. It slid into his neck with ease, and he crumpled without a sound.

I dragged the body into the darkness, my heart pounding. I needed to move faster. Every moment that ticked by was another second she suffered, and I would not -- could not -- fail her.

My progress through the mansion was a dance with death, each step measured, each breath calculated. I avoided the light, sticking to the blackness that pooled in the corners and crevices. More guards met the same fate as the first, their lifeblood a testament to the lengths I'd go to save her. Not just her. I knew this man had tormented other women before Ares. This was revenge for all of them.

With every inch gained, fear filled me. Was Ares still all right? Had she managed to survive without losing her mind? She needed me, and I would tear this place apart, stone by stone, if that's what it took to free her from the clutches of the monster who dared claim her as his property. She was mine. Had been mine for over a year now, even if I hadn't been able to officially make her mine.

I was coming for her, and hell itself wouldn't stop me.

I made it to the door I hoped would lead me to Ares. My fingers worked deftly, coaxing the tumblers into submission. The adrenaline in my veins sharpened my focus to a razor's edge. A soft click, barely audible over the hammering of my heart, signaled success. The door yielded, swinging open with a reluctant groan.

Beyond lay a dimly lit hallway, oppressive and lined with doors like silent sentinels. Whimpers leaked from the cracks, the soft sounds of shattered spirits. They were the cries of the damned, and they fueled my resolve. Ares was somewhere here, her pain a phantom ache in my own chest. I stepped over the threshold, the shadows embracing me like an old friend.

I couldn't save them all, but I would get my woman out of this hell no matter what it took. The rest of the men with me would have to take care of the other women.

A man emerged -- a hulking beast who looked more like a devil than a human. The guard was monstrous, a towering mass of muscle and malice. I tensed. As the club's Enforcer, I'd faced down death more times than I cared to count, but each time was a roll of the dice with the reaper. Would I be lucky this time too, or would this be my last fight?

With no room for hesitation, I summoned the training that had been drilled into me. I twisted away from his lumbering grasp, my body operating on instinct. His size was his downfall. Power meant nothing without the grace to direct it. And grace was something I had in spades when the stakes were life and death.

A feint to the left, and he took the bait. Like a viper, I struck -- my blade striking his side, his stomach, and finally slicing across his neck. And as he fell, I felt a surge of grim satisfaction. This was for Ares, for every tear she shed, for every scream muffled by these walls. And I wasn't finished yet.

I stepped over the inert behemoth. Ahead, another door beckoned -- the door I hoped would lead me to her, to the end of this nightmare. I moved forward, my breaths shallow. A tomb-like silence hung heavy around me. The dim light flickered, casting sinister shadows. Through each door I passed, I heard the muffled sounds of despair.

I paused by the last door. The cries behind this door were familiar to me. Ares. I didn't know what I'd find on the other side, but I knew she was inside. The sounds of her agony ripped into me and I steeled myself. Drawing in a breath, I kicked the door, shattering it on impact.

The man who'd purchased Ares stood before me, his twisted grin a sickening slash across his face. Wire had texted me an image of him, one he'd taken from a still off the cameras inside the house. But even without it, the evil rolling off this man would have been enough to tell me who the fuck he was. Our gazes locked -- two predators fighting for dominance. The air was charged with the electricity of impending violence.

"Prophet," he oozed, his voice slick as oil. "You are Prophet, right? Ares talks about you so much, when she thinks no one is listening. So good of you to join us."

"End of the line, asshole." My words were ice, my gaze locked onto him with unwavering intensity.

He laughed, a sound that scraped against my nerves like barbed wire. I didn't dare stop to look at Ares. If I did, I might break. First, I needed to deal with this bastard. I could use my gun and end him quickly, but what would be the fun in that? He needed to suffer for all he'd done to Ares, not to mention the other women.

I gripped the knife tighter and charged at him. He danced to the side, but I'd anticipated his move and slashed the blade along his ribs. The man snarled, eyes narrowing. He swung his fist at me, but I kept out of range. The two of us circled one another. We each wanted to destroy the other.

I landed a few more blows, the blood flowing from the man's wounds. I watched the crimson drops splatter on the floor and knew it wasn't enough. Pulling one of the guns from the holster behind my back, I took aim and shot both of his knees, forcing him to the ground. He cried out as he collapsed, his face going pale. Now that I knew he wouldn't be able to escape, or fight back, it was time to make him pay.

I approached, kneeling down. His eyes went wide with fear, as if he suddenly realized his life was over.

"Don't worry. You won't die right away." I smiled, flashing my teeth. "I'll make sure you suffer first. Although…"

I still couldn't look at Ares. I knew she was there.

Not only did I hear her, but I could feel her presence in the room. Holding my hand out to her, I beckoned her closer. If anyone deserved to get revenge on this man, it was her. I'd once thought she'd been forged from iron, but I had to wonder if she still felt as strong as she had before. How much damage had this man done to her? Not only physically, but emotionally and mentally as well.

I felt her hand close around mine, and when I finally looked her way, I wished like hell I hadn't. I didn't know how she was standing, or how the fuck she'd survived. The woman was stronger than anyone I knew, even though I didn't think she realized it. All I had was my bike, and it wouldn't be an easy ride for her to get the fuck out of here, but I'd need her to pull through. For Ares' sake, we needed to put as much distance as we could between this house of horrors and her.

"Ares, is there anything you want to do or say to him before I continue?" I asked.

"He stripped me naked. You should do the same to him." Her voice was barely a whisper and I heard the ragged pain behind her words.

I didn't want to hear the answer, but at the same time, I needed to. "Did he touch you? Did he…"

"Yeah. He raped me."

I closed my eyes and fought for control. Using my knife, I shredded his clothes. The pathetic dick hanging between his legs wasn't anything to brag about. It didn't even look big enough for me to slice it off. I tapped the head of his cock with the flat side of my knife and he flinched.

"Is this why you hurt women? None of them want you without being forced?" I asked. "Ares, can you pick the locks on the doors in the hall?"

"With the right tools," she said.

I handed her my lockpicks. "Go free the women and tell them if anyone wants vengeance to come in here."

I stood and gripped a handful of the man's hair and hauled him over to a wall with leather cuffs hanging from it. I fastened them onto his wrists and wondered what those women would do to him. Glancing around the room, I noticed a locked cabinet.

Ares returned, two young women following behind her. None of them had on clothes. I made sure not to look anywhere other than their faces.

"Ares, go unlock the cabinet. Maybe there's something in there they want to use on this sorry excuse of a man," I said. She made her way to the cabinet and used the lockpicks to open it. Once it swung open, I let out a whistle. Various sex toys were inside, including floggers and strap-ons. I eyed Ares, wondering if he'd used those on her. She gave a subtle shake of her head and relief flooded me. One less trauma to overcome.

"Ladies, I'm going to hand him over to you, with only one caveat." I handed the revolver to one of them. "When you're done making him suffer, make sure he's dead."

The younger of the two tipped her head to the side and stared at the man. "If I shoot him in the dick, will he bleed out?"

"Guess it depends on if you can hit a target that small." I heard Ares snicker behind me, and the sound filled me with joy. She might be badly beaten, and she'd suffered in the worst way, but at least she hadn't been completely broken.

I looked at Ares again, and I wished like hell I hadn't. I wasn't one to cry, but the sight of her battered body was enough to make my eyes sting with unshed tears. My heart shattered at the sight of her. I swept her into my arms, her body trembling against mine.

"Shh, baby girl, I've got you. You're safe now. You're going home," I murmured, pressing a kiss to her forehead.

Her arms wrapped weakly around my neck, holding on as if she feared the world would rip us apart. But nothing would take her from me again. Nothing.

"Take me away from here, Prophet. Please," she pleaded, her voice cracking with the weight of her ordeal.

Once we'd walked out of the mansion, I paused only long enough to remove my cut and pull off my T-shirt. I tugged the shirt over her head before sliding my cut on once more. It wasn't ideal, but at least it covered her.

"Do you think you can ride?" I asked.

"If it meant leaving this place, I could walk without stopping for the next week."

"Come on." I took her hand and led her to my bike. I swung my leg over the seat, and she settled behind me, pressing against my back.

I didn't wait to speak to anyone or thank them for their help. Right now, she was my priority, and I had a feeling they all understood. I rode, not stopping until we'd gotten far enough away that I hoped Ares would feel safe. I pulled into the parking lot of a cheap motel and got a room. I didn't know if we'd stay until morning, but she needed a chance to get cleaned up, and I needed to buy some clothes for both of us.

The place didn't even offer toiletries, and the towels looked questionable. Yeah, we sure the fuck wouldn't be here long. I just needed a place to keep her while I got what we needed. She couldn't very well go into a store like this. If I hadn't wanted to get as far as I could from the place where I'd found her, I wouldn't have even made her ride on my bike in her current state of undress. Maybe if I hadn't reacted the moment I saw her on Wire's screen, I'd have taken the time to get her a change of clothes and shoved them into my saddlebags.

"I need you to wait here while I grab some supplies. We'll get back on the road after we've both showered and changed."

She looked up at me, tears slipping down her cheeks. "I worried you wouldn't make it in time. I didn't know how much longer I could hold on."

I cupped her cheek. "I will always come for you, Ares. Always."

She nodded and wiped the tears away. "Hurry back. This place gives me the creeps."

I kissed her forehead, then rinsed off my hands and face, making sure I didn't have any blood spatter on me. Once I thought I didn't look like I'd just committed murder, I headed to the nearest store that would have the basics we needed. I bought a package of panties for her, a shirt, and pair of leggings, then grabbed a cheap pair of tennis shoes and some socks. All I needed was a shirt for now. I'd buy more things when we got to our final destination, which I'd already decided wouldn't be the Dixie Reapers compound. She wasn't ready.

Once I got back to the motel, I helped her wash and dress. I tugged on my new shirt, forgoing a shower for the time being. It was more important to get out of here right now.

"If you could go anywhere while you heal, where would you go?" I asked.

"The beach." She smiled a little. "But I also want to go home to Alabama."

"Then we'll find a place along the Gulf." I used an app on my phone to locate a home we could rent by the month and made the payment. The owner sent the info for accessing the house, and I checked out the quickest route to get there.

"Only time I'm stopping is if you need food or need to pee. You all right with that?" I asked.

She nodded. "Just… Don't leave me."

I leaned down, pausing a moment before my lips brushed over hers. It was technically our first kiss, and not the way I'd wanted it to happen. But it felt like we both needed this. "I should have said this before now. You're mine, Ares. I'm not going to ask anyone for permission. You've been mine for the last year."

She leaned into me, wrapping her arms around my waist. "I know. I'd planned to ask what was taking you so long."

"Stupidity."

She laughed softly. "Take me to our temporary home, Prophet."

I'd take her anywhere she wanted to go. No matter how far or impossible, I'd find a way.

Chapter Five

Ares

The roar of the engine settled into a purr as Prophet cut the ignition, and we coasted to a stop in front of the beach house. The air was thick with salt and promise, but it felt like a world away from the one I'd been living in -- a world of darkness and pain.

"Here we are, Ares," Prophet said softly, his voice a balm to the chaos churning inside me. He didn't know, couldn't know, how my insides were a twisting mass of snakes. A silent scream echoed in my head.

"Looks quiet," I managed to say, forcing what I hoped was a reassuring smile as I stepped off the bike. My shoes crunched on the crushed shells, the sound too loud for such a peaceful night.

Prophet slung an arm around my shoulders, ushering me toward the house -- our temporary sanctuary. His touch was meant to comfort, but it felt like a lifeline. Agony, fear, and rage burned inside me. I wanted to cry, scream, and hit something. I leaned into him, needing his strength because mine was long gone.

"Let's check the place out," he said, and there was a lightness in his tone that told me he was trying for both our sakes. The shadows in his eyes told a different story. I knew he was worried about me.

We walked through the house, and I noted the exits, the locks on the windows, the way the furniture could be used as barricades. I froze, realizing what I was doing. I was safe now. Not to mention, Prophet was beside me. He wouldn't let anyone get to me. He watched me, his gaze both warm and concerned.

"Need anything?" he asked once we'd finished

our inspection. "There's a store not far from here. We could stock up. I only got you the one outfit earlier."

"Sure." Shopping. Such a normal thing to do, yet it felt like we were talking about scaling a mountain without ropes. I wasn't sure I was prepared yet for *normal*.

Prophet's hand found mine, our fingers lacing together. We walked to his bike, and I climbed on behind him, feeling the rumble of the motorcycle beneath us as we took the short trip to the store. I knew we wouldn't be able to buy a lot since we didn't have a vehicle with four wheels and more space. Even still, he'd been right about us needing certain things.

The fluorescent lights of the store were too bright. I wanted to shrink from them and hide, but I forced myself to remain by his side. I followed Prophet down the aisles, my gaze skittering over the racks of clothes. I could feel others watching me, hear them whispering. I knew how I looked, and what they must think. If they'd bothered to ask, I'd have told them Prophet would never harm me. Of course, I doubted they'd listen. They'd just see a big, tough biker and draw their own conclusions.

Prophet picked out two pair of jeans and a handful of shirts for himself, glancing back at me every now and then, a question in his eyes that I answered with nods and half-smiles. It was clear he worried about me, and I loved him for it, but even his silent *Are you okay?* was starting to wear me out. I didn't want to pretend I was fine when I wasn't.

After he got the items he needed, he led me to the women's section. He found a modest swimsuit for me, as well as some comfortable outfits and a casual dress. By the time he'd gathered enough to last us several days, I had to wonder how he was getting it back to the house. He must have realized the same thing because he grabbed a duffle bag and bungee cords.

The aisles seemed to stretch into infinity, a mundane gauntlet that I stumbled through. My hands trembled as I reached for a pair of flip-flops. Prophet's hand steadied mine, his touch grounding even as everything else spun out of control.

"Let's get you home," he murmured, his voice low and laced with concern.

I nodded, unable to find words, my throat constricted by a fear that refused to ease its grip. The normality of shopping felt suffocating, and wrong.

Prophet quickly paid for our things, then shoved them into the bag. When we got to his motorcycle, he strapped it to the back fender. We'd still need more things, and laundry detergent. At least the house had a washer and dryer. I climbed onto the bike behind him, putting my arms around his waist. There had been a time I'd loved riding with him. Right now, I felt too exposed. Every little sound or shadow made me jump.

Back at the house, my feet dragged across the threshold, each step heavier than the last. Prophet's presence was the only thing keeping the tide of panic at bay.

"Stay with me," I whispered, my voice barely audible over the roaring in my ears.

"Always," he vowed, his arms folding around me as if he could shield me from the horrors etched into my soul.

He made a call, his words a low rumble that I clung to. "Yeah, delivery."

He rattled off an order for basic food items and drinks. It would be enough to hold us for now. It wasn't like he could carry a case of water and a week's worth of groceries on his bike anyway. Delivery was the only option.

Hours passed, marked only by the arrival of boxes and bags at the doorstep. Prophet brought them inside, but never strayed more than a few feet from where I sat, curled on the couch. I tracked his movements, my breath hitching whenever he moved out of my line of sight.

"Can't lose you again," I confessed, the words spilling out raw and edged with desperation. Because not being with him made me feel like I might lose myself. He was the glue holding me together right now.

"You won't," he assured me, settling beside me with an arm draped protectively over my shoulders.

I leaned into his warmth, the steady beat of his heart beneath my ear having a calming effect on me. It reminded me we were both alive, and we were together. And this time, he didn't seem like he'd let me go. I could only imagine how much our lives would change when we got back home. Right now, he was my anchor. The one constant in this fucked-up world I knew would never change.

The phone in Prophet's hand glowed. His thumbs danced across the screen, and though I couldn't see the words he typed, the tension in his shoulders told me enough. He was reaching out, casting a lifeline back to the club -- to my father. Or possibly Wire. Either way, they would know I was safe. I was glad my dad wouldn't have to worry anymore. This had to have been hard on him.

"Done," he murmured, slipping the device into his pocket. His eyes found mine, a storm of emotions swirling within their depths. "Savior knows you're safe."

"Thank you," I whispered. I knew he'd needed to let the club know I was alive, yet the thought of returning, of facing the questions and the pitying stares, splintered something inside me. I couldn't face them yet.

"Hey," Prophet said softly, pulling me close. Despite his strength, his voice and touch were gentle. I focused on the rhythm of his heartbeat. It was steady, reliable -- everything I needed right now.

"I just... I can't go back yet." The truth tasted bitter on my tongue. How could I return to them, fractured and shadowed by memories that refused to fade, and new nightmares I hadn't had time to process?

"Then we stay here for as long as it takes," he replied, his voice a rumble that resonated within me. "I already booked the place for a month. If it looks like you need it longer, I'll see if it's open again next month. If not, we'll find another place."

I wanted to be brave. I knew the club had to be more than a little concerned about me. If I could get strong enough, we could go home. But right now...

"Prophet," I started, my voice barely audible, "I'm so scared."

"Shh," he soothed, pressing a kiss to the top of my head. "Fear is just a sign we've got something worth fighting for. And, Ares, I'll fight with you, every step of the way. I'm confident the men who stayed behind at the mansion made sure that evil bastard was dead. They wouldn't have left until they confirmed he wasn't breathing."

I nodded and closed my eyes. I wondered if those women had made him suffer horribly. As much as I wanted to know, I didn't ask. Prophet could have most likely found out if he'd checked with the other men who had been there. I hadn't even paid attention to which of the Dixie Reapers had been with him. It made me feel guilty. They'd helped save me too, and I hadn't bothered to thank any of them.

"You seem to be stuck in your head," he said. "Why don't we take a short walk on the beach? If it's too much, we'll turn around and come right back."

"All right." It wasn't like I could hide in the house the entire time we were here. The sooner I tried to find some semblance of normalcy, the better.

The sand was a warm cushion beneath my bare feet as I walked alongside Prophet, the rhythmic wash of waves a soothing sound. The beach stretched out before us. The sun had already set, and I didn't see another soul out here. Stopping at the edge of the water, I closed my eyes and tipped my head back. The soft sound of the ocean sliding across the sand, then retreating once more, eased some of the tension I'd been carrying. This place was peaceful.

Unlike my mind. Inside, I still felt like I was screaming, begging for someone to find me, to get out of that hellish place. Even now, if I blocked out the sounds around me, I could almost hear that man's voice, as he told me all the things he'd do to me. Hear the slide of his zipper before he violated me. A shiver raked my spine and I wanted to go inside and take the hottest shower, scrubbing my skin until I finally felt clean. Except, experience told me, soap and water wouldn't help in that regard.

There would be nightmares. I'd had them before. I doubted this time would be any different. Reliving the moments when that bastard cut me, whipped me, used his fists on me… The feeling of him forcing his way into my body. None of it would go away overnight.

I'd be okay. I wasn't right now. Far from it. But I

could be, with enough time... and with Prophet by my side.

"Look," Prophet murmured, nudging me gently with his elbow.

I followed his gaze to the neighboring beach house where two familiar figures lounged on the deck. Dr. Myron, with his gentle eyes and ready smile, sat beside Dr. Sykes, whose sharp intellect often hid behind a facade of humor. The Dixie Reapers' trusted healers, unexpected in this place of retreat.

"Hey, Ares," Dr. Myron called, waving us over. "Small world, huh?"

"Seems like it," I replied, the words catching slightly in my throat.

"Are you okay?" Dr. Sykes asked, his tone careful. I wondered if they'd heard what happened to me. Or was he asking more because of my cuts and bruises?

I glanced at Prophet, seeking reassurance in his steady presence. He nodded, as if giving me permission to not be okay.

"Been better," I admitted, the weight of my confession threatening to drag me under.

Dr. Sykes rose from his seat, closing the distance between us with a few measured steps. His gaze studied me, and something told me he saw far more than I'd wanted him to.

"If you need to talk, we're here," he said, his voice low and even. "But we won't push you. Just know the offer is there."

"Thank you," I whispered. Tears burned my eyes, but I blinked them back, refusing to cry.

"I think I'm going to grab a beer and join Dr. Myron," Prophet said. "I think the two of you may need a little privacy."

It seemed he understood there were things I needed to confess that I didn't want to say to him. He'd always been perceptive, especially where I was concerned.

I sat across from Dr. Sykes, hoping this was the right decision. I kept Prophet within view, which settled my nerves a bit. I'd known Dr. Myron and Dr. Sykes for years, and knew neither of them would hurt me, but panic flared inside me if I couldn't see Prophet. I wondered if I had PTSD or something from my recent ordeal.

"Start wherever you want," Dr. Sykes encouraged. "This isn't an official session, so I'm not keeping notes, recording, or anything else. It's just you and me having a conversation."

"Wherever" felt like standing at the edge of a chasm, peering into the abyss. I took a deep breath. The smell of the sand and water calmed my mind a little. Should I start with being kidnapped? Talk about what it was like to be sold, yet again?

"It's like… I feel hollow and at the same time I'm full of pain and anger. I'm not sure that makes any sense. I have no idea how to describe everything going inside my head right now."

"Trauma can feel like a living thing," Dr. Sykes interjected softly. "It has teeth and claws, and it's hungry. But you're not alone in this fight, Ares. Prophet loves you, and so do your family and friends. You have a support system if you choose to use it."

I knew he was right, which was part of why I felt so guilty hiding in Gulf Shores when I knew my family had to be waiting for me. I wasn't the only one hurting right now. No doubt, Dad had blamed himself for me being taken from the compound. That was just the sort of man he was.

"Will I ever be whole again?" The question slipped out before I could think better of it.

"That's the goal," Dr. Sykes said with a reassuring nod. "But 'whole' doesn't mean unchanged. It means accepting the scars and finding strength in them. You went through something similar before, Ares, but it doesn't mean you're going to feel the same things or heal the same way. Let's start with why this time was different."

"I have people who care about me," I said. "They're worried and were probably scared they'd never see me again. There's a man who loves me enough to kill to protect me."

Dr. Sykes nodded. "You're right on all counts, but is that all?"

I shook my head. "No, I wasn't the same as I was the first time. I knew what was going to happen to some extent since I'd lived through it before, but this time, I chose to go with them."

He froze for a moment and I knew I'd taken him by surprise. Did no one realize how the men had managed to take me from the compound? It hadn't occurred to me until now that they'd thought I'd been taken against my will.

"Yeah, I went willingly," I said. "Surprised?"

"A little. Can you tell me why?"

"Junie, Judd, and Marnie. The man who caught me outside the house threatened to take them instead. I knew they'd die if they had to go through being sold and owned by pedophiles. What other reason would adults buy children on the dark web?"

He leaned back, relaxing his posture. "So you were protecting your family by sacrificing yourself."

"I did, and while I worried I'd be broken beyond repair this time, I knew it was better for me to go with them than to let my little brother and sisters face those monsters."

"You've been through counseling before, so you know this is all confidential. However, I think your family needs to know why this happened. It might help give them closure and blame themselves a little less."

"Or it could make them feel even worse," I countered.

"I'm not going to tell you what you should or shouldn't do. And I'm not going to force you to talk about anything. I'm here to listen, and to help."

I knew all that. Like he'd said, this wasn't my first time going to counseling. At the same time, I wasn't sure I was ready to talk. Glancing at Prophet, I felt my stomach clench. We had the chance to be together, and I knew I needed to work through everything I'd gone through. It was the only way we'd be able to move forward.

Taking a break, I started slow… I told Dr. Sykes about the trip in the van, being locked up in the cage, and what happened after I'd been sold and met my owner for the first time. The entire sordid tale spilled from my lips, and at some point, I realized tears were falling down my cheeks. He listened, not stopping me or interjecting. Patiently, he waited until I reached a point where I couldn't continue.

"Do you need to be tested, Ares? Not just for an STD, but also for pregnancy."

I shook my head. "He wore condoms."

"For peace of mind, would you *like* to be tested? Dr. Myron could draw your blood and get a local lab to process it. If things were to progress with Prophet, can you say with any certainty you wouldn't infect him with something, or if you were to find out you're pregnant, would you be positive it was his child?"

I hated his questions, but he was right. "I'll let Dr. Myron draw some blood. I think it's too soon to tell anything, though. At least, as far as a pregnancy goes."

He nodded. "I'll ask him to expedite the results. We should know something in three to five days. In the meantime, you know where we are if you need us. And if you're right, he can always test you again when the time is right."

"Thank you. For everything."

He smiled and we stood, then joined Prophet and Dr. Myron. The four of us talked a bit longer before Prophet and I returned to the home we'd been renting.

Chapter Six

Ares

The darkness clung to the corners of the room despite the moonlight coming through the windows. I lay there, my back flush against the cool sheets, eyes wide open, staring at the ceiling. Since my talk with Dr. Sykes a few days ago, I'd had trouble sleeping. My thoughts were chaotic and never seemed to shut off. The silence around me felt oppressive, and I shifted restlessly.

If I'm not going to sleep, I might as well get some water.

Getting out of bed, I slipped down the hall and into the living room. Something outside the living room windows drew my attention. I stepped out onto the deck, breathing in the cooler night air and closing my eyes.

The moon hung low and heavy in the sky, casting a silver glow over the beach, painting the world in monochrome shades. I leaned on the railing, seeking solace in the rhythmic crash of waves on the shore, the scent of salt in the air. I scanned the beach, and that's when I saw them -- two shadows down on the sand, moving together in an intimate dance. My cheeks warmed when I realized it was Dr. Myron and Dr. Sykes, unaware of my gaze from above.

A sharp twist of embarrassment knotted in my stomach. This wasn't meant for my eyes -- this private moment. Backing away, I crept across the deck. The sounds of their grunts and groans reached my ears, spurring me to move faster.

With the image of their embrace seared into my memory, I retreated to the safety of the darkened interior of the house. Right before I reached the door, my foot caught on the edge of an unnoticed chair, and it scraped against the deck. There was no way they hadn't heard me. I froze, feeling the blood drain from my face. I glanced at the beach, seeing both men staring at me.

I stood there, flustered. *Shit.*

They stood, wrapped towels around their waists, and headed in my direction. My heart pounded and I wondered how angry they'd be. Their presence loomed over me as they stepped onto the deck.

"Sorry," I managed to mutter, though the word felt inadequate, hollow in the wake of my clumsy interruption. "I... I didn't mean to -- just needed some air, and... I'm sorry."

My cheeks flamed hotter. I'd never been so embarrassed in my life.

"Hey, it's okay," Dr. Sykes said gently, his voice cutting through my panic. He and Dr. Myron shared a look that spoke volumes of their bond -- a silent conversation passing between them before they turned their attention back to me.

"We understand, Ares. No harm done." Dr. Myron's eyes were kind. He had every right to be furious with me, and instead he was trying to console me.

"Thanks," I whispered, the word barely more than a breath. "Can I... can I talk to you about something?"

"Of course, Ares," Dr. Sykes said. "You can tell us anything."

I twisted my fingers together, the knuckles white. Talking about this, laying bare the fears gnawing at me, felt like peeling back the layers of my skin.

"It's Prophet," I started. "I mean, it's not him, not really. It's me. We're getting closer, and there's stuff we haven't done yet… because I'm scared."

Neither man said anything for a few minutes, almost as if they were weighing my words and trying to find the best answer they could give. Knowing them, that's exactly what they were doing.

"Scared?" Dr. Myron prompted softly, giving me the nudge I needed to keep going.

"Ever since… since what happened, both recently and when I was younger, being intimate… I've never felt comfortable doing that with anyone. I can't say I'm a virgin because of my past, but I've never willingly had sex with someone. I want to -- with him -- I really do, but… What if I freak out? What if I can't trust my body not to remember… not to go back to that place?"

I felt their gazes on me, but I couldn't look up. I stared at the wooden planks under our feet. They didn't say anything and I wondered if I hadn't conveyed my emotions very well. Everything in my head felt jumbled.

"Every time I think about being with him, really being with him, my heart starts racing, and I feel like I'm suffocating. It's stupid, right? Prophet would never hurt me. But what if I panic? What if all those old wounds open up again, and I can't --"

"Hey," Dr. Sykes interrupted, his voice a soft command that forced my eyes to his. "It's not stupid. Your fears are real, and they matter. *You* matter."

Dr. Myron nodded in agreement, his eyes reflecting the moonlight. "This is about survival, Ares. You've been through hell, but you're here, you're fighting. That takes courage. More than most people have. And if anyone would be understanding and give you the time and space you need, it's Prophet."

"Courage," I echoed. I didn't *feel* courageous. Far

from it.

"Prophet cares about you," Dr. Sykes added. "He'll understand. He'll never push for more than you're willing to give."

"Will I ever be ready?" Perhaps that's what worried me the most. How could I say I'd be with him the rest of my life if I didn't know what sort of relationship I'd be able to give him? It wasn't fair to him.

"Only you can answer that," Dr. Myron said. "But don't rush yourself. Healing takes time."

"Time," I murmured. No. I felt like the longer I waited, the worse it would become. Maybe this was like ripping off a bandage. "Thank you. Both for listening, and for not getting mad at me for…"

"It wasn't intentional, Ares. Besides, we were out in the open. No one to blame but ourselves. Sometimes we like the thrill of possibly getting caught." Dr. Sykes smiled a little. "I'm sorry we made you uncomfortable."

"Prophet… How do I tell him?" The question came out jagged, spiked with anxiety. "How can I make him understand without pushing him away?"

"Communication," Dr. Sykes advised, his eyes locking onto mine. "Open, honest communication. Prophet cares for you deeply. He'll want to understand, to be there for you. But he can't do that if you don't let him in."

I nodded, but the idea of talking to him about this stuff terrified me.

"Take it one step at a time," Dr. Myron added, his hand reaching out as if to offer a lifeline. "There's no rush. And remember, we're here for you too. You're not alone in this."

"Thank you," I managed to say. "I'll try."

Turning away from them, my feet carried me across the wooden planks to the door. I turned the knob and went inside, wondering if I had the courage to have a real relationship with Prophet, the kind my parents shared, and countless others at the compound. Making my way to his bedroom, I paused outside the door. He hadn't shut it, and I could see him sprawled on the bed, one arm flung over his eyes, the sheet down around his waist.

The moonlight caressed his bare chest, and I had to admit he looked beautiful. My cheeks warmed at the thought. Could I really use that word for someone like him? My fingers twitched as I wondered what it would feel like to run my hands over him. A mixture of curiosity and fear filled me.

Swallowing hard, I took one step, then another, drawing closer to his bed.

"Prophet," I whispered. I moved even closer, until my knees brushed the side of the bed. Watching him sleep, I couldn't resist any longer. Reaching out, I lightly ran my fingers over his hair. My hand trembled, and part of me wanted to run away. But the other part…

* * *

Prophet

I felt her before I saw her, the slight shift in the air, the scent of her skin. Her presence filled the room.

"Prophet…" Her voice was little more than a whisper, and I heard her drawing even closer. When she reached out and brushed her fingers through my hair, I felt the way her hand shook and knew this was a huge step for her. I didn't want to scare her away, but I couldn't pretend to be asleep any longer.

"Come here," I murmured, tugging gently.

She resisted for a heartbeat, then yielded, climbing into bed next to me. I pulled the sheet over her and held her close to my side.

"Are you all right?"

She was silent for a moment. I wondered if she was going to answer, but I gave her time. I didn't want to push. "I've felt so broken. Useless. Like I'm not even really a woman anymore. All the progress I made went away in an instant. At the end, I wasn't sure I'd last long enough for you to find me. He was so close to breaking me."

"Hey, look at me." I cupped her chin, turning her face toward mine. "You're one of the strongest people I know. Don't let this shake you. I'll do whatever it takes for you to feel like yourself again."

I saw tears mist her eyes and wondered if she'd cried any of the times we'd been apart. Had she been holding back all this time? Didn't she know how much I loved her, and that I'd do anything for her?

"None of us are perfect, Ares. Everyone has a battle they're facing. You're still you. Even if it doesn't seem like it."

"Thanks, Prophet," she whispered.

My heart was a heavy thud against my ribs, each beat a reminder of how much I needed her. "Ares, I love you."

A tear slid down her cheek, and I wiped it away. She was my everything, and I thought I'd proven that to her over the past year, but maybe I hadn't. She'd been too young, and then… I'd been an idiot and tried to wait for the perfect time. I knew better. The right time wasn't something that came around by itself. We had to create those moments.

Her eyes flickered with a fragile hope. "Can we… maybe just kiss? See what I can… handle?"

A rush of heat surged through me, desire knotting in my gut, fierce and insistent. My body's reaction was immediate, a carnal response I gritted my teeth against. Could I keep myself in check? For her, I had to.

"Only if you're sure," I managed to say, my voice rough with the effort it took to remain still, to not scare her with the intensity of my need. If things were different, I'd have pinned her to the bed, kissed her breathless, and gotten both of us naked as quick as possible. But that wasn't what she needed from me.

Her nod was almost imperceptible, but it was enough.

Leaning in, our lips met in a tentative brush. A shiver ran through me, from my lips down to my cock, as the taste of her filled my senses. It was like finding water in a desert, precious and life-giving.

My breath caught as her fingertips traced my tattoos, mine exploring the curve of her jaw. The connection was electric, a current that sang through my veins. I'd never wanted anyone as much as I did Ares. Since the moment I'd decided she'd be mine, I hadn't touched another woman. It had been more than a year since I'd last had sex.

My tongue traced the seam of her lips, begging entrance, and she parted for me with an eager shudder. The kiss deepened, our mouths moving in unison. Her lips were soft, yet firm, parting under mine, welcoming me. Her breath mingled with mine in a sweet exchange. I couldn't help but let my hands wander down her back, feeling the gentle curve of her spine, pulling her closer. Our bodies pressed against each other.

Her fingers tangled in my hair, urging me on, and I gave in to the desire I'd been holding back. Our tongues met in a tangle of desire and need. It felt so right holding her like this in my arms after everything we'd been through.

Ares' heartbeat raced against my chest as our kiss grew more urgent. Her nails dug lightly into my skin, sending pleasure coursing through me. Her scent invaded my senses, making me hunger for more of her. I could feel the heat rising between us. It was intoxicating and addictive at once.

I pulled back from the kiss. She looked up at me with eyes full of longing and need, blinking slowly as she tried to catch her breath. "This... this is okay?"

Was it okay? More than. I was worried about how she felt and if I'd pushed her too far, and yet it seemed she wasn't quite finished yet. At the first sign she was going to dark place in her mind, I'd stop.

"Can I?" I murmured against her lips, asking for permission that I wasn't sure I deserved.

"Please," she breathed, and it was all the consent I needed.

My hand trembled as it slipped beneath the soft cotton of her pajamas, skin on skin igniting sparks. But as I touched her, something changed. Her body tensed, the easy rhythm of her breath hitching in her chest.

I froze, pulling back instantly. This was Ares -- my sweet Ares -- and I'd die before I caused her an ounce of fear.

"Sorry," she whispered, a crack in her voice. My heart felt like it had just shattered. I'd moved too fast.

"Shh, no apologies needed." I moved away, putting space between us. "You have nothing to be sorry for."

She curled toward me. I wrapped my arms around her, feeling the tremor in her small frame. She nestled into me, her head against my chest. I wondered if she could hear my heart -- feel it -- It only beat for her. When I'd told her I loved her, had she understood the depths of my feelings? They hadn't been empty words.

"Stay with me," she murmured, and in that moment, I knew there was nowhere else I'd rather be.

Chapter Seven

Prophet

The world outside was a palette of blues and grays, the ocean churning as if it shared my unrest. But the kitchen was warm with morning light, and Ares moved around it with ease, a plate of scrambled eggs in one hand, toast in the other. I watched her, noting the more relaxed look on her face, the way her eyes seemed to shine brighter than they had been.

"Breakfast's ready," she said, setting down the food in front of me on the small table that overlooked the beach.

"You didn't have to cook," I said.

"Yeah, I did. It was something I needed."

I couldn't argue with her. If making breakfast made her feel better, then she could cook as much as she wanted. I took a bite of the eggs and gave her a wink. Her cheeks flushed, but I saw the spark of pleasure in her eyes.

She seemed better this morning. Not quite her old self, but she'd definitely taken a big step in healing from her ordeal. I hadn't dared ask the details of what happened to her. The simple fact he'd tortured and raped her was enough to give me nightmares.

Dr. Myron had called yesterday to let me know her lab results were in. He'd given her the all clear, but she hadn't seemed to be in the right frame of mind at the time to hear the news. As much as I wanted to blurt it out right now, I worried it would cause her to retreat again. Still… she needed to know.

I cleared my throat. "Um, Dr. Myron got your labs back."

She froze, her hand gripping her fork tighter. "And?"

"All clear."

The tension drained from her and she flashed me a quick smile. "Good. I figured as much, but hearing it…"

"Why don't we go out today?" It had been a while since we'd done anything more than hang around the house or walk on the beach.

"Out?" She paused, her brow furrowing. Had I asked too much too soon?

"Yeah. I thought we could explore a bit. Maybe play some mini golf or visit the tourist shops. I know this isn't exactly a vacation, or at least it wasn't intended as one. Doesn't mean we can't have fun while we're here. Unless you aren't ready."

She shook her head. "No. I need to leave the house more, and I know it. As long as you're with me, I'll be fine."

"Then as soon as we finish eating and get cleaned up and changed, we can head out. The main strip is only a few blocks away, if you'd prefer to walk?" There were also bicycles in the shed, but I wasn't about to ride one. Only two wheels I wanted under me was my Harley.

We finished eating, and I rinsed the dishes before loading them into the dishwasher. I didn't hear the shower running when I went to check on Ares and found her in the bedroom she'd been using. She dug through the clothes we'd bought since we'd arrived in Gulf Shores. There weren't a lot, but I'd picked up a few more things for us shortly after we got here.

"You care if I shower first?" I asked. She paused, her back tensing. "Ares? Everything all right?"

She gave a jerky nod. "Fine. I just…"

I entered the room and put my arms around her, giving her a quick hug. The fact her cheeks were flushed made me wonder what she'd been thinking about.

"You know you can tell me anything, right?" I asked.

"It's more of an ask," she mumbled. "Never mind. I'm not ready."

What the hell was she talking about? "If there's something you want or need, tell me. How am I supposed to help you if you hide stuff like that from me?"

She turned to face me, her cheeks flushing even more. "The only naked men I've seen were the ones who've hurt me. After seeing you shirtless last night, and touching you, it made me wonder what the rest of you looked like. But as much as I want to see, I'm scared too."

My cock started to harden at the thought of stripping my clothes off and having her soft hands touch me in other places. It twitched, and I knew if I didn't get my mind off those sorts of thoughts, I might damn well come in my pants. It had been far too long since I'd had sex with anyone or had a hand touching me that wasn't my own.

"Want to do this in baby steps?" I asked. I waited for her consent, then slowly tugged my shirt over my head.

She stared at my chest and reached out to touch me. Her fingertips lightly grazed my skin, and when she ran them over one of my nipples, I sucked in a breath and clenched my teeth. My dick got even harder and was now throbbing. No one had ever discovered that little secret about me... my nipples were even more sensitive than the head of my cock.

"Have you ever watched porn?" I asked.

"A few times, mostly because I couldn't fathom

anyone enjoying sex." She winced. "Although, a few of the movies were a little too much for me. Are there really things that go in your butt with tails attached?"

I coughed to cover my laugh. "Yeah, there are."

Her nose scrunched in the most adorable way, and I could tell she didn't understand why someone would be into that sort of thing. Although, now that she'd brought it up, I suddenly wanted to see her with a fox tail and a pair of ears. Jesus. I'd watched one too many anime movies. I blamed Royal. He'd gotten me hooked on the damn things. Some of them were essentially animated porn.

"Um. Probably not a good idea for me to remove anything else," I said.

"Why?"

I glanced down where my cock was pressing against my pants. She gasped and I looked up, seeing her eyes go wide. At the same time, there didn't seem to be any fear in her gaze. "Do you want me to take my jeans off? I have on underwear."

She nodded. "Wait. Is that all right? I don't want you to do anything you don't really want to do."

"Ares, if our situation was different, I'd already be balls-deep inside you, making every inch of you mine. You have no idea how much I've wanted you, *still* want you." I swallowed hard. "But I can control myself. I'm not going to pounce on you suddenly."

She reached for me, her hands trembling. She opened the button on my jeans, then slid down the zipper. I let her tug the denim over my hips and down my thighs. I wasn't sure if it was my own heartbeat or hers I could hear. With the gentlest touch ever, she reached out and traced a line down my cock. Even through the fabric of my boxer briefs, I felt the heat of her touch.

"Fuck! You have no idea how good that feels." She placed her entire hand over me, cupping both my cock and balls. I damn near exploded. "Ares, sweetheart... I think you better stop."

"Why?" she asked.

I ground my teeth together. "Because I'm really fucking close to coming."

She gave my cock a squeeze. *Shit!* I stumbled back a few steps, then bolted to the bathroom, nearly falling from my pants getting stuck around my knees. I couldn't even bother closing the door. Kicking off my pants and shoving my underwear to my ankles, I gripped my cock, tightening my hold around the base.

It pulsed in my hand, the head turning purple and pre-cum leaking from the tip. I was too damn close. There was no holding back right now. Bracing one hand on the vanity and stroking my dick with the other, I got myself off in less than fifteen seconds. Nothing to be proud of. Over my ragged breaths, I heard a sound in the hallway. Turning my head, I saw Ares... watching me.

Closing my eyes, I wondered how badly I just fucked up. *Way to go, asshole. You just had to push her for more, then scarred her for life by jerking off in plain sight.*

Not my best moment.

"Fuck, I'm sorry, Ares. You shouldn't have seen me like this."

"I feel strange," she murmured.

I glanced over at her and saw her nipples were hard and poking through the fabric of her pajamas. She pressed her thighs together, shifting from foot to foot.

"This is probably not a good question to ask right now, but have you ever made yourself come?" I asked. She slowly shook her head. "Do you sometimes touch yourself intimately?"

"Never," she said.

My next question could either get her one step closer to being whole again or send her a million miles back. It was a gamble, and I wasn't sure it was one I should take.

"Do you want to try?"

Her gaze dropped to my cock, which still hadn't gone completely limp. "Like what you did just now?"

"Something like that. Do you not know how?" I asked.

"Is it like they do in those porn movies?"

"Jesus. You're killing me." I shook my head. "None of that stuff is realistic, but if you were curious about anything you saw or want to try it, then there's no reason you can't."

"I don't even know how to start."

I was going to hell. Straight to fucking hell. Do not pass Go. Do not collect two hundred dollars.

"Close your eyes." She did as I said, and I kicked off my underwear before moving closer. I tugged her into the bathroom, and she came willingly. Standing behind her, I positioned her in front of the mirror over the sink. "Imagine you're the star in a porn movie. Your lover is behind you. The heat of his body pressing against yours. It's one of those cliché ones about the shy virgin, so you aren't ready to undress."

A little whimper escaped her lips and I saw the way her cheeks flushed and her lips parted. Looked like she was enjoying this. Maybe it was a good start to building a different sort of relationship with her and replacing her nightmares with happier memories.

I took her hands and placed them over her breasts. "Using his palms, he teases your nipples in slow circles, letting the fabric of your shirt scrape against them."

She felt stiff as I tried to help her move in the way I'd said, then she suddenly dropped them to her sides. "C-Can you do it?"

Every muscle in my body tensed. Was she serious right now? What if doing this hurt her more? It was one thing for her to touch herself, and another for me to do it. "Are you sure?"

She nodded and leaned into me. My dick started to harden again, and I hoped it didn't freak her out. I gave her breasts a light squeeze, testing the waters, so to speak. I didn't get any indication I was scaring her, so I rubbed my palms across her nipples the way I'd described.

"Does that feel good?" I asked.

"I… I feel weird."

"Good weird or bad weird?"

"Good, I think. I like the way it feels when you touch me like that, but I'm starting to tingle between my legs."

She was going to kill me. Seriously. The innocent way she talked about being turned-on made me want to yank her panties off, bend her over, and fuck her in front of the mirror. I wanted to see every expression she made, hear every cry of pleasure. I pinched one of her nipples, and she gave a little yelp, but I noticed she was arching her back and shoving her breasts into my hands.

"I can't do any more, Ares. I want to, but… I'm worried I won't be able to control myself. I refuse to do anything that might hurt or scare you." I dropped my hands from her breasts and stepped away from her. "If you still want to do this later, then we'll see how far you can go before it's too much. Right now, I think I need to shower so we can leave."

She wouldn't meet my gaze as she scurried from

the bathroom. I hoped like fuck I hadn't made her feel like I didn't want her. At the same time, I wasn't sure how to explain how dangerous this was without terrifying her.

Way to go, Prophet. You just treated that damaged girl like she was your own personal toy.

Sometimes, I really hated myself.

* * *

Ares

I still felt embarrassed over what we'd done earlier. No matter how many shops we went into, or fun things we tried, I couldn't get my mind off Prophet running from me so he could get himself off. That alone made him so different from every man who'd ever touched me. They would have forced their way into my body, made demands of me, and left me bleeding and wishing I were dead.

Feeling his hands on me had been a little scary, but also thrilling. I already knew I wanted to try again. Sex wasn't wrong if it was between two people who wanted it, right? Clearly, Prophet wanted me in that way, and I thought I wanted him too.

I shook the thoughts from my head as we stopped at a park. Prophet found a picnic table and carried over the bag of food we'd just picked up from a nearby deli. A breeze made the leaves of the trees rustle, and I watched the families and couples enjoying their time together.

We ate our food in silence, and I sipped my lemonade. It felt peaceful here. I didn't know how I'd feel once we went back home, but in Gulf Shores, I felt like I was healing one day at a time. After we finished, Prophet threw our trash away, and held out his hand to me.

"Ready to lose at mini golf?" he teased, drawing me to my feet with a tug on my hand.

"You wish," I shot back, and the challenge in his eyes made something inside me flutter to life. I'd missed this. We'd once bantered this way frequently. Did it mean I was slowly becoming the Ares I'd been before the Lathems took me? I hoped so.

The mini golf place wasn't far. Prophet paid for our game, and I lost. Not that it mattered. Doing something fun with him was the important thing. Afterward, we went to a few more stores before heading back to the house.

We changed into our swimsuits and walked down to the water. I still felt self-conscious, but I'd discovered people weren't staring at me the way I'd thought they were. Everyone minded their own business, and I managed to relax and enjoy myself.

Prophet chased me into the shallows, and I turned to face him, my heart pounding in a way that had nothing to do with fear and everything to do with the excitement I felt when I was with this man. He smiled, and it held a world of promises. I knew he'd wait, however long it took, before I was ready to completely be his. I didn't know how I'd gotten lucky enough for someone like him to want me.

He charged at me, and I squealed, running off. It didn't take him long to catch me, his arms going around my waist.

"Gotcha!" He spun me around, then lifted me and dropped me into the water.

"Hey!" I protested, slinging my wet hair out of my face. "No fair!"

As the sun began to dip below the horizon, I realized I'd been having fun and hadn't thought about the suffering I'd experienced. Right now, I wasn't the

Ares who'd been kidnapped and held captive. I was just… the woman who loved Prophet.

"Thank you," I whispered as we walked back to the house, leaving wet footprints in the sand.

"For what?" Prophet asked.

"For this," I said, gesturing at the fading light, the beach, the ocean. "For today. Everything."

He squeezed my hand, and I knew without looking that he was smiling. "Anytime, Ares. Anytime."

Chapter Eight

Prophet

"Prophet?" Her voice trembled, and I wondered what she was going to ask. "Can we… can we go to the bedroom?"

I'd worried I'd gone too far earlier. Now it seemed like she wanted more. Was she pushing her boundaries, trying to see what she could handle before she broke? I'd give her whatever she needed, but I wasn't sure I liked the idea of her trying things she wasn't quite ready for yet.

"Only if you're sure." Did she even know what she was asking for? Or was I reading too much into her request?

She nodded and stood. I switched off the TV and took her hand, lacing our fingers together. Leading her to the bedroom I'd been using, I fought the urge to ask once more if this was really what she wanted. If she changed her mind, she knew she could tell me. I'd told her often enough I wouldn't take more than she wanted to give, and that we'd go at her pace.

The room was dim, the moonlight filtering through the windows. I hadn't bothered to make the bed this morning and the covers were tossed to the end of the mattress. I turned to face her, reaching up to cup her cheek. I brushed my thumb over her bottom lip.

"Ares, you can still walk away."

"Kiss me," she said, sounding desperate. I didn't know what was driving her right now, but I wouldn't tell her no. She could have whatever she wanted.

I nodded and leaned in slowly, my lips brushing against hers gently. The kiss was soft, tentative, and she closed her eyes as we explored each other's mouths. I felt her shudder slightly as I deepened the kiss, sliding my tongue against hers. Her hands went to my chest, then she eased one up to my neck, pulling me closer. Her small frame pressed against mine as if she needed the contact as much as I did.

I moved us over to the bed, sitting down with her in my lap. Her legs wrapped around my waist, and I groaned at the feel of her soft skin against mine. The moment it felt like she was starting to panic, I'd stop. It amazed me she'd made this much progress already. As much as I wanted this moment to never end, I didn't want her to feel pressured to be intimate.

"Still okay?" I murmured, trailing my lips down her neck, sucking lightly on the sensitive skin there before moving to her collarbone. She smelled like strawberries and vanilla.

"Prophet," she moaned, arching into my touch. "I'm fine. Please don't stop."

I saw the desire in her eyes, and grinned. Her fingers dug into my hair as I placed featherlight kisses along her ribcage, making my way toward her breasts. My right hand cupped one of them through the thin fabric of her tank top, finding the nipple already hard beneath it. She gasped as I rolled it between my fingers teasingly before pulling away to remove her top entirely.

I froze, wondering if I'd taken things too far. The flush on her cheeks, and the warmth in her eyes were reassuring. I tried really fucking hard to ignore her beautiful breasts. My mouth practically watered with the need to taste her.

"I'll let you know if it's too much." She bit her bottom lip. "But I really want this, Prophet."

"You know my name. When are you going to call me Hunter?"

"Hunter," she said softly.

She was absolutely stunning. Her small breasts with their pink nipples stood proudly against my touch as I ran my tongue along them and then teased one with my teeth for a moment before sucking hard enough to make a soft noise escape from her throat. A shudder racked her body, and she gave a soft cry.

Ares moaned softly as my lips met hers again, my tongue teasing her bottom lip before sliding inside her mouth. She opened up for me, as if she needed the connection just as much as I did. Her hands raked through my hair, pulling me closer. I held her tightly, feeling an urgency I'd never experienced before.

We broke apart, both of us in desperate need of air.

"More," she whispered.

It was a demand I couldn't ignore. I trailed kisses down her jaw and neck until I reached the hollow of her throat. She arched into my touch, gasping softly when I sucked on her skin. She whimpered softly, the sound of her need filling the room.

"Do you really want this?" I asked between breaths. "Because I'll stop if it's too much."

She nodded. Her lips parted and her breath came out in little pants.

"Prove it," I murmured before stripping off my shirt and tossing it aside. It wasn't the first time she'd seen me without a shirt on, but the appreciation in her eyes still made me feel like a fucking king.

I tossed her onto the bed and settled over her, wondering how I'd gotten so lucky.

"You're so beautiful," I whispered against her skin, before returning to kissing my way down her body. My tongue danced around her belly button before I moved over the soft skin of her hips and into the waistband of her panties.

Slowly, I eased them down her legs, giving her ample time to stop me. When she just stared at me with complete trust, I removed them completely and let them drop to the floor.

I pressed a soft kiss to her inner thigh. "I love you so much, Ares."

She gasped when I parted the lips of her pussy and teased her with my tongue. She tasted like paradise, sweet and sour all at once. My fingers found her entrance, slipping inside and finding how wet she was. She was ready for me, more than ready. But I knew she'd never experienced pleasure before. I wanted her to come before I took things any further.

Ares's hips bucked. "More! I can handle more. I'm not scared, Hunter. I know it's you, and I want this so much."

I added another finger, and she took it all, moaning softly. She looked like a fucking goddess. My other hand found her mouth, feeling her warmth on my fingers as I brought them to her lips. She didn't pull away and sucked gently, eyes meeting mine.

"Oh fuck," I groaned, feeling a mix of emotions washing over me. Pure lust, fear at what we were doing, and love for this woman beneath me. She kept surprising me, in the best of ways.

I positioned myself at her entrance, my cock hard against her pussy as I pushed inside. She gasped as I started to thrust slowly, watching her face for any signs of distress. Her skin was flushed and sweaty. I took my time, savoring the moment, and trying to draw out the pleasure for her.

She cried out softly when I changed the angle, the head of my cock rubbing inside her in a different spot. Her nails scratched lightly at my back as she lifted her hips, taking me in deeper. I felt her tighten around me, then the heat of her release as she cried out my name.

I devoured her lips with mine, my strokes becoming erratic as I neared my own climax. I broke the kiss and watched the emotions playing over her face.

"You feel so good, Hunter. Don't stop." She met me thrust for thrust, her hips undulating with each stroke. Our kisses were heated and sensual, with just the right amount of bruise to them.

I took her harder, no longer holding back. As I pounded into her, she clung to me, making the sweetest sounds. I couldn't last another second and I groaned as I came inside her, filling her up. We hadn't discussed kids, but she was mine and I knew she wanted a family. The thought of her round with my child made my cock twitch inside her.

Pulling out, I fell to the bed beside her and tugged her into my arms. "Still doing okay?"

"I'm fine, Hunter. That was perfect."

"I didn't trigger any past memories or cause you any pain?" I asked.

She lightly touched my chin. "No, you didn't. I love you. More than anything in the world, and I'm so glad I'm yours."

I kissed her softly. "I'm never letting you go, Arcs. You're mine now and forever."

I held her close and listened as her breathing eventually slowed and she fell asleep. I'd taken a gamble, and this could have backfired in the worst way. My woman was so strong and amazing. I'd never met anyone like her before.

When she was ready, we'd go home. Until then, we'd enjoy our time at the beach. If she had any setbacks, or panicked, we could always pay a visit to the doctors next door. They'd decided to extend their vacation until we left, in case Ares needed them. I really owed them for this.

"Hunter," she whispered. I looked down and noticed her eyes were still closed.

"Sleep," I murmured.

She nestled closer, her warmth seeping into me. She looked peaceful, and I hoped she wouldn't have any nightmares. I wish there were a magic pill she could take that would wipe away all the ugliness in her past. Since there wasn't, I'd do my best to help her in whatever way I could.

Chapter Nine

Prophet

Days melded into each other, a blend of salt and sun, as we found solace in the beach and one another. We swam until our limbs grew heavy, basked in the sunlight until our skin turned shades darker, and strolled through the nearby town, hand in hand, as if we were just any other couple seeking summer's simple joys.

I could feel the sand clinging to my toes, grains rough against the soles of my feet. I felt at peace here, and I thought Ares did too. I knew we couldn't stay forever. The days had turned into weeks, and then months. We'd been here far longer than I'd anticipated. There were times I'd wondered if Ares would ever be ready to go home. The club knew why we were gone, and they supported the both of us. Although, Savior probably wouldn't be happy to hear I'd claimed his daughter. He'd known it was coming, but I still should have given him a heads-up or asked his permission.

My gaze settled on a vendor nearby, an old man with stooped shoulders and wrinkled hands. He sold oysters, their shells gritty and raw, plucked from the depths of the sea that morning. An inexplicable urge took hold of me, a need to gift Ares something symbolic of our time here.

"Hey," I called out to her, nodding toward the stall. "What do you think about taking a bit of the ocean back home with us?"

I'd already been in touch with Wire, letting him know we'd be returning soon. It was time. I knew Ares felt apprehensive about it.

Ares approached, her stride confident. I'd never thought I'd see the sight again. Warmth filled me as I watched her. She inspected the oysters, turning one over in her palm, her fingers tracing the rugged lines.

"Sure," she said with a half-smile.

I picked up an oyster, its surface mottled and slightly iridescent, and handed the vendor some bills.

"Here," I said, offering the oyster to Ares. Her hand brushed against mine as she took it, and the jolt of contact sent shivers up my spine. Since the first time she'd given herself to me, we'd been intimate countless times. In fact, I had a hard time keeping my hands off her.

"Thanks, Prophet," she murmured, looking at the oyster as if it was a treasure. She had no idea I intended to do something with it later. It wasn't like she could take an unopened oyster home. The thing wouldn't last more than week, even if she put it in water.

"If you're only getting the one, I'm going to assume you don't plan to eat it. Do you want me to open it?" the vendor asked. "Some have a pearl inside."

"That would be great," I said. Ares handed it back to him, and he sliced it open.

He'd been right. There really was a pearl inside. A pretty pink one. Rather large at that. He gave the empty shell back to Ares and leaned in to whisper to me.

"You could take it to the local jeweler. He can shine it up and put it in a ring or necklace for your wife."

Wife. I liked the sound of that. I glanced at Ares. Maybe I could turn the pearl into an engagement ring.

"Thank you," I told him, sliding the pearl into my pocket.

"Isn't that mine?" Ares asked as we walked off.

"I'll give it back later."

We continued our walk and returned to the house a short while later. I convinced Ares to shower and take a nap, and while she dozed, I quietly left the house. I knew which jeweler the vendor meant. I'd seen their shop in town.

I entered the small store, the bell jingling over the door.

"Can I help you?" asked the jeweler, a middle-aged man with a balding head and friendly eyes.

"I need a ring made," I said, voice low, my usual confidence faltering at the admission of my intentions. She'd agreed to be mine, but in our world, that didn't always mean marriage. What if she didn't accept an engagement ring from me?

"Let's see what we're working with," he responded, professional interest replacing any surprise at my appearance -- tattooed arms and all.

I drew the pearl from my pocket, feeling its slightly bumpy surface one last time before placing it on the counter. It didn't look very impressive on top of the glass cabinet housing diamonds, rubies, and other precious stones.

"An engagement ring," I clarified, knowing full well the stakes. If this went wrong, if Ares said no, I wasn't sure how I'd come back from it. Regardless, she was mine, and I was hers.

"Unique," I added, almost as an afterthought.

The jeweler picked up the pearl, eyes narrowing as he examined it closely. The longer he studied it, the more nervous I became.

"We can do unique," he finally said, a note of respect in his voice -- I wasn't sure if it was for the pearl or the task, or maybe for the love behind my request.

"Thank you," I said.

The jeweler leaned in, studying the pearl some more. My nervousness spiked again, as I worried something was wrong.

"Remarkable," he finally whispered. "Could make something… exceptional."

"Show me," I said, eager to see what he envisioned for the ring I'd give Ares.

He sketched rapidly on a pad, lines flowing into curves, the design taking shape before my eyes. He added etchings of flowers, which I assumed he planned to engrave on the band.

"Like this," he said, holding the drawing up. "A band that echoes the pearl's strength and purity."

I stared at the design. It resembled Ares. Her soft side, and her strength. "Perfect. Let's do it."

"Give me a few days," the jeweler said, his own excitement a mirror to mine.

"Thank you," I managed, the weight of the moment settling over me. This ring -- it was a vow, a pledge to face whatever hell might come, together.

I returned to the house, slipping back in before Ares woke. She'd never know I'd been gone, or what I'd been up to. Not until the time was right.

* * *

Days slipped by, and I kept myself busy. Ares laughed more, her guard lowering with every sunset we watched bleed into the horizon. And yet, I could feel the tension coiling within me. It was time. The ring was supposed to be ready today, which meant I'd be proposing to the woman I loved.

"Is it ready?" I asked the jeweler. His nod was all the confirmation I needed. He unveiled the ring, and it was like gazing upon a reflection of Ares herself. The pink pearl sat nestled among tendrils of silver, strong yet delicate. I couldn't have imagined a more perfect ring for her.

"Beautiful," I whispered. I lifted it from the box, admiring it from every angle.

"May it bring you both joy," he said, and I could see the glint of respect in his eyes. "If it's not too bold of me to say so, I don't get many bikers in here. I'm glad to see a hardened man such as yourself still has a softer side when it comes to the woman you love."

"Thank you," I replied. Perhaps I should have felt offended by the way he viewed men like me, but I understood where he was coming from. Not everyone in a leather cut had the same values as the Dixie Reapers.

I left the shop with the ring burning a hole in my pocket. What if the scars of Ares' past were too deep? What if my love wasn't enough to eclipse the darkness that still lingered in her eyes every now and then? She'd healed, and was doing so much better than before, but I wasn't sure she was entirely whole, and I knew she might never be.

But her smile had brightened, and her laughter sounded full of joy. She'd been carefree most days this month. She'd been to hell, but perhaps she'd finally made it back to me. It had been a while since she'd had a nightmare.

I prayed to every known god that when I asked her to marry me, she'd say yes.

I pulled to a stop in the driveway of the beach house and turned off the engine. Making my way up to the deck, movement on the beach caught my attention. I saw Ares, staring out across the water. I removed my boots and socks, rolled up my jeans, and walked down the steps, my feet sinking into the sand with every step I took.

"Come on," I urged gently, reaching for her hand. Our fingers laced together, fitting as perfectly as I hoped our lives would.

"Isn't it beautiful?" she asked.

"More than you know," I answered, my throat tight as we walked. I knew she'd meant the water, but I'd meant *her*. Before we made our way back to the house, I paused.

"Prophet?" Her voice, tinged with curiosity, pulled me from my thoughts.

"It's nothing," I lied, squeezing her hand a little tighter. "Just enjoying the moment."

The salty breeze, the cries of the gulls, the endless blue -- it all faded into the background. Only Ares and the ring burning in my pocket mattered. This was it. The perfect moment.

My heart hammered against my ribcage, every beat a drumroll to the moment I had been steeling myself for.

"Let's stop for a second," I said.

She turned toward me, a question in her gaze. "Prophet, are you sure you're all right?"

I steadied my breath, reaching into the pocket of my jeans. I dropped to one knee, opened the jewelry box, and showed her the ring inside.

"Ares, you've walked through hell and came out the other side with a fire that burns so bright, it puts the sun to shame. Your strength has always amazed me. *You* amaze me. There are so many reasons to love you. You've faced everything head-on, never backing down or giving up. Ares... Will you join me on the adventure of a lifetime? Will you be my wife?"

Tears gathered in her eyes and her lips trembled. I worried she was about to reject me, but she let out a soft sob before dropping to her knees in front of me.

Her hand shook as she held it out. "Of course, I'll marry you. I love you, Hunter."

I slid the ring onto her finger and brushed my lips against hers. I drew back and smoothed her hair from her face. Ares' hand trembled as she admired the ring on her finger.

"It's beautiful," she whispered.

I cupped her face in my hands. "Not nearly as beautiful as you."

Her eyes misted again and she threw her arms around my neck. "I love you so much, Hunter."

Ares admired the ring again. "I can't believe we're doing this. I never thought…"

I tucked a strand of hair behind her ear. "You deserve all the happiness in the world, Ares. And I intend to spend my life giving it to you. I know in our world marriage isn't really necessary. But this was something I wanted to give you. I want you to be mine in every way possible."

She smiled warmly. "I don't need anything except you."

I kissed her again, then we returned to the house, hand in hand. She led me to the bedroom and slid the cut off my shoulders. After gently putting it aside, she worked on the rest of my clothes, removing them one item at a time.

I groaned as her fingers teased down my spine, her nails raking against my skin. I growled, unable to control myself any longer.

"Ares," I breathed in her ear, "I want you so damn bad."

"Good," she murmured low. "Because I want you too."

Her lips met mine, and we fell into a ravenous kiss. It was rough and messy, but it felt like coming home. I pulled at her clothes until she was bare, before pushing her against the wall. Our bodies fit together like two halves of the same whole.

She led me to the bed, and pushed me down onto the mattress, tasting every inch of my skin. I couldn't believe this woman was now mine. My Ares... She'd become so bold since our first time together, and I looked forward to what our future would hold.

She straddled my hips and braced her hands on my chest. Reaching between us, I lined my cock up with her pussy, and she slowly took me into her body.

Ares moaned as she rocked against me. I gripped her hips and surged upward, controlling her motions. She tossed her head back, her hips undulating as she rode me.

Within minutes, she came, her pussy gripping my cock as the heat of her release triggered my own orgasm. I thrust up into her, taking what I wanted. My balls drew up, and I urged her to ride me faster as I came inside her.

We lay entwined afterward, breathing hard, our chests rising and falling in tandem. Ares smiled at me. "Do you have any idea how happy you make me?"

"Hopefully it's at least as half as happy as *you* make *me*." I kissed her again, then held her close, wanting the moment to last forever.

"We should go back," she murmured. "It's time I faced everyone."

"If you're ready, then we can pack tonight and head out in the morning. I'll let the owners of the house know, as well as the doctors next door." I didn't know how the club had managed to convince them to stay this long, but I knew they had to have had a hand in it. Both men had been a big help in getting Ares back on her feet.

She pressed her lips together. "There's something I need to confess."

I leaned up on my elbow and looked down at her. "What is it? Whatever you have to say, you know I won't be mad, right? You make it seem like you've committed some horrible sin."

She took a breath and slowly let it out before holding my gaze. "I'm pregnant, Hunter. I asked Dr. Myron to do a pregnancy test, and he confirmed the results yesterday. I just didn't know how to tell you."

I placed my hand on her belly, and marveled at the fact our child was growing inside her. "You've made me the happiest of men, Ares."

She reached up and placed her hand on my cheek. "You're the one who makes me happy, Hunter. I will love you until the day I die."

I hoped that wasn't going to happen for a long, long time. The day she'd disappeared from the compound, I'd nearly lost my mind. All the time it took to track her down had felt like agony. I knew I wouldn't be able to survive without her. She was my entire world, and if she were to leave me, I'd have no reason to keep living.

Chapter Ten

Ares

We were home. Passing through the gates of the Dixie Reapers compound, I felt anxious over seeing my family again, and terrified people would look at me differently. Logically, I knew they would, but I didn't *feel* like the same person I'd been before. Too much had happened.

My heart hammered against my ribs. I could feel the eyes on us before I even swung my leg over the bike, the weight of their stares pressing down on me. The scents and sounds of the compound should have felt familiar, relaxing even, but today it was anything but.

"Easy, Ares," Prophet murmured as he steadied me with his large hands. His touch was meant to be reassuring, but it couldn't chase away the coiling tension in my gut. I'd thought I was ready to come back. What if I was wrong?

We walked side by side toward the clubhouse, boots crunching on the gravel. I knew every face that turned our way. Yet now, their gazes bored into me, sharp and probing, sending shivers skittering across my skin.

"Prophet." The voice cut through the murmurs around us. My father, Savior, stood framed in the doorway of the clubhouse, arms crossed over his broad chest. His stern expression was one I knew all too well -- the one that spelled trouble.

"Pres," Prophet said, his voice respectful but firm. He released my hand to stand alone, facing down the President of the Dixie Reapers.

"Good to see Ares home safe," Savior said, his tone flat, eyes drilling into Prophet's. "But you took your sweet time getting back here. Care to explain why?"

I wanted to speak up, to defend Prophet, but the words tangled up in my throat. Fear kept them locked tight, fear of what admitting the truth might bring upon us both. I hadn't reached out to my family even once while we'd been gone. I knew Prophet had been in contact, which made me curious why my dad was acting like this. He'd known I wasn't in any sort of shape to be here until now. Unless he hadn't trusted the things Prophet had told him.

"Needed to make sure she was okay," Prophet replied. "Wasn't going to rush her after --"

"Enough!" Savior snapped, cutting him off. The air and my pulse raced. Why was my dad so angry?

"I assure you --" Prophet started again, but a hard look from Savior silenced him.

"Assurances don't mean squat to me, boy. Actions do." Savior's gaze flicked to me then, and the unasked questions in his steely gray eyes set my blood to ice. Somehow, he knew things had changed between me and Prophet. He'd seemed okay with Prophet claiming me once I became of age, but now I had to wonder if he was really all right with it. It didn't seem like he was.

The compound felt like it was closing in around us. I wanted to hide behind Prophet or beg him to take me somewhere else. This was too much too soon.

"Let's go inside," I finally managed to say, the shakiness of my voice belying my emotions. "We can talk there."

Savior held Prophet's gaze for a beat longer, then nodded once, sharply, and turned back into the clubhouse. Prophet reached for me, his touch a lifeline. Together, we followed my father into the belly of the beast, where our fate waited. It had never occurred to me Savior might disapprove of our relationship. What if he tried to tear us apart?

The three of us sat at a table in the corner. I scooted my chair closer to Prophet's, which had my dad's eyes narrowing.

"You know how I feel about Ares," Prophet said. "I love her, and I haven't made it a secret. Everyone here is aware of my feelings. I'm not sure why you're so angry, Pres."

"You never once let me talk to my daughter while the two of you were gone. When you said she needed some time, I thought you'd be gone a week, maybe two. Not over two fucking months!" He slammed his fist on the table. "Do you have any idea what it's been like? Dessa and the kids keep asking about her, and want to know when she's coming home, and all I could do was tell them *I don't know*."

"That's my fault, not his," I said. "Even after I told him I was ready to come home, I nearly changed my mind once we got here. Even now…"

I held up my hand, showing him how badly I was shaking. My dad closed his eyes and pinched the bridge of his nose. This wasn't like him. He'd never acted this way, except for the time I got caught texting Dylan. He'd nearly blown up then.

"I need you to calm down, Pres," Prophet said, his voice low and easy. "It's not good for her to be stressed out like this. And it's definitely not good for the baby."

A hush fell over the place. My dad's face started to turn purple, I wondered how many pieces of broken furniture would be left in his wake. He didn't lose his temper often, but when he did, he went all out.

Tempest stood and came closer, his gaze locked

onto Prophet. "Do you really think you played fair? She had no choice but to rely on you. It was just the two of you all that time, which meant it was inevitable she'd grow even closer to you, and now she's pregnant? I thought she needed to heal. If you fucking took advantage of her…"

Tempest let the threat hang in the air, and I knew without a doubt if Prophet had truly harmed me, no one here would hesitate to lay him out. Especially Tempest. He might not always like the women who came here and ended up being old ladies, but I was the daughter of not only a patched member, but the club's President. Tempest had always been overly protective of me. Same with the other kids.

"Shut it, Tempest," Royal said, standing and moving closer. "Prophet has been by her side for over a year. He's taken care of her, and I'm sure the two got close long before this happened. If you ask me, it was inevitable. Hell, I doubt I'm the only one who thinks that. Pretty sure most of us figured he'd claim her and they'd live happily ever after. Just without all the extra bullshit she's had to endure."

My dad slowly stood, bracing his hands on the table. "You go after my girl, take her someplace where none of us can see her, and bring her home pregnant? Are you fucking kidding me?"

The air crackled with the kind of tension that spelled trouble in big neon letters. I needed to get my dad to calm down, except I didn't know how. Fumbling with the phone in my pocket, I sent a text to my mom. *Dad is about to lose it in the clubhouse.*

I saw she read the message, but she didn't respond. I hoped that meant she was on her way, although I knew she couldn't get here quickly. Her wheelchair made it difficult for her to hop in the car. It wasn't impossible. Just harder than it was for people with working legs. Even all these years later, she had trouble transferring. Dad always helped her when he was around.

The clubhouse doors swung open a few minutes later, and I stared with wide eyes as I watched Wire and Lavender come in, with my mom clinging to Wire's back like a monkey. I bit my lips, trying to stifle the laugh that bubbled up.

"Savior, so help me, if you scare our daughter off when we haven't seen her in months, you're going to sleep outside," she said as Wire eased her down into the chair beside my dad.

"What the fuck, Dessa?" He narrowed his eyes at Wire, but the hacker just shrugged and took a step back. Lavender came over to me and patted my shoulder. I reached up to take her hand, grateful for the support.

"Our daughter sent a text that you were about to lose your shit," she said.

My dad stared at her. "Did you just cuss?"

"It seemed appropriate. Besides, it's not like I never say bad words."

My dad glared at me before turning back to Mom. "Did she also tell you that she's pregnant?"

Mom paled, and I knew she'd jumped to the wrong conclusion. I glanced at Prophet who gave my hand a squeeze.

"It's mine," Prophet said. "And no, I didn't take advantage of her. I asked her repeatedly if she was sure. The last thing I'd ever do is hurt Ares. I also asked her to marry me."

The color came back to Mom's face, and she gave us a smile. "Well, in that case, this is good news, isn't it? The two of you have been close since before Ares turned eighteen. I was honestly surprised you didn't try to claim her the second she was of legal age."

"Will you stop?" Dad growled as he looked at Prophet again. "I gave you permission to hang out with Ares, and to date her when she was ready. No one said a fucking thing about you knocking her up. Considering the amount of trust I gave you when it comes to my daughter, couldn't you have at least attempted to play things by the book? My permission didn't extend quite that far."

"Dad, you do realize he's not the only one to blame, right? It's not like he forced me to have sex with him."

Dad held up a hand. "No. Just… no. I don't want to hear that word in relation to you. Ever. When you give me grandchildren, I'd like to think the stork dropped them off. If I think about the real reason you have kids, I may murder that boy sitting next to you."

I rolled my eyes, all the tension draining from me. "Dad, seriously? First of all, he's not a boy. And secondly, should I ask where Junie came from? Because I doubt she was grown in a cabbage patch or delivered by a bird."

"That's different."

No, it really wasn't. I got it, though. I was his little girl, and he didn't want to think about me doing naughty things with a man. Didn't matter if that guy happened to be an officer in the club and one of his most trusted men. When it came to me, no one would ever be good enough.

"He helped me heal, Dad. You have no idea what I went through, and I really don't want to tell you. I felt so broken I wasn't sure I'd ever be the same Ares you once knew. Prophet helped me put the pieces back together and helped make me strong again."

Prophet leaned in and kissed my temple. "No, sweetheart. You were already strong. All you needed was a reminder."

"Are you taking Ares to your house?" Mom asked. "You haven't been there in two months. Does it need to be aired out? Fridge cleaned?"

"I took care of it already," Lavender said. "Once we knew they were heading back, I went over to make sure everything would be ready for them. We might have hacked into his shopping apps to figure out what sort of items they'd been buying."

I felt Prophet tense next to me and I leaned into him. The amused look Lavender shot me told me she'd realized something had been missing off the list -- condoms.

"Dr. Myron and Dr. Sykes were vacationing in the house next to ours," I said. "Dr. Myron already checked me over, ran some blood tests, and he's the one who confirmed my pregnancy. And Dr. Sykes gave me unofficial counseling during the two months we were there."

My dad sighed. "Fine. I can see I'm outnumbered. But you need to come by the house if not tonight, then tomorrow. The kids need to see you. They've been worried."

"Pres, I know you aren't happy about this, but please know Ares is everything to me. Her and our child. I'd walk through fire for them, go straight to hell and fight the devil, or die if that's what it took to keep them safe."

My dad stared at him for the longest time. I wanted to chime in that I didn't like that last part about him dying for me. If he did that, what would be the point of me living? Placing a hand over my still flat belly, I realized I'd have to push through the pain because I now had someone depending on me.

"Words are cheap, boy," Dad finally responded, his voice low and controlled. "Love isn't worth a damn without action to back it up. I realize you care for my daughter, and you put a lot on the line to go rescue her. Even took care of her for two months. But your job doesn't end there. Two months compared to a lifetime? That's nothing."

"Then watch me," Prophet challenged, his jaw set. "Watch how I protect what is mine. You've known me a long time now, Pres. You know I'm not a man who bends or breaks. I'll stand by Ares, today, tomorrow... forever."

Wire sighed. "Pres, I think it's time to stand down on this one. You did your job by raising Ares and protecting her. Now it's his turn. Got to let her go."

Lavender elbowed him. "Will I have to remind you of those words when it's Livvy's turn?"

Wire glared at his woman. "I will examine every inch of that man's life, and if he's found lacking in any way, I'll fucking crush him before he gets a chance to make a move on our girl."

She shook her head and laughed softly. "All right, Papa Bear. Take it easy. Besides, you aren't the only one who plans to thoroughly check out the guys she brings home. Don't forget, your wife is rather skilled with a computer too."

Wire tugged her against his side, his arm going around her waist. "Never said you weren't."

"Then let our actions speak for us," Prophet said. "We've already faced a lot. Whatever comes our way, we'll handle it together. Ares isn't someone who will stand in my shadow. Her place is beside me."

Mom smiled. "I knew I liked him. Come on,

Savior. Take me home, and let these two get settled in. Ares, I'll gather some of your things and have someone drop them off within the hour. You can come pack the rest tomorrow."

Chapter Eleven
Prophet

Our return home hadn't gone quite the way I'd thought it would. I'd expected Savior to hug his daughter and give her a warm welcome. Instead, he'd been pissed at me, which had upset Ares. I'd do whatever it took to make her feel safe again. I worried all the progress we'd made was about to go down the drain.

"Let's go home, Ares," I murmured, giving her hand a squeeze.

The farther we got from the clubhouse and Savior, the less tense Ares became. I drove us straight to the house and let her go inside while I unstrapped the duffle from the bike and carried it to the bedroom. We'd washed everything before we packed it, so all we needed to do was put them up.

I hoped this house would be a sanctuary for her. It had been in the past. Even if the rest of the compound put her on edge right now, I needed this space to be a place she could stay without feeling as if she was being judged.

Ares stood in the living room. Everything remained the same as it had been the last time she came over. I winced when I realized it was *exactly* the same, which meant I'd need to change the bed and wash the sheets. Lavender may have stopped by, but I doubted she'd gone quite that far. Dusting, mopping, cleaning counters, and stocking the fridge had probably been more along the lines of what she'd taken care of. Once Ares had gone missing, I hadn't really thought about general housekeeping things. Besides, I'd liked the fact my bed smelled like her. Not that we'd shared it before, but she'd taken a nap here more than once.

"Safe," she whispered, looking around the house. My heart ached for her. If her dad wasn't the club president, I'd go back and kick his ass. Did he have any idea the damage he'd done to his daughter today? Fucking asshole!

"Always," I said. "No one will ever hurt you in this house, Ares. It's our place. Yours and mine."

I gently led her to the couch and made her sit. Handing her the remote, I went to the bedroom and quickly stripped the bed and remade it, I went to toss the sheets into the washer before I joined Ares again. Taking a seat next to her, I pulled her against me. A motorcycle drove past the house, and she immediately tensed, her gaze shooting over to the front door. I hated that she felt so unwelcome. Yeah, I definitely needed to hand Savior's ass to him. What the fuck was wrong with him?

Another engine came by the house, but this time, it sounded like they were pulling into the driveway. If I wasn't mistaken, it was one of the club trucks. What the fuck was it now? I hoped it was only the clothes Dessa said she'd send over for Ares, but after the welcome we'd received, I couldn't be sure.

"Stay here," I said, standing and heading to the door.

When I opened the door and saw Sam on the other side, I relaxed. If anyone here would be supportive of Ares, it would be him. While his daughter hadn't gone through quite the same thing, she'd been a victim just like Ares.

"Sorry to interrupt," he said. "Just dropping off a box of stuff for Ares."

"Thank you," she said softly from where she sat in the living room. I wasn't sure he heard her, until he flashed a smile in her direction.

"Where do you want me to put it?" he asked. "Or would it be better if I didn't come inside?"

"It's okay," Ares said, her voice still so low I could barely hear her.

I motioned for him to come inside, and he carried the box to the hall. I told him which room was mine, and he placed it inside the door. He gave Ares a little wave as he left the house, and I shut the door behind him, twisting the lock. I'd never really locked the doors here before, but I thought it was best for Ares.

"You don't have to deal with that stuff right now. We can just relax tonight."

She shook her head. "Better to get it out of the way."

I held her hand on the way to the bedroom, then opened the box to see what Dessa had sent over. On top lay a picture of Ares with her family. She quickly looked away and I realized it was too soon to put the photo out. Instead, I tucked it in my bedside table drawer.

We worked in silence, sorting her items and putting them into the dresser or closet. When Lavender had checked my fridge, she'd apparently come in here too. I hadn't had a drawer emptied before, or the closet organized in a way that would leave room for Ares' items. But both were ready for her. I really did owe Lavender and Wire a lot.

Right after we put away the last of her things, Ares looked around the room, her hands trembling. I lifted her into my arms and she buried her face against me. Carrying her to the living room, I sat with her on the couch again, giving her the remote. I didn't care what we watched. She could put on whatever would make her feel less stressed over being here.

She cuddled closer, and I wondered if the situation with Savior was going to cause more of a setback in her recovery than I'd thought. Not that she didn't like being close to me even when she was having an amazing day. This time it felt more like she needed me to comfort her. Much like she had in those first days we'd been in Gulf Shores.

I didn't know if she was actually watching the TV or not, but I let the movie play. She'd chosen a romantic comedy, and I figured she needed something lighthearted like that. As long as we were spending time together, I didn't really care what we watched.

I shifted my hand so I could trace lazy circles over her arm. At the beach house, I'd discovered doing things like this seemed to help her. It would pull her from whatever dark thoughts were haunting her. She leaned in closer, practically gluing herself to my side, and I used my other hand to trace patterns on her thigh.

She sighed and closed her eyes.

"Better?" I asked.

"Getting there," she whispered. "You seem to always know exactly what I need, even before I do."

I wasn't sure what to say to that. While I liked knowing I could offer that to her, I hated the fact she needed me to. If I could go back and change things, I'd have stopped her from going home that day. Maybe if I'd been there when she left Joker's house, I could have walked her home, and I'd have noticed the cut in the fence. It would have allowed us to take the Lathems down then and there. Or I could have invited her over to my place.

But I couldn't time travel, and I couldn't erase the things that happened to Ares. All I could do was be here for her, give her my support, and make sure she knew she wasn't alone, no matter how bad things got.

"Thank you," she said. "For everything. Saving me. Giving me time to process what happened to me. Just… thanks for being you."

"That's not something you should say thank you for. I love you, Ares. Everything I've done is because you're my other half, the one person in this world who means the most to me. Seeing you happy makes *me* happy. So don't make me out to be some angel or some shit. I was being selfish and nothing more."

She smiled a little and turned her face into me, breathing me in. "Can we stay like this a while longer?"

"I don't have any plans. You?"

"No."

"Then I guess you have your answer." I watched the movie she'd put on, and when it was time to start the next one, I realized she'd fallen asleep.

I went ahead and watched a second movie to make sure she was actually sleeping. When she didn't budge the entire time, even though I'd put on one of her favorites, I knew it was time to turn off the lights and head to bed.

I stood and lifted her into my arms, carrying her to the bed. After I placed her on the bed, I stripped off her leggings, managed to somehow remove her bra without waking her up, and left her to sleep in her T-shirt and panties. I smoothed her hair back from her face, then kissed her forehead.

"I'll be right back."

I quickly went back to the living room to shut off the TV, turned off any lights we'd switched on, and double-checked the doors and windows. Even though the compound was safer than your average neighborhood, we'd all learned just how easily it was for someone to distract us and sneak inside. I hadn't said anything to Ares, but I'd noticed some of the fence had been replaced with a brick one while we'd been gone. I wondered if Savior was going to do the entire compound like that. From a distance, it had looked like there were spikes along the top of the bricks. I still didn't think that would be enough to keep anyone out.

I'd have asked Savior about it if he hadn't been such a dick when we got here. Plenty of time to check-in with Saint tomorrow. I knew he'd tell me what was going on, without the extra drama. Although, I hoped Dessa had made her point tonight. If anyone could make Savior back down, it was her.

Returning to the bedroom, I stripped down to my underwear, then slid under the covers, pulling Ares into my arms.

"Thank you," she whispered. I didn't know what the hell she was thanking me for now. I just kissed her on the forehead again, and hoped she had a good night's sleep. Her breathing evened out, and her body relaxed against mine.

I stayed up, keeping watch over her for a while longer, making sure she wasn't going to have any nightmares. With the stress she'd endured today, anything was possible. She hadn't had one in weeks, but... I knew she wasn't completely over what happened to her. Hell, she might never get completely over it. All we could do was take it one day at a time.

When she rolled away from me, I eased out of bed. Pausing, I waited to make sure she wouldn't wake up. She continued to sleep, so I grabbed my phone and slipped from the room. I went to the kitchen, where I paced as I called Savior. It was late, and he'd probably be pissed I was calling, but I didn't care right now. There were things that needed to be said.

"This is Savior," he said when the call connected.

"I need you to listen and not talk. Think you can do that, Pres?"

He sighed. "What do you want, Prophet? I already got an earful from Dessa."

"Do you have any idea what you did today? Between me and the doctors, we'd gotten her to a good place. She wasn't as anxious, stopped having nightmares, and she no longer jumped at every little thing. I didn't worry as much about her suddenly wandering off in a dark direction in her mind. Until now."

"What's that supposed to mean?" he asked.

"The shit you pulled when we got here. That was the last thing Ares needed. I know you were mad she'd been gone for so long and hadn't bothered to reach out to you or accept your calls when you tried to reach her. I get it. But none of that was an excuse for you to be a dick today."

Savior growled. "Watch it! I can still kick your ass out of here."

"Yeah, you can. And guess what, your daughter would go with me."

"Are you threatening me, you little shit?" I could tell he was getting twice as pissed as earlier. I needed to bring him back down, but honestly, he wasn't going to like hearing what I had to say.

"Look, Pres. My priority is your daughter. What she needed today was for you to welcome her with a hug, maybe a few of our brothers or their women coming to greet her in a peaceful and calm environment. Instead, you picked a fucking fight." It was quiet for a little too long. I glanced at the phone to see if the call had dropped, or if he'd hung up. "Pres?"

"I'm here. And you're right. Is Ares okay?" he

asked.

"She wasn't in the best shape when I brought her home, but I think she's doing okay right now. The sound of motorcycles passing made her tense up again. I think she worried you would come to the house. Or that someone else would decide to make her feel unwelcome in her own home."

"Ouch. That fucking hurt," he muttered.

"Good. It was meant to."

"I'll keep my distance until you tell me Ares is ready to see me," he said. "It's going to fucking kill me, but I want what's best for her. As much as I hate to admit it, I think that's you."

"Thanks for saying that, Pres. Means a lot."

"Go take care of our girl. And let me know if there's anything she needs. Looks like I have a lot to make up for."

We ended the call and I went back to bed. Ares hadn't budged, and I curled my body around hers. I hoped things would be better for her tomorrow. If she wanted to hole up in the house for a few days, then I'd let her. Eventually, I'd have to give her a nudge to venture out around the compound at the very least. There were plenty of people here I knew would be happy she was back.

Maybe I needed to call Lavender tomorrow and see if she'd get in touch with some of Ares' friends and have them stop by. I didn't know what else to do to prove to her she belonged here, and people were on her side. "Love you, Ares. And so many others do too. You're going to be okay." I kissed her shoulder. "We've got your back."

She mumbled something in her sleep, and I hoped she'd heard me... I'd rip the moon from the sky and give it to her, if that was what she wanted.

Chapter Twelve

Ares

The moment we pulled up to my dad's house, I wondered if I'd made the right choice. Anticipation had been building ever since we'd decided to come home, and now it twisted into a tight knot of anxiety in my stomach. It had been a few days since we'd come back home. Our welcome had been far from what I'd hoped for, but I'd thought maybe things were better now. It had been three days since my dad blew up at Prophet. Maybe we shouldn't have come here. Was I trying to do too much too soon?

"Ready?" Prophet's voice was soft, reminding me he was here and I wasn't alone.

I nodded, unable to find my voice. My fingers clenched and unclenched at my sides as I took a step toward the front door. I could feel my entire body starting to shake as I scanned the area and realized I was standing in the exact spot I'd been in when the kidnapper came up behind me.

"Hey," Prophet said gently, reaching out to touch my shoulder. "Take your time. If you can't handle this, then I'll ask them to come to our place. Until I can install a ramp for your mom, I can always help her into the house if your dad doesn't come with her."

I drew in a deep breath, trying to steady myself. I'd lived in this house with my family, made happy memories. If I let the Lathems take all that away from me, then they won. It didn't matter that I'd been freed. Part of me would be caged for as long as they controlled my thoughts, actions, and emotions.

Stepping onto the porch, I paused, my heart pounding so loud I could hear it echoing in my ears.

Prophet stood close behind me, near enough I could feel the heat of his body. I raised my hand, hesitating as it hovered over the doorbell. A shiver ran down my spine. I could do this!

"Whatever happens," I whispered, more to myself than to him, "we'll face it together, right?"

I had no idea if I'd fall apart when I got inside, or if things would be better. Was this the PTSD Dr. Sykes had mentioned?

"Always," he replied, his voice a firm promise.

With a shaky exhale that did nothing to calm my racing heart, I pressed the doorbell. Before now, I'd have just entered without even knocking. But this wasn't my home anymore.

The door swung open, and the familiar face of my father, Savior, filled the doorway. Surprise etched his rugged features for a fleeting second before his expression settled into something unreadable. I managed a tremulous smile, but it felt like it might shatter at any moment.

"Hey, Dad," I murmured.

"Girl, you're a sight." He didn't make single move, and I noticed he seemed more tense than usual.

It felt like my feet had cemented to the porch. A cold sweat broke out on the back of my neck, and nausea welled inside me. I couldn't bring myself to go into the house. Even though the kidnapper had caught me outside, I had no way of knowing if they'd gone into the house at some point. I wondered if Prophet had made me close my eyes and carried me inside, if I'd have been fine if I hadn't seen the area where it had happened.

"Prophet, I…"

Prophet's arm wrapped around me, his presence a solid reassurance. "Easy. I've got you, Ares. You going to be all right?"

"Trying to be," I admitted. My dad stood silently, observing us.

"Let's take this slow," Prophet said. "We can stay here like this until you're ready. Just squeeze my hand when you think you can go inside."

"Damn it, Ares! What's wrong with you?" My dad sounded more hurt than angry. I knew he had to be frustrated with me. "Can't you see I'm here for you? Look at me!"

I swallowed hard, my lips parting as I tried to force the words out. Tears burned my eyes, and my chest felt like it was tight. "P-Please…"

It felt like I was drowning and couldn't get any oxygen. The world spun, and I leaned back into Prophet, not sure my legs would hold me up.

"Savior, she's not -- It's not what you think." Prophet glanced at me, pain etched across his face, before locking eyes with my father. "She needs space. It's not about you or her not wanting to be here."

My dad's jaw clenched, his body rigid. Prophet stood his ground. His hold on me was gentle, even as he faced off against his President.

"Prophet --"

He held up a hand. "Give her a moment. Let her breathe."

"I… I don't know if…" I couldn't even get the words out. It wasn't that I didn't want to see my dad and the rest of my family. I'd missed them.

"You're okay, Ares. I'm right here." Prophet squeezed my waist.

"Enough!" The word burst from Dad like a gunshot. I flinched, bracing for the anger I knew so well, the disappointment I feared. But as his stern gaze met mine, something shifted in his hardened features.

The lines around his eyes softened, the set of his mouth loosened with an emotion I hadn't expected -- regret. The fire in his eyes dimmed, replaced by a dawning realization that cut through his fury like a knife.

"Shit," he muttered, the word rough and low. He raked a hand through his beard. "Ares... I didn't... I'm sorry."

The simple apology hung between us. It was an olive branch, a small gesture, and yet I knew what it cost my dad to say those words. He wasn't one to say sorry very easily. I watched the man who had taken me in when I had nowhere else to go, who had saved me. In that moment, I saw not just my father, not just the President of the Dixie Reapers, but a man wrestling with his own demons -- fighting to be better for the daughter he claimed as his own.

Dad took a step forward, his gaze locked on mine. I read the silent plea for forgiveness, and the hope he hadn't made things worse for me.

"Let's talk inside," he said.

I nodded, a tentative acceptance, and allowed Prophet to guide me into the house. As long as I had him with me, I knew I'd be okay. I just had to get over my initial fear of being here.

"I'm so sorry, Ares." My dad's voice broke. "I guess I hoped when you came back, things would go back to normal. I know you're struggling to find your way here as Prophet's woman now and not just my daughter, but I'm having a hard time too. I want you here, back in your room, and to see you smile the way you used to."

"Time." I swallowed hard. "I need more time."

He nodded. "All right. I've been too scared to hug you, so let me know that will be okay."

"Where's Dessa and the kids?" Prophet asked.

"I asked them to give me some time with Ares first. If the children had seen her like this, it might have scared them."

It had been the right thing to do. Even now, I wasn't sure how much longer I could stand being in this house. And going outside would be even worse.

"I think I need Dr. Sykes," I said. "I thought I was better, but I was wrong. I need his help getting through this."

Prophet squeezed my hand. "Then you'll have it. You're not alone, Ares. I'm not going anywhere."

"I thought I was finished with counseling, but I think I need more sessions. Official ones this time," I said.

"Okay." He kissed the top of my head. "We'll get you whatever help you need."

He laced his fingers with mine. My hand trembled as I reached for my phone and called Dr. Sykes' number. He'd made sure I'd be able to reach him at any time of day. Even though he hadn't charged me for therapy, I had a feeling the club made sure he'd been compensated. I'd found it odd they'd extended their stay until I was ready to return home. How had they been able to keep their practices closed for that long without some sort of payment? The call connected on the third ring.

"Dr. Sykes speaking."

"It's Ares. I need to see you. Regular appointments. I'm not over everything like I'd thought I was. I'm not only having a hard time, but it's causing problems with my family too." I bit my lip so I wouldn't cry. "I feel like I'm going to destroy everything important to me because of how screwed up I am."

"We'll set something up. We can meet as often as

you need to. I'll have my assistant call you back in a little while and figure out what days and times will be best for you. Do you need to see me right now? Do you feel like this is an emergency?" he asked.

"No, I think I can wait." I ended the call, and slowly exhaled the way he'd taught me to do. I leaned into Prophet. "Thank you."

"Anything for you," he replied.

"The two of you should go home," Savior said. "I'll let Dessa know she should take the kids to your place if they want to visit."

I felt like my dad was dismissing me, and it broke my heart. Prophet led me to the door, glancing over his shoulder once, before taking me outside. I closed my eyes, thinking it might be better if I didn't see the place where I'd been abducted. Prophet lifted me into his arms and carried me to his bike. He eased me down onto the back of it and leaned in to kiss my temple.

"Keep your eyes closed a little longer," he said.

I nodded and felt him get onto the motorcycle in front of me. I placed my hands on his waist and pressed my forehead to his leather-covered back. It wasn't until he stopped at our house that I finally looked up. If I'd known I would panic like that, I wouldn't have offered to go to my dad's house. It wasn't that I didn't want to see him, or the rest of the family. I just couldn't handle going to that house right now. I worried I'd never be able to.

"We're home, honey," he said, patting my thigh. "You want me to run a hot bath for you?"

"Dr. Myron said it couldn't be too hot. But yes, that sounds nice."

I got off the bike and waited for him, then we went into the house together. I went straight to the bedroom and took off my shoes. Sitting on the edge of the bed, I waited for him to run the bath. I could have easily done it myself, but Prophet seemed to like doing things like this for me. When I'd tried to tell him I could do it on my own, he'd glowered at me and done it anyway.

"You want any help?" he asked.

"I think I want to be alone." I reached out a hand to him. "I'm sorry. It's just... today has been a lot, and there are things I need to process."

"Mind if I stay in here in case you need me? All you'll have to do is call out to me."

I gave him a brief smile. "I'd appreciate it."

Before I got cleaned up, there was one other thing I needed to do. Call Dessa. She'd been a mother to me, and also a good friend. I pulled out my phone and quickly selected her name off my contacts list.

"Ares?" she asked the moment the call connected. "Are you okay?"

"No, but I think I will be, eventually." I pressed my lips together. "None of this is your fault, and I'm sorry I can't come to the house to see you."

"Oh, honey." I heard her sigh. "I did blame myself the day you disappeared. If I'd been more vigilant, or talked to you on your way home..."

"No, and I'm glad you and the kids weren't there when it happened."

"I had been. Junie forgot a toy at Delphine's house. She'd been over there playing with Jae, and you know how she gets about her favorite things. I wasn't gone for very long, and I knew I shouldn't have wheeled my way over there with the children, but..."

I understood. "Junie was crying and you felt like you might lose your mind before anyone else got home to help?"

"Exactly. Your dad read me the riot act once he got home. And I've felt like complete crap about everything."

"No, Mom. If you'd been there, then you and the kids would have been in danger. In fact, they may have taken Junie, Judd, and Marnie instead of me. You know they wouldn't have survived." I swallowed hard. "I was strong enough to handle it, or so I thought. If I had to make the choice again, I'd still sacrifice myself for them."

Prophet reached out to squeeze my hand.

"I love you, Ares. You know that, right?" Dessa asked.

"I know, Mom. Love you too. I need to go, but I hope you can come to our house to visit."

We didn't make definite plans, but I still felt better after speaking to her for a moment. I hung up the call and headed into the bathroom. I partially closed the door and quickly stripped out of my clothes. Easing down into the tub, I leaned back and closed my eyes. It would have been nice if it could have been hotter, but this was better than nothing. If only the water temperature were all I had to worry about... When would I feel normal again?

* * *

Prophet

I hung my head and stared at the floor. She'd been doing so well before we'd returned home. I worried this wasn't something we could easily fix. While I wouldn't go so far as to say that she'd been as happy as she'd been at the beach, she hadn't freaked out until she got to Savior's house today.

It made me wonder if there was something we could do specifically for his house or that area of the compound that could help Ares. If not, did I need to consider the fact we might need to move? Living outside the compound wouldn't be safe. Too many chances something would go wrong and she'd be put in danger again. I'd been a Dixie Reaper for so long it was a part of who I was.

If it did come down to it, I didn't think Savior or the other officers would make a fuss over me leaving. I could always declare myself a Nomad if I didn't want to leave the club entirely. Or I'd have to consider possibly moving out of this area and patching into another club.

I glanced at the bathroom door and knew I'd do whatever Ares needed me to. If that meant we left this place, then that's exactly what would happen. I knew this had to be hard on her. She'd smiled more, laughed, and even been playful toward the end of our stay in Gulf Shores. Now it almost felt like we were back to the beginning in her healing process. Would it have been better to come here after I got her out of that hellhole? Had I only messed up by taking her somewhere else? I'd done what I thought was best, and she hadn't seemed ready to go home.

"Ares, you all right in there?" I called out, thinking it was a little too quiet. She didn't answer and my stomach knotted. "Ares?"

Still nothing. I got up and went to check on her, only to see she'd fallen asleep in the tub. Thankfully, she hadn't slipped beneath the water and drowned. It looked like I'd have to keep a better eye on her for now. I drained the water, grabbed a towel, and lifted her from the tub. There was no way to dry her without laying her on the bed, so I'd change the sheets later. Good thing I'd started using a waterproof mattress pad after I'd spilled one too many beers while watching TV in bed.

All right. So, maybe I hadn't *only* been watching TV those times. I'd been in love with an underage young woman. My hand was the only way I was going to get any relief, or I'd have walked around with blue balls.

I managed to pull her nightgown over her head and decided not to worry about panties. Tugging the sheet over her, I kissed her brow and left her to get some rest. The visit to her dad's house must have been too stressful for her body to handle.

"Love you, Ares," I whispered before I shut the bedroom door.

I went into the kitchen and wrote a note letting her know I would be at the clubhouse in case she woke up before I returned. Leaving it in the center of the table, I went out to my bike and decided to see if Savior was in his office. It looked like we needed to have a more in-depth conversation about his daughter, before things got any worse.

Chapter Thirteen
Prophet

My boots echoed through the empty clubhouse, each step a heavy beat in the quiet before the storm. I was going to confront Savior. I couldn't think of any other way to handle this. I didn't know if his emotions kept getting the best of him, if something else was going on that was causing him to be moodier than usual, or if he just really had no damn clue how to deal with his daughter now. Either way, something needed to change. I'd thought we'd had an understanding, but clearly not.

I paused by his office door, my hand hovering over the worn metal handle. Inhaling deeply, I opened the door.

Savior didn't look up, not yet aware that I'd entered his private sanctum. Either that, or the bastard was ignoring me on purpose. He looked exhausted even though it hadn't been more than an hour since I'd been at his house. Did this thing with Ares weigh on him that much?

"Prophet," he finally acknowledged, without looking up.

"Savior," I replied. "We need to talk. Again."

Closing the door behind me to shut out the world, I watched as his gaze slowly lifted, meeting mine. There was a challenge in his stare, a silent demand for me to speak my piece and get the fuck out. I could see this was going to go over well.

"It's about Ares," I said, then paused. I didn't know how to phrase what I needed to say.

"Go on," he prompted.

The next words needed to be spoken, no matter how much we both wished they could remain unvoiced. He needed to know what his daughter had been through. It sucked, and I didn't want to give him those nightmares, but I thought he might better understand Ares.

I let the silence linger a moment, then decided to dive in. Standing here wasn't going to get this resolved any faster. "She's been through hell, man. You know it. I know it. But it's more than just knowing. It's about facing the ugly truth of it."

Savior's eyes narrowed, a silent command to continue. Was he really prepared to hear what I had to say? I glanced around his office, wondering if everything in here was about to be destroyed.

"Every night, she fought demons in her sleep. Nightmares about what she endured. She's gotten better. But the Ares I saw this morning is closer to what she was like when I first found her. The extent of her trauma… it's not just physical scars. Those wounds run deeper, carving into her very soul. She may have survived trafficking before, but this time was different."

"What the hell aren't you saying? Just spit it the fuck out," he demanded.

Speaking the words out loud nearly ripped my heart in half. I knew Ares didn't want her father hearing what she'd been through. It felt like I was betraying her, but I needed him to understand the extent of what she suffered.

"The man who bought her took pleasure in breaking her down. He tied her up. Beat her. Cut her. Starved her. And… he raped her. When I found them, he was in the room with her. Fucker taunted me. He was so certain he was safe, that I wouldn't be able to touch him."

Savior's hands fisted on top of the desk. "And

did you kill the bastard?"

"No. I left him alive, then handed him off to some of the women he'd been abusing. The club who helped get Ares out of there let me know the man was dead. The women hadn't been able to finish him off, so their club took care of it. He's buried in about ten different graves spread all over the state." He still looked pissed as hell, but hopefully he wouldn't destroy his office. "In case you're curious, the Wild & Reckless crew are taking care of the other women. I didn't really ask for updates, and Ares hasn't seemed curious. She was kept separate from them, so it's not like they bonded."

Savior still didn't say anything, but I'd noticed his face started to turn a startling shade of purple. If he erupted in here, there'd be no saving the office or anything in it. The man looked seconds away from ripping apart or smashing everything in sight.

"Creating a safe environment for Ares -- it's critical," I said. "She needs to feel secure, not just when we're around, but in every corner of this place she calls home."

I hoped he understood what I meant. Being at his house this morning sent her spiraling. It was where she'd been abducted. I was a fucking idiot for not considering that before I took her over there. It didn't even occur to me she might have an issue with being in that location.

"Prophet, I --" He sighed. "What do I need to do? I want my daughter back in my life. She's here but not here, if you know what I mean. And I'm sure that's at least somewhat my fault."

Now was my chance. "Speaking of... Something going on with you, Pres? You've been acting a bit out of character since we came back. I get that you're pissed I asked her to marry me without discussing it with you first, and that she's pregnant. But it seems like something more is happening."

"You're right. And it's something for me to worry about, not you or Ares. I'll try to do better."

That wasn't going to cut it. If there really was a problem, then I wanted to help. He wasn't just my club President anymore. "You do realize you're going to be my father-in-law, right?"

"I just have some health shit going on. Turns out I'm diabetic, and I can turn it around with the right diet but I feel like I'm fucking starving all the time. It makes me grumpier than usual. I've been lashing out at everyone for no damn good reason for weeks. Dessa threatened to hit me with a skillet if I didn't stop." He ran a hand down his face. "I'm fine. Or I will be. I go back next month for more blood work. They'll tell me then if what I'm doing is actually working, or if I need medication. One way or another, it will resolve itself."

"Fine. But if you need someone to talk to, or need help with anything, let me know. As for Ares… I think being in front of your house took her back to the day she was abducted. I'm not sure what to do, in all honesty. I've wondered if we'll eventually have to leave this place in order for her not regress. She was doing so much better until we returned from Gulf Shores. She's stronger than anyone I know, but even the strongest steel can fracture."

"All right." He leaned forward. "We need to come up with a way to give her that safe space. If that means I need to tear down my house and rebuild it elsewhere, then so be it."

"Let's not get quite that extreme. Why don't we start with a makeover for the outside? Change enough stuff that the house doesn't look the same, and maybe that will keep her from panicking."

"Want to help me come up with a plan?" he asked. "Or do you need to get back to Ares?"

I hesitated only for a moment. "She was taking a nap and I left a note telling her I'd be at the clubhouse. She can either find me here, or call me if she needs something, so I can stay for a bit."

"Let me grab a pen and pad of paper. Let's head to a table in the main area and discuss this over a beer."

I went out to the bar and grabbed two cold longnecks before claiming a table. There weren't many brothers in here right now. None of them came over, even though Tank gave me a nod. I enjoyed coming to the clubhouse more these days. The club whores who used to hang around had been a troublesome bunch, and I for one was glad they were gone.

Savior joined me at the table and slapped the pad and pen down. "I don't even know where to start."

"Well, think about what the outside of your house looks like. Not just the house either but the yard, driveway, all of it. She didn't even make it to the door before she tensed up."

"Go on," he said, picking up the pen.

"What about putting in a garden? You have the backyard for the little ones to play. No reason you can't landscape alongside the driveway and up across the front of the house. Add some flowers or shrubs. Whatever."

"A garden full of green. Maybe a koi pond too. The sound of water can soothe the soul, and the kids would love feeding the fish." He wrote down the ideas then did a rough sketch.

"Exactly," I said. "Maybe some flowers. Something to add color to the place. Make it cheerful."

He nodded and added more to the sketch, along with putting more into his notes. I hadn't realized before the Pres actually knew a few things about this shit. He even listed types of plants he'd want to use.

"Maybe put up a different style of fence around the backyard?" I suggested. "Or put in a wood one instead of chain link? That would change the look of the place too."

"All right." Savior stood abruptly, his chair scraping back against the floor. "Let's do this. For Ares."

I rose with him, wondering if he literally meant he was starting the project right this second. I mean, if he was motivated, then why not? It just seemed a bit abrupt.

"Let's give her a place that will help her heal," I said. "I'm assuming you want to start right now."

"No time like the present. I'll call a few others. At the very least, we can dig out the grass in the areas I plan to put the garden, and I can get one of those pond inserts. As long as I know the dimensions, we could dig the hole for it."

"What's going on?" Tank asked, coming over.

Savior showed him the sketch and list. "Going to change up the outside of my house. Ares froze up when she came by earlier. Prophet said she was probably reminded of her abduction. But if the place looks completely different…"

Tank nodded. "Good idea. Should probably paint the outside a different color too, unless you just really love the color it is."

"Better ask Dessa before you go that far," I said. "Hell, you need to show her all this before you start digging up the yard. It's her place too."

"She won't care. If it's for Ares, she'll tell me to

do whatever is needed. She loves that girl like her own." Savior headed out the door and over to his bike. "I'll still run this by her. Meet me at the house in a few minutes. If you see anyone you can convince to volunteer for this, bring them with you."

Savior rode off and I shook my head. "Do you think he realizes this isn't getting finished in just day or two?"

Tank snorted. "Not likely. If he could, he'd have it done before dinner."

"You're not wrong." I went over to my bike. "Want to lend a hand?"

"I'm too old for this shit. But I'll round up some youngsters."

I stared at him for a moment. "By youngsters…"

"Foster needs to make amends for some shit. And where Foster goes, so does Owen."

I frowned. Had I missed something while I'd been gone. "What did Foster do this time?"

"Oh, shit. She never said anything?"

"Who? Ares?" I got off the bike. "What the fuck did he say or do?"

Tank held up a hand. "Easy. It was before the Lathems got her. Foster tried to lure her out of here, saying his buddies wanted her to hang out with them. She got pissed at him, which is understandable. Sometimes I wonder what exactly is in that boy's head other than air."

I pinched the bridge of my nose. I couldn't be entirely pissed off about it. For one, Foster was known for saying and doing the wrong thing, especially when it came to women. He'd gotten in trouble so many times I'd lost track.

"When the hell is he going to grow up?" I asked.

"No idea. That's between him and his dad. I stay

out of it. Unless he comes near my girls. Then he'll be going home with my boot print on his ass, and possibly his face."

I snorted. "Yeah, even Foster can't be that stupid, right?"

Tank shrugged. "I wouldn't bet on it."

"All right. I'm going to Savior's place. If Ares comes here looking for me…"

He waved me off. "I'm heading out, but I'll let someone inside know. You could always text her."

"Yeah, I may do that. See you later, Tank." I got back on my bike and drove over to Savior's house. I noticed he'd roped Saint, Flicker, and Royal into this project as they were all standing in the yard talking to him while looking at the paper in his hand.

Saint waved at me as I walked over. "You help him come up with this?"

"Somewhat. I made a few vague suggestions, and he just ran with it," I said. "But I think this will be good for Ares."

"I'm really fucking glad my woman would rather me buy her a new motorcycle than put in a garden," Flicker said. "Otherwise, this might give Pepper ideas."

"I already know I'll be asked to make the yard as pretty as Savior's," Saint said. "But if that's what Sofia wants, then it's what she'll get. But I may force the Prospects to do it."

"I brought two cans of white spray paint," Royal said. "Had some in the garage. I thought we could use it to mark off the areas Savior wants dug up."

"Good idea," I said. "Let's see what we can get done. I don't want to be away from Ares too much longer, though."

Savior slapped me on the back. "Go on home to

her. I have enough help for now. Just keep her away from this area as much as possible until it's done. I want it to be a surprise."

"All right, Pres. Keep me posted and let me know if you need me."

I got on my bike and watched them for a moment. Dessa wheeled out onto the porch and gave me a wave, as well as a forced smile. Anyone could see she felt like shit over Ares being abducted. I hoped the two of them would be able to find peace again. Neither deserved this shit.

I waved back, then headed home. There were times I really loved being part of the Dixie Reapers. Of course, like any family, we didn't get along one hundred percent of the time. Still, we usually overcame our issues. Our bond was tighter than blood. We were family by choice.

Chapter Fourteen

Ares

I hadn't been to the clubhouse in a while. For some reason, Prophet had said I wasn't allowed anywhere near my dad's house, and not because I'd freaked out. I had to wonder what was going on. At least I could come here when I wanted to visit with everyone. Now that the club whores were gone, the place was open to the women too.

And as an added bonus, there was a ramp here, so Mom could hang out with everyone whenever she wanted. Now that the place was family friendly all day every day, the kids were also able to come inside. Although, most of them didn't except the smaller ones who came with their parents. The teens, however, were another matter. It made them feel grown-up to be in here unsupervised.

I couldn't drink since I was pregnant, so a Prospect had given me a bottle of water. I accepted it and took in everyone either sitting at tables having conversations, or dancing to the beat of whatever song played through the speakers. I'd only half paid attention to it. Being in here still left me feeling a little overwhelmed. Not because anything bad happened to me in this place, but I was still adjusting once more to being in crowded spaces. At the beach, we'd only been around crowds in restaurants or out in the open. This was... different. For one, the only windows were at the front of the room, which left the place rather dreary even when the sun was at its highest peak.

I wondered if it was the darker atmosphere that bothered me. After being locked up in a room with no windows, a place like this made me feel like I was still confined. I knew I could get up and walk out whenever I wanted, but my body still had a fearful response to places like this.

Part of me wished Mom was here. I hadn't had a chance to spend a lot of time with her since my return. The little ones needed her, and she really did struggle to leave the house some days. Prophet's house wasn't close enough for her to wheel herself over there. I needed to call her more often at the very least.

Wraith's woman Rin plopped down on the stool next to mine. She was quite a bit older than me, but I'd heard she was around my age when Wraith claimed her. I'd always thought she was rather beautiful, even with the scars covering her body.

"Hey." She flashed me a quick smile.

"Rin," I acknowledged. We'd spoken often over the years I'd been here, but I wouldn't have considered her one of my friends. I didn't have anything against her. I'd just mostly hung out with those closer to my age.

She reached out, her hand warm and steady as it enveloped mine. "You looked slightly freaked out, and I thought you could use someone to talk to."

I forced a smile. "It shows, huh?"

She shrugged shoulder. "I know you've been through this before. Different story, same kind of hell. And you know my past wasn't the greatest. I just wanted you to know I'm here for you. Don't feel rushed to be the same Ares you were before. In all honesty, you'll never be her again. I'm not saying you won't heal, because you will, but the experiences you had will make you stronger -- eventually."

"Thanks, Rin. I appreciate it." I really did too. There were several women here who'd survived sexual assault and more. Rin was only one of them. The men here had a tendency to take in the broken birds and mend their wings. And yeah, I'd just called the two of us fucking birds. Maybe they'd given me more than water. I sniffed the contents of the bottle. Nope. Not vodka, just straight-up water. Maybe the stress was affecting me more than I'd realized.

"Wraith didn't let me drown in my nightmares. Didn't look at me like I was something dirty. We didn't have the smoothest start to our relationship, but he loves me and I love him. I can see you have that with Prophet, but I know there are times you need a woman who will understand. I just wanted to remind you that you have several here who would be willing to listen or hold you while you cry or scream about the unfairness of it all. We've been there, done that."

"Seems impossible some days," I admitted. "Living a normal life again. You'd think I'd be able to shrug this off after going through it before. I don't know why this time it's hitting me harder. And Mom… I can tell she feels guilty even when she shouldn't. It makes me wonder if our relationship will ever go back to what it was before."

"As far as Dessa is concerned, she's a grown woman and has to deal with her issues. You have enough on your plate. Focus on getting better. Maybe you didn't properly process everything before because of your age," she suggested. "But you're seeing Dr. Sykes, right?"

"Yeah. I had counseling with him before, but this time it feels like he's digging deeper. Guess I need it since I'm such a basket case some days."

She squeezed my hand. "Don't think that way."

I held her gaze and realized there were times she still felt the pain of what she went through. It resonated with me, and perhaps that more than anything else reminded me I really did have plenty of people to help me through this.

"Thank you," I said. "Really."

"Anytime," Rin said with a small smile, releasing my hand. "We're all in this together, remember? That's what makes us stronger."

"Family. I get it." I looked across the room where my dad sat with Saint, Tank, and Venom. I could tell there something going on with him, but no one had said anything. But maybe... "Hey, Rin. Do you know what's up with my dad lately? He's been quick to anger and even got mad at me over stuff I couldn't control. You know that's not like him."

"Wow, okay then." She blew out a breath. "I see they're keeping you in the dark."

I jerk my head around to stare at her. "What? Is something really wrong with him?"

She lifted her hands. "No. I mean, it's not life-threatening as long as he does what he's supposed to, and I think he's trying. Honestly, I thought you'd know already. Didn't Prophet..."

"Oh my God! Why haven't they said anything to me?" I stared at my dad again, trying to see if I could figure out what illness he had. Was it cancer? A bad heart? A tumor? My mind started spinning with one horrible scenario after another. And Prophet had kept it from me? Did he think I was so fragile I couldn't handle it?

"Easy, Ares." Rin placed her hand on my shoulder and gave it a squeeze. "I think we need some backup. Just breathe in and out, slowly."

I felt her waving at someone, even though I didn't see who. Next thing I knew, Lavender and Mara were standing with us. I did a double take as it registered Mara was really here. It was a rare thing to find her at a gathering like this. She'd been with Rocky since long before I came here, and yet, she mostly stayed in her house. I'd always thought she was just too shy, but maybe it was more that she preferred the peace and quiet. She seemed at ease right now.

"What's up?" Lavender asked.

"They haven't told Ares about Savior, and now she's panicking," Rin said. "I shouldn't have said anything, but she was worrying about the way he's been acting."

Lavender sighed. "Let's get to a table."

I followed them to an empty table on the opposite side of the room from my dad. Once I'd sat down, Lavender took the chair beside me with Rin on my other side. Mara sat across from me.

"You know he probably wanted to protect you, right?" Mara asked. "It's why he didn't say anything. You've been through a lot, and he most likely didn't want to burden you with anything else."

"Burden? I'm his daughter! How could he not tell me if there's something wrong?" I asked.

"It's not as awful as you probably think." Lavender nudged my bottle of water closer to me and I took a swallow. "He's been diagnosed with diabetes. They're giving him time to correct it by changing his diet and lifestyle a bit. If the next test still says he's diabetic, they'll put him on meds most likely."

"I don't know anything about diabetes," I said.

"He's had to cut out carbs, sugar, increase his protein intake. He also has to lay off the beer. He can still enjoy one, just not several a day. I think the change in what he can eat, and the stress over checking labels for carb and sugar content, has stressed him to the point he's a bit snippy. Dessa said he's always complaining he feels like he's going to starve to death, so that's not helping matters either." Lavender glanced at him, then back at me. "Maybe you should talk to him about it?"

I shook my head. "I'll wait and see if they bring it up first. At least I now understand why he's been acting out of character. Thank you for telling me."

"Do you know how far along you are?" Lavender asked, changing the subject.

"Um. Dr. Myron did a blood test to confirm the pregnancy, but we haven't really narrowed down when it happened. I go see Dr. Myron again in a few weeks. Maybe he can tell me more then."

Mara reached over to lightly touch my ring. "Interesting choice of engagement ring. Is there a story behind it?"

I nodded. "We were staying at a house on the beach in Gulf Shores. One of the vendors nearby sold oysters. Prophet bought one, had the guy cut it open, and there was a pink pearl inside. He took it to a jeweler and had it made into a ring. The day I decided it was time to come home, he proposed to me."

"It's unique, and beautiful," Rin said. "An unpolished pearl has a rougher, bumpy exterior. I bet the pearl reminded Prophet of you, and everything you'd been through."

"He said something along those lines. I guess I'm supposed to be the finished pearl once I'm done dealing with what happened." It had been rather sweet of him, but then, he'd always been kind to me. Even when he sounded gruff, he was usually forcing me to do something that was for my own good.

"Since you've been gone, and you've had some… trouble… readjusting, you probably haven't heard." Lavender leaned in closer. "Joker and Cleo have a son now. I think they've been keeping their distance in case their presence bothers you. They took in a little boy named Caspian. He's a cutie."

"None of this is Cleo's fault. Her family did this to me, not her. She had a bad heart, right? Did that get resolved?"

Rin nodded. "Yeah. She got a transplant, and while she's not running a marathon anytime soon, she's definitely much improved."

"I heard Joker still sticks to her like glue, though," Mara said.

"You'd see it for yourself if you came out of your house more often," Lavender said. "But you've always been quiet and preferred being home."

"I know. Sometimes all this is a bit much for me," Mara said, waving her hand at the people gathered in the clubhouse. "Although, it's much better now those women are gone. They always made me feel uneasy, and with all the trouble they kept causing, I didn't understand why they were here."

"Um, because men think with their dicks?" Rin asked.

I'd just taken a swallow of water and spewed it all over the table. "True, but I can't believe you said that."

They laughed and Lavender handed me a napkin. I used it to clean myself up, then mopped up the water on the table. They'd always treated me like a child before. I guess getting engaged and being pregnant changed things. I wasn't just one of the kids now. I was going to be one of them. An old lady.

Of course, now that I thought about it…

"Why am I the only one at the table without a property cut?" I asked.

"Oh, shit." Lavender put her hand over her mouth. "I didn't even realize it. I bet Savior hasn't ordered it yet."

"But you know where they get them, right?" Mara asked Lavender.

"I do, but... That request should really come from an officer or their old lady. And Wire is awesome, but he's just the club hacker. It's not like he has an official title around here."

"I always thought he was a bit like God -- he could see you anytime he wanted and track you too."

Lavender threw back her head and laughed. "That's fucking perfect! I'm so telling him that."

"No!" Rin looked appalled. "He already thinks he's the most amazing thing on earth. Can you imagine the size of his ego if he knows someone thinks he's a god?"

"You make a good point," Lavender said.

Prophet came over, squatting beside my chair. "Looks like you're having fun now. Do you need anything?"

"She needs her property cut," Lavender said. "Did you not ask Savior to get her one?"

Prophet winced. "Actually, I didn't. With everything going on, it didn't seem like the right time. Everyone knows I've claimed her, that we're engaged, and expecting a baby. The cut is important, and I know that, but... it's not the *most* important thing."

"I guess things are a little different now," Mara said. "Before, it was the only way to keep the club whores away from our men, or at least it stood as a warning those guys were taken. Now we don't have to deal with those women."

"Not to mention Ares was part of this club already," Prophet said.

"Fine. But I'd like to have mine before my stomach is too big for me to wear it properly." I leaned in to kiss him. "Deal?"

"I can manage that." He smiled and stood. "Let me know when you're ready to head home. I don't want to cut your time short since you seem to be enjoying yourself, but I also don't want you to overdo it."

"I know." I watched him walk off and realized the women were smirking at me. "What?"

"I'm deciding if he has you wrapped around his finger, or it's the other way around," Rin said.

"I think it's a bit of both." Lavender smacked her hand on the table. "And I don't know about you, but I'm getting hungry. I'm going to ask a Prospect to make us some fries. Anything else for the table?"

"Loaded potato skins," Rin said. "But tell them to put the sour cream on the side this time. Last time they loaded the tops of them and I couldn't handle it."

"All right. Back in a minute," Lavender said.

She hadn't been gone more than a few seconds before someone dropped into her seat. I stared at Foster, wondering what the hell he was up to. Nothing good ever happened when he was around. How the hell had someone like Bull had a kid like this one?

"Are you lost?" I asked.

"I needed to apologize to you," he said.

Mara sighed. "Child, you might as well print off apology cards and just hand them out on a daily basis. You're at my house enough I feel like you're my kid, but when are you going to grow the hell up? If Owen fucked up as much as you do, Rocky would have buried him somewhere already."

Foster winced. "I know. And actually, I'm more scared of Mom than Dad, but don't tell him I said that."

"You act or run your mouth before your brain has the time to tell you that you shouldn't do whatever it is you're jumping into," I said. "It's exhausting, and often insulting, to a lot of us. You ran Leigha off all the way to the Reckless Kings."

"And I learned my lesson. If a woman says no, or tries to politely turn me down, then I know she's really not interested and isn't just playing hard to get." He leaned in closer, giving me puppy eyes. "I'm really sorry, Ares. I didn't get to apologize because of what happened, and then you were gone for two months. If there's ever anything I can do to make it up to you, or to prove I'm trying to change, then tell me."

Lavender was back and smacked him on the top of his head. "You can start by getting your ass out of my seat. Then bring our food to the table and some fresh drinks."

He shot up out of his chair and took a hasty step back. "You got it!"

Rin looked amused as she watched him run off. "Don't think I've seen him move that fast before."

"He knows I can erase his entire existence if he makes me mad," Lavender said. "I already had his license revoked once. I fixed it two days later, but he learned his lesson when he got pulled over for speeding."

I stayed another hour, enjoying my time with the ladies. For the first time since I'd come back home, I felt like I belonged here. These women were incredible, and I owed them so much. They'd given me the one thing I'd been missing -- confidence, and hearing that it was okay to *not* be okay. I hoped one day I could be like them and give advice to those younger than me.

I definitely want to be like Lavender when I grow up. Well, minus the hacking because I wasn't that great with computers.

Right when I was about to ask Prophet if we

could go home, the doors opened, and Mom wheeled her way into the clubhouse. She glanced around the room, and the moment she spotted me, she came over. The women scooted their chairs to make space for her. She pulled up next to me, and before she said a word, she pulled me in for a hug.

"You looked like you could use one of these," she said. "And I definitely did."

"Thanks, Mom."

"Your dad texted that you were here. I asked Delphine to watch the kids long enough for me to come see you." She squeezed my hand. "I've missed you, Ares."

"Same here. I'm sorry I haven't been able to come visit at the house. It's just been too hard," I said.

"And I'm sure they don't blame you for that," Rin said. "Right, Dessa?"

Mom nodded. "Right. You're the victim in all this, Ares. Or rather, the survivor. My strong, beautiful girl."

"All right, Mom. Enough or I'm going to think you've been drinking." I laid my head on her shoulder. "But I'm really glad you came tonight."

"Me too. So, catch me up on the all the gossip."

Lavender told her about me calling Wire a god, and before I knew it, I'd been sucked in to another hour of conversation. But spending time with everyone like this made me truly feel like I was back where I belonged.

Epilogue

Ares
Five Months Later

The morning light seeped through the curtains, casting a warm glow over the room. A profound sense of peace settled over me as my hand instinctively found its way to the gentle swell of my belly. So much had happened since I'd returned home, but I was in a better place now. I saw Dr. Sykes once a week, or more often if I needed to, and I felt like I was truly a part of the club again.

"Hey, darlin'," Prophet's voice rumbled from the doorway.

I turned toward him, my heart skipping a beat at how sexy he looked with a half smile on his lips, and his eyes lighting up. He came closer, and I admired his ink as he sat on the edge of the bed, leaning in to kiss me on the forehead. He was also so gentle with me, even though I'd seen him beat the shit out of people multiple times. Even though he had that darker, rough side, I knew he'd never be that way with me.

"How are my girls?" he asked.

"We don't know for certain yet. Remember, Dr. Myron said the baby wasn't in the best position. It's possible it's a boy."

He scooted closer and put his arm around me. "Yeah, but I'm hoping for a cute daughter who takes after her mom."

"Why? So you can run off the boys like Foster? And considering the age differences around here…"

He growled. "Don't even joke about that! I'd be fine if she wants to fall for Atlas. He's the most levelheaded kid I've seen around here. Out of the boys anyway."

"He's not even old enough to drive yet. He could change a lot the older he gets," I said. "I bet Foster wasn't so bad when he was smaller."

"Fine. She can have a girlfriend instead of a boyfriend. Wait. No, she could end up with someone like a club whore. Shit."

I couldn't help but giggle at him. "You're too much. Come on. We're going to be late."

"Every morning I wake up next to you, I realize this is the closest to heaven that I'll ever be. I love you so much, Ares."

"I love you too, Hunter. Can you believe we're going to be parents?"

He grinned. "Can you believe your dad is going to be a grandpa?"

"Yes, and you love reminding him of that every day. One day you'll go missing, and I'll discover he fed you to the giant koi in his pond."

Dad had really outdone himself. Prophet had told me about the original plan for the house, but Dad had gone above and beyond. He'd ended up moving the pond farther to the side of the house and tripling the size of it. There was a bench beside it, so I could go and watch the fish whenever I wanted. Junie and Judd loved to sit there too, but Marnie was scared of the water.

He'd created a beautiful garden, even though he'd used part of the lot beside the house. One he'd intended to give to someone in the future. The club had convinced him to use it to create a safe space for me, and I loved all of them for it.

"Is Jackson back yet?" I asked. He'd left for a rodeo shortly after I returned, and he hadn't been back since. It worried me because he should have been home months ago.

"No, but I wouldn't worry too much. You know if something had gone wrong, Cowboy would have said something. Man seems chill as ever, so I think Jackson is okay."

I hoped so. With his sister gone, the two of us had grown close before my abduction. I thought of him like an older brother.

I got out of bed and Prophet helped me into the shower. While I rinsed off, he got our things together. The club had set up a picnic near the clubhouse, and I couldn't wait to go. It was near enough to the playground for the little ones to have fun, close enough to the clubhouse in case the men needed more beer or anyone needed a bathroom, and the pavilion provided ample shade. Although the weather would have normally been much too cold for something like this, we'd had an odd heatwave recently. Instead of the usual forty-degree temps, it was nearly seventy outside this week.

I put on one of my maternity dresses and slipped on my canvas flats. Prophet had already stored the potato salad I'd made and tossed a clean blanket in the back of the car. He helped me into the passenger seat, then drove us over to the picnic area. Before being pregnant, I'd have enjoyed the walk. But these days, my ankles were swelling and I felt like I'd swallowed a watermelon. Walking wasn't my favorite thing to do right now.

By the time we pulled up and parked, it looked like half the club was already present and accounted for. I could hear the squeals of the little ones on the playground. I saw Lavender, Mara, Ridley, Isabella, Darian, and several others already setting up the picnic tables. When I got closer, I stopped in my tracks.

"Um, Prophet. Why is there an armchair here?" I

asked.

"Because your dad wanted to make sure you'd have a comfortable place to sit. He said the wood bench wouldn't be good for you."

I sighed. Yeah, sounded like something he'd do. I would sit at the table to eat, but it looked like I'd be holding court in the only padded chair here. Some days my family was so damn embarrassing. Did he really have to go that extra mile in this particular instance?

"I'll carry the potato salad over to the food table. Find a place to sit that gives you easy access to get up and down," he said, kissing my cheek.

I took the end seat at the nearest table, and Darian came to sit beside me. She looked like she had something on her mind, so I waited for her to speak first.

I gave her a nudge with my elbow. "What's wrong?"

She shook her head. "Nothing. Just… my son being his usual self. He hasn't caused you any other problems, has he?"

My brow furrowed. "No. He's actually not spoken to me much since I returned. Why? Did something happen?"

"I'm probably seeing issues where there aren't any. Bull thinks I'm overreacting. If you happen to see or hear anything, let me know? I just have this feeling he's in trouble again."

It wasn't like I'd be the one Foster would confess to. If anything… "You should ask Owen. Those two are really close."

She nodded. "You're right. I'll see if he knows anything. For now… How are you doing? Feeling all right?"

"Yeah. I've finally settled back into life here, and things with Prophet are going really well." I smiled. "I'm not quite as broken as I was before."

She patted my shoulder. "I'm glad. If you ever need anything, let me know. You have your mom, of course, and a lot of others but... just know you can call or stop by anytime you want."

"Thanks, Darian."

Of course, now that she'd brought up Foster, I scanned the area looking for him. What the hell had he gotten himself into now? I really wished, not only for his sake but for everyone's, that he'd grow the hell up. How Bull and Darian had a kid like him was beyond me. He wasn't anything like either of his parents.

By the time everyone else arrived, I was beyond starving. I ate my food, enjoyed good conversation, then moved over to the padded chair. A few of the ladies had packed folding chairs and joined me, so at least I didn't feel quite so alone. I was still the only one with a living room chair at a picnic, but I was rather grateful for it right now.

I'd finally found a way to be at peace again. To feel like part of this big family once more. It wasn't just thanks to Dr. Sykes and Prophet, but to all the amazing people in my life. Now that Dad had gotten his blood sugar issues under control, he was back to his usual self. Everything that had felt like it was upside down, was now right side up once more.

"What's that smile for?" Ridley asked.

"I'm just happy. We have a really amazing life here, don't we?"

She nodded. "We do. Can't imagine living anywhere else. These men might be rough around the edges, and willing to kill if it's needed, but they would walk through fire for us. That's not easy to find in this world these days. They're a special breed."

"And all ours," I said.

I might have walked through hell -- twice -- but I'd come out the other side much stronger. I couldn't wait for what came next in our lives. The thought of being a mom scared me, but I also wanted to hold my little baby in my arms. My life was about as perfect as it could get.

"When's the wedding?" Ridley asked.

"Actually, I decided to let Lavender use her skills to marry us before the baby arrives. Preacher offered to give us an actual wedding ceremony when I feel up to it." I placed my hand over my baby bump. "But I don't think I need one. I already have everything I could ever want."

"Spoken like a true old lady," Ridley said. "You're going to do just fine, Ares. And we're all here whenever you need us."

"I know." I smiled. "Thank you. I love all of you so much."

Ridley hugged me. "We love you too."

One chapter of my life was slowly coming to a close, but the next one would be even better.

Cowboy Up (A Bad Boy Romance 6)
A Dixie Reapers MC Spinoff
Harley Wylde

I never planned to be anyone's hero – until Mia needed one.

Mia -- I ran away from home when I was seventeen and attached myself to a too-old-for-me cowboy. Then he knocked me up, slapped me around, and left me. My baby and I would have had nowhere to go, but the sweetest cowboy I've ever met threw me a lifeline. It was only supposed to be a marriage of convenience. I wasn't supposed to fall in love with him. When life keeps throwing us one obstacle after another, I have to wonder if I made the right choice. What if I'm ruining Jackson's life?

Jackson -- I have really big shoes to fill. Not only is my dad a retired rodeo national champion, but he's also part of the Dixie Reapers MC. He saved my mom, and he's been my hero ever since I was a kid. So when my friend starts yelling at his girlfriend and slaps her around, I know I have to step in. Now I have a family I didn't plan for, and I have no idea how to tell my parents. But with trouble following us no matter where we go, there's only one place I can turn -- to the Dixie Reapers -- because I'll do whatever it takes to keep my family safe.

Chapter One

Jackson

"Jackson! Jackson!" The roar of the crowd assaulted my ears as I settled over the bronc in the chute. My heart hammered in my chest, adrenaline zipping through my veins. Every ride was different, but this part remained the same.

"Jackson! You got this!" Carter Bales, my longtime friend, was shouting encouragement from the sidelines. With one hand gripping a cold beer and the other waving wildly in the air, he seemed to be enjoying the event almost as much as I was. I couldn't help but grin. I already had sweat dripping down my face, and soon I'd have the dust from the arena coating me.

"Come on, Adler! Show 'em what you're made of!" another voice chimed in, joining Carter's cheers. The energy of the crowd was infectious, and I found myself feeding off their excitement.

I caught glimpses of my fellow rodeo cowboys watching from the sidelines. They were a motley crew of rough-and-tumble men, each one of them a seasoned rider with countless bruises and scars to show for it. And yet, despite the dangers that came with the sport, there was an undeniable camaraderie between us all. We were more than just friends -- we were a family bound together by our shared passion for the rodeo.

Although, we each hoped the other would fall off before the buzzer. Each of us wanted the top spot in our events.

"You'll get the top spot, Jackson!" Carter called out again, his voice barely audible over the din of the crowd. I could see the excitement in his eyes, the thrill of watching me push myself to the limit. And for a moment, I allowed myself to bask in the glory of it all -- the adrenaline, the cheers, the sheer exhilaration of being a rodeo cowboy.

Making sure my hat was smashed down far enough it wouldn't fly off, I gripped the rigging and gave a nod to the men waiting to open the chute. Once the doors opened, the bronc burst from the chute, twisting and bucking.

Eight seconds, just eight seconds. I tried to focus on the rhythm of the ride, to stay one step ahead of the animal's frantic movements. It was a battle of wits and strength, a test of endurance that had become second nature to me over the years. Holding on tightly, my knuckles turned white with the effort. The bronco beneath me bucked and kicked like a beast possessed, desperate to unseat me from its back. But I held on, every muscle in my body working together to keep me anchored to the wild creature.

Five... four... three... I counted down the seconds in my head, willing myself to hold on just a little bit longer. The bronco beneath me seemed to sense my determination and redoubled its efforts to unseat me, but I held fast, refusing to give in.

Two... one!

And just like that, it was over. The buzzer rang out, signaling the end of my ride, and I released the reins, allowing myself to be thrown from the bronco's back and onto the dirt floor of the arena. I landed in a crouch, then stood and waved my hat to the crowd. The cheers from the audience washed over me like a tidal wave as I stood there, panting and covered in sweat, but victorious. I didn't know if I'd earned enough points to make the top three, and I watched the scoreboard.

"Jackson! That was amazing!" Carter said as I climbed the rail to exit the arena. "You really showed 'em who's boss out there!"

"Thanks," I replied with a weary grin, feeling the ache in my muscles already beginning to set in. But it didn't matter -- the pain, the exhaustion, the risk -- none of it mattered when I was on the back of a bronc, doing what I loved most. And with friends like Carter by my side, cheering me on every step of the way, I knew that nothing -- not even the wildest bronco -- could keep me down for long.

The announcer said my score, and I watched as my name took the top spot on the scoreboard. I couldn't hold back my smile. Today had been an excellent day, and as the final ride, I knew no one was knocking me from that position.

I leaned against the railing, catching my breath and wiping the sweat from my brow. The next event would start in a few minutes. Bull riding. I'd done my fair share in the past, but broncs were my passion, just like my dad. He'd been a national champion, and that was my goal as well.

The rodeo was in full swing, the electrifying atmosphere filling every corner of the arena with energy and excitement. As I watched the cowboys compete, a strange mixture of pride and envy washed over me -- pride for my fellow riders, who threw themselves into the fray with reckless abandon, and envy for the adrenaline that coursed through their veins, propelling them toward victory or defeat.

"Hey, man, you did great out there," Carter said, clapping me on the back and taking a swig from his beer. "You'll be back on top in no time."

"Thanks," I responded with a half-hearted smile, my attention still focused on the action unfolding before us. I might have come in first this time, but I needed to place in the next three rodeos to make it to nationals.

"J-Jackson?" a voice whispered hesitantly from behind me. Surprised, I turned around to find Mia Cox standing there, her face pale and her eyes brimming with tears. A flash of concern shot through me. It was unusual to see her without her usual bright smile and infectious laughter.

"Hey, what's wrong?" I asked gently, drawing her away from the chaos of the rodeo and into a quieter corner.

Mia swallowed hard, her eyes darting between me and Carter, who had grown silent at her appearance. "I... I need to talk to Carter. Could you..."

The way her voice trembled, and she couldn't meet our gazes, made me think she had bad news. Clearly, something private between the two of them. I hoped like hell he hadn't fucked up. Everyone knew Mia was only seventeen. Even though she'd left home to chase after Carter, I'd told him to keep things platonic. Why did I get the feeling he hadn't done that?

"All right." I nodded, stepping back to give them some space. I saw Carter's expression shift from curiosity to apprehension as he set his beer down and turned to face her.

"Talk to me, Mia. What's going on?" he asked.

He hadn't even given me a chance to move far enough away I wouldn't overhear them. And her next words stopped me in my tracks.

"I'm... I'm pregnant, Carter," she blurted out, tears streaming down her face. "And it's yours."

Holy. Shit! I stared at him, wondering if he'd realized yet just how badly he'd fucked up. Forget the fact they were going to have a kid, he was in his twenties and she wasn't even legal yet. One phone call from her or her family, and he'd be locked up for statutory rape. What the hell had he been thinking?

The noise of the rodeo seemed to fade into the background as the weight of her words settled upon us. I glanced at Carter, searching for some sign of emotion -- joy, fear, anything -- but his face remained impassive.

"Are you sure?" he asked quietly, his eyes never leaving hers.

Mia nodded, wiping away her tears with the back of her hand. "I've taken three tests, Carter. They all came back positive."

A heavy silence hung in the air between them, filled with unspoken questions and fears. As I watched from the sidelines, my heart ached for both of them -- for Mia, who had been thrust into a terrifying and uncertain future, and for Carter, whose life had just been turned upside down in an instant. Although, to be fair, if he'd kept his dick in his pants, which in this case he definitely should have done, then they wouldn't be having this discussion right now.

"All right," Carter finally said. "We'll figure something out."

"Thank you," Mia whispered, her shoulders sagging with relief as she leaned against him, seeking comfort in his embrace. As they stood there together, their lives forever changed by the revelation of a single secret, I couldn't help but feel a strange sense of foreboding, an icy chill that crept up my spine and whispered of dark days to come. When had Carter ever acted this way? He was always loud, obnoxious, and quick to anger.

For now, all I could do was offer my support and stand by their side, no matter what the future held. I should have listened to that inner voice and stuck to Mia like glue. If I had, then things might have turned out differently.

* * *

Two Days Later

Carter's face twisted into a snarl, his grip on the beer in his hand tightening until I feared the bottle might shatter. I should have known things would turn out this way. Although, I'd never seen him act like this with a woman before. I remained tense and ready to intervene the moment I thought he was going too far.

How many beers had he had? Five? Six? He looked completely plastered. I was thankful I'd decided to come to this rodeo. At first, I'd thought to pass and go to a different event, but when I found out Carter was heading here, something told me to follow.

Why the fuck was he doing this right by the arena? I could barely focus on my upcoming ride. A quick glance showed I needed to get moving if I wanted to make this ride count.

"You stupid little whore," he spat, his words laced with venom and rage that made my blood run cold. "You think I'm gonna stick around and play daddy to some brat? You're out of your Goddamn mind!"

Mia recoiled, her eyes wide with terror. Shit! If he took a swing at her, I'd have to forget my damn ride and go help her. *Hold on just a bit longer.*

"Jackson, it's now or never," said one of the cowboys waiting for me. I pulled my attention away from Carter and Mia, hoping I wasn't making a mistake. I knew I'd ride like shit if I sat here worrying about her.

Closing my eyes, I cleared my mind, blocked out

all the noise around me, adjusted my grip and gave the cowboy a nod. He opened the chute and the bronc beneath me bolted in a straight line. Bastard didn't start bucking until we'd reached the other end of the arena. If I got a shitty score for drawing this horse, I was going to be pissed.

The horse's hooves would pound into the dirt, then he'd go airborne again. He did his best to scrape me off on the arena fencing when he couldn't seem to throw me. Sweat dripped into my eyes and I held on, hoping for a high enough score to at least keep my place. I was gunning for nationals and needed every point.

As the buzzer sounded, I jumped off the bronco. The moment my feet hit the arena floor, I took off for the fence. My body still hummed with energy from the ride, every muscle tense. I cleared the fence and closed the distance.

I'd never seen my friend act like this before, and it sickened me.

"Please, Carter," she begged. "I didn't want this to happen either, but we have to do something."

"Then get rid of it!" he bellowed, causing heads to turn in their direction. "I don't give a damn how, just make sure it's gone!"

The bond between us as friends had shattered in an instant, and I couldn't let Carter hurt Mia any further.

"Hey!" I shouted, my voice firm and commanding. "Leave her alone, Carter!"

He whipped around to face me, his eyes blazing with fury, and for a moment I saw the man I'd once considered a brother. But that fleeting glimpse disappeared as quickly as it had come, replaced by the monster he'd become. I'd like to hope it was only the alcohol, but I worried I might be seeing his true self for the first time.

"Stay out of this, Jackson!" he snarled, his hands clenched into fists at his sides. "This ain't your business!"

"Like hell it isn't," I shot back, my heart pounding in my chest as I positioned myself between him and Mia. "You don't get to treat her like this, not while I'm still breathing."

My words hung heavy in the air between us, a testament to the line we'd crossed and the friendship we'd just left behind. We stood there, two men who'd once been closer than brothers, now locked in a battle neither of us could back down from. I'd never let him, or any man, hurt a woman. Not in my presence. I'd been raised to take care of those weaker than me, and Mia definitely qualified.

"Get the hell away from her, Carter!" I demanded, my voice unwavering. She trembled behind me. I heard her suck in a breath and sniffle, which meant she was most likely crying. I felt her shaky hands press against my back.

"Who the hell do you think you are?" Carter seethed, his bloodshot eyes filled with rage. He threw his beer to the ground, the glass shattering against the dirt, and clenched his fists.

"Someone who won't stand by and watch you hurt a woman," I replied, my pulse racing, knowing the situation was spiraling out of control.

"Stay out of it, Jackson!" Carter spat, his face contorted into a snarl. "I told you this ain't your business!"

I shook my head, refusing to back down. "It became my business when you laid a hand on her. Or are you trying to tell me one side of her face is redder than the other for a reason besides you hitting her?"

Carter's nostrils flared, the alcohol and anger fueling him like a wildfire. He lunged at me, swinging a wild punch aimed straight for my face. I could feel the heat of his fist as it narrowly missed me, my instincts and years of rodeo reflexes kicking in as I expertly dodged the blow.

"Is this how you want to handle things, Carter?" I asked, my heart pounding even faster now, adrenaline coursing through my veins. But before he could answer, I retaliated with a powerful punch of my own, connecting with his jaw.

"Son of a bitch!" he cursed, stumbling back a few steps, clearly stunned by the force of my blow.

"Leave her alone or I swear, I won't hesitate to knock some sense into you," I warned, my eyes locked onto his, showing him I meant every word.

He glared at me, his face reddening with humiliation and fury, but he didn't make another move. His hands fisted at his sides, and I wondered if he was going to take another swing at me. The sweat dripped off my brow as I stared into Carter's rage-filled eyes, preparing for his next move. I couldn't afford to let my guard down -- not with Mia's safety on the line.

"Is that all you got?" Carter snarled, wiping blood from his mouth.

"Leave her alone, Carter," I warned, my chest heaving with the effort it took to keep my emotions in check. "This ends now."

"Over my dead body," he spat back, throwing another punch. But I was ready. With practiced ease, I sidestepped his attack and landed a decisive uppercut to his jaw.

He came after me again, but in his drunken state,

he was no match for me. As much as I hated to hurt the man who'd once been my friend, I landed blow after blow to his ribs, gut, and face. If he'd backed down, I'd have let him go. He charged me again. I slammed my fist into his cheek.

Carter's body crumpled to the ground like a rag doll, the fight finally drained out of him. Silence fell over the rodeo arena as everyone held their breath, waiting to see what would happen next. Shit! I hadn't even realized everyone was watching us. Didn't surprise me no one was stepping forward. They all wanted to watch the drama unfold, but no one wanted to take responsibility for whatever happened.

He groaned and struggled to get to his knees.

"Stay away from her, Carter," I warned.

"Think you can tell me what to do?" he spat, his voice slurred with alcohol.

"About Mia? Yeah, I do," I replied. "Someone needs to protect her from you. When did you become such a mean drunk?"

"Who are you to decide what's best for her?" Carter sneered, wiping the blood from his lip as he advanced.

"Someone who won't lay a hand on her in anger." The alcohol had completely pickled his brain. "Go sleep it off, Carter."

He staggered to his feet and disappeared into the crowd. I had a feeling he'd come for her again. Maybe not today, but sometime in the future. I trusted my gut, and it was telling me Mia was still in danger.

"Jackson, please," Mia whispered, her hand on my arm. Suddenly, the noise of the surrounding chaos seemed to fade away, and all I could hear was her voice, her fear and vulnerability plain for me to see. In that moment, I realized this wasn't just about teaching

Carter a lesson. It was about showing Mia she had someone in her corner, someone who would protect her no matter what.

"Okay," I said. "It's over."

I took her hand in mine, leading her away from the crowd. I might not know a lot about pregnant women, but the stress couldn't be good for her or the baby. She needed somewhere quiet, and we both needed time to think.

"Where are we going?" Mia asked, her eyes still brimming with fear.

"Somewhere safe," I assured her. "Away from all this. Just trust me, okay?"

"Okay," she agreed, her voice barely more than a whisper.

I could feel her body trembling as we moved through the sea of people, and I wished more than anything that I could take away her pain. But for now, all I could do was guide her toward safety, one step at a time.

"Almost there," I murmured, my eyes scanning the area for any sign of danger. "Just keep holding on."

Not knowing what else to do, I led her toward the motel nearby. I'd walked here this morning, or I'd have put her in my truck. The motel was on the outskirts of the rodeo grounds. It wasn't glamorous, but it appeared clean enough.

"Jackson…" Her lower lip trembled. The sight of her like that made my heart ache, and I vowed to do everything in my power to ensure she never had to feel this kind of fear again.

"Hey," I whispered, reaching out to lightly touch her chin. "Are you okay?"

"Y-yeah," she stammered, offering me a weak smile as I lead her inside. "Thank you, Jackson… for everything. I don't know what he'd have done if you hadn't intervened."

"Of course," I replied, meeting her gaze with a reassuring grin. "I'll always be here for you, Mia. No matter what."

She sniffled and a tear rolled down her cheek. I grabbed some tissues from the box on the counter by the sink and handed them to her. She dabbed at her eyes and blew her nose. Even now, she seemed so small. How could Carter have ever hurt her like this?

"Are you okay?" I asked, my voice soft with concern.

Mia hesitated. "I... I don't know. I'm scared, Jackson."

"Hey," I said gently, reaching out to take her hand. "You're not alone in this. I've got your back. I meant it when I said no matter what."

I didn't know a lot about Mia, except that she was now entirely on her own. With Carter out of the picture, she'd have nowhere to go. Shit. He probably had her things. Although, now that I thought about it, I'd never seen her in more than three different shirts. She always wore jeans and boots. Did she not own much?

"Thank you," she whispered, her grip tightening around my hand. "It just feels like everything's falling apart. I never thought Carter would react like that."

"Sometimes we don't really know people until they show their true colors," I replied, anger simmering beneath my words as I thought about what Carter had done. "But he'll never hurt you again. I promise."

"Can we really be sure of that?" Mia questioned, her fear palpable.

"I won't let him," I answered firmly, my resolve

unwavering. "No one gets away with hurting someone I care about. We're friends, right?"

Even though I hadn't known her as long as Carter, she'd been at every rodeo since they'd started dating. We'd watched Carter's events together, and the three of us had gone out to eat many times. Mia had always seemed like a sweetheart, and I'd hoped she'd be good for Carter. Guess I should have worried more about him being an asshole to her.

"Yeah, we are." Mia looked up at me. "I don't know what I'd do without you, Jackson."

"Let's not think about that," I suggested, giving her hand a reassuring squeeze. "We'll figure this out together, all right?"

"Okay," she agreed, swallowing hard.

I had no idea how I should help her right now. We'd have to take things one step at a time. For the moment, I just needed to keep her away from Carter.

"We need to talk about a few things," I said. "Come up with a plan. Are you up for it?"

"Okay," she said softly. "I was staying with Carter."

"What about your things? Do you want me to try and get them for you?"

She shook her head. "It was only a few shirts and some panties."

"Then we'll get you some new things before we leave town. And don't even try to argue. I have the money to cover the expenses." I studied her for a moment. "I think you need to come with me when I check out and move on to the next event. With some luck, Carter won't be there."

"I don't want to be a burden," she said.

"Hey, you're not any trouble, Mia. I want to help you, all right?"

She nodded and leaned into me, letting me hug her close. I didn't know what the hell was going to happen going forward, but I'd make sure she was okay. Whatever it took.

Chapter Two

Mia

I clung to Jackson, my knuckles white as I gripped the fabric of his shirt. My body trembled against his, betraying the fear that seeped into every crevice of my being. The scent of leather and horse filled my nostrils, a soothing reminder of the man holding me tight. It had been a few weeks since I'd told Carter about the baby. Even now, I was worried he'd try to hurt me or the baby.

"Hey," Jackson murmured softly, his breath warm on my ear. "It's going to be all right, darlin'."

I wanted to believe him, but fear had its claws in me, and it refused to let go. I couldn't shake the feeling that Carter was lurking somewhere, waiting for the right moment to strike. And with our baby on the way, the stakes were higher than ever.

"Jackson, I… I don't know what to do," I whispered, my voice so low even I could barely hear myself.

He pulled back slightly, just enough to look me in the eye. His gaze was steady, full of determination and something else I couldn't quite name. But it made me feel a little more grounded, like maybe there was hope after all.

"Listen, Mia, I've been thinking," he began, his drawl comforting me like a warm blanket. "I know things are tough right now, and this whole situation with Carter is far from ideal. But there's something we can do to make sure you and the baby are safe."

"Anything," I said, desperate for any solution that would keep us out of harm's way. Thanks to Jackson, I'd earned my GED, but I didn't feel very much like an adult. With all the moving around, chasing one rodeo after another, I hadn't had the chance to get a job. Right now, I had nothing to my name. No bank account. No cash. The clothes I had were the things Jackson bought me.

"Marriage." Jackson's declaration hung in the air between us, heavy with meaning and unspoken promises. "If we get married, it'll give us some security. We can build a life together, a good one, for us and the baby. *Our* baby."

The way he'd said *our* made my heart race. Would he seriously claim the child as his own? We'd never been more than friends. I'd been so focused on Carter, I'd never really noticed the other men around me.

The thought of marrying Jackson, of becoming a true family, sent a shiver down my spine. It wasn't that I didn't like him -- I did, more than I could ever put into words. But the idea of tying ourselves together in such a permanent way felt like a leap of faith, one that had the potential to either save us or drag us both under.

More than likely, he'd be the one to suffer for it. I knew what people would think when they saw us together. I'd been underage when Carter got me pregnant. While I'd just recently turned eighteen, Jackson was six and a half years older than me.

"Jackson, are you sure?" I asked, searching his eyes for any hint of doubt. "I don't want you to feel trapped or like you have to do this because of the baby."

He shook his head, his expression resolute. "No, Mia. I want this. I want the baby to grow up knowing they have two parents who love them. I'll do whatever it takes to keep the two of you safe."

My heart swelled at his words. Maybe this was

the answer we'd been searching for, the key to keeping Carter at bay and ensuring a stable future for my child. And as I looked into Jackson's eyes, I realized that I couldn't imagine facing this journey with anyone else by my side. He'd already done so much for me.

"All right," I whispered, daring to let myself believe that things could work out. "Let's do it. Let's get married."

Since Jackson and I had never shared more than a hug, I had to admit to feeling anxious over the idea of having an actual relationship with him. I had no idea what his expectations would be. I should have asked, but part of me was too scared. What if he wanted a true marriage? Was that something I could give him?

"Come on," Jackson said. "I rented us a cabin near the next rodeo. It won't start for another week, but we can get there early and have a bit of a break. I'm sure you're tired of motel rooms."

"A cabin sounds perfect. Thank you, Jackson."

He flashed me a smile, and I felt a fluttering in my stomach. If I wasn't careful, I'd end up falling in love with him… which wouldn't be awful, unless he never felt the same about me.

* * *

The sun dipped below the horizon as I stood on the porch, the evening breeze carrying with it a hint of jasmine from the nearby flowerbeds. The scent calmed me, if only for a moment, before my thoughts inevitably drifted back to Carter and the danger he posed. I could feel the weight of the decision Jackson and I had made settling heavily on my shoulders.

The rodeo started in two days, and I'd spotted Carter in town earlier. I didn't think he'd noticed me, but if he did… I didn't feel safe knowing he was nearby.

"Hey," Jackson said softly, stepping up behind me and wrapping his arms around my waist. "You okay?"

I leaned back against him, grateful for his support. "Just thinking."

"About what?" he asked, his breath warm on my neck.

"Everything. Carter, the wedding, the baby..." My voice trailed off as I tried to find the words to express the whirlwind of emotions inside of me.

"Hey, look at me," he urged, turning me gently to face him. His eyes searched mine with a tenderness that made my heart swell. "We're going to get through this, Mia. I promise."

His certainty was contagious, and I found myself nodding. "I know. It's just... hard not to worry, you know?"

"Of course," he acknowledged, pressing a gentle kiss to my forehead. "But we're taking control of the situation. Getting married will hopefully give you a layer of protection from Carter. We'll make sure our baby has a safe, happy life. Maybe if he realizes I'm going to claim the kid as my own, then he'll realize he doesn't have anything to worry about."

As the next two days passed, my fear of Carter intensified. Every shadow seemed to hold the possibility of him lurking there, every creak in the house sent shivers down my spine. I knew it was irrational, that he couldn't be everywhere at once, but the thought of him coming after us consumed my every waking moment.

"Jackson, do you think he knows?" I asked one night, unable to keep the worry from my voice. "About the baby, I mean. He told me to get rid of it, but I didn't."

"Maybe," he sighed, his arms tightening around me. "But we can't let that control our lives, darlin'. We'll take whatever precautions we need to and stand up to him if it comes to that."

"I just don't want anything to happen to you or the baby," I whispered, my eyes filling with tears. "You've been so good to us. I feel like I don't have anything to contribute."

"Hey now," he murmured, brushing my tears away with his thumb. "We're going to be okay. Remember, we've got each other, and if I think he's going to make a move, we can always go back to my hometown. I told you my dad is part of the Dixie Reapers MC. I know they'll help watch our backs."

"Thank you, Jackson," I said through the tears, allowing myself to soak in the comfort he provided. I knew marriage wouldn't magically make everything perfect, but it would give us a fighting chance against Carter's potential harm. And for now, that was enough.

* * *

I gripped the steering wheel tightly, my knuckles turning white. The rain pummeled down on the roof of the truck, each drop sounding like a tiny drumbeat and nearly blinded me as it came down hard on the windshield. I glanced at the rearview mirror and shuddered. All I could see was darkness swallowing the road behind me.

The rodeo had been rained out, which ended up being a good thing. Jackson had a fever so I'd left him at the cabin and ventured out to find medicine for him. If only I'd realized how bad the weather would be, I may have asked him to ride with me. I heard a sudden *pop* and the wheel nearly jerked from my hands. Squinting, I looked in the sideview mirror and realized the tire was now flat. Had I run over something?

Frustration welled up inside me. I hadn't had any issues going to the pharmacy. Was this really just an accident? At least the rain had eased up.

"Need some help?" a voice called out, startling me. Carter approached from the darkness, I hit the button to make sure the doors were locked. "Don't have your guard dog with you?"

Why had I never noticed the evil lurking in his eyes? The man was a monster. He banged his fist against the window, smiling at me.

"Go away, Carter!"

"Is that any way to talk to your boyfriend?"

Was he serious right now? "We broke up. I'm not yours anymore."

The smile slid from his face. "You might want to rethink the way you speak to me, Mia. We're all alone in this storm, and it looks like the truck isn't going anywhere. Guess you better let me give you a ride."

I shook my head. I had a bad feeling he'd hurt me if I got out. But since I had Jackson's truck, he didn't have a way to come look for me. How was I going to get back to the cabin?

Right when I was contemplating the best way to get away from Carter, I saw another set of headlights. A familiar red truck stopped beside me, leaving Carter between the vehicles.

"Hey, Bales! That's not your girl. Think you need to move along." The cowboy glaring at him was a friend of Jackson's, and relief flooded me. I knew Cooper wouldn't leave me alone with Carter.

"This isn't your business," Carter said. "Move along."

"I don't think so. Jackson won't be happy about the fact you're harassing his fiancée."

Carter faced me again, his eyes narrowing. "What the fuck is he talking about?"

"Jackson and I are getting married, Carter. I need you to leave me alone."

He slammed his fist against the window again and I yelped, shrinking back. Now I was certain the flat tire wasn't an accident. Carter must have put something in the road, then waited for me to come back through here.

Cooper got out of his truck, then dragged Carter off by his collar. After landing two punches, he used his booted foot to shove Carter to the ground, then spat on him. When Cooper knocked on my window, I rolled it down partway.

"Come on, Mia. I'll give you a ride to the cabin, then come back and deal with the flat tire. Most likely, it's going to need a new one."

"Thank you, Cooper." I rolled up the window, shut off the engine, then got into Cooper's truck. I hit the button on the key fob to lock the doors, and eyed Carter as we drove past him. Would this be the end of it? Was I finally done with Carter?

"You need to tell Jackson what happened," Cooper said.

I held up the bag from the pharmacy. "He's sick. It's why he didn't go with me."

"He still needs to know, Mia. If you don't tell him, then I will."

I sighed. "All right."

We pulled up to the cabin, and I rushed inside. Jackson still slept on the couch, and I hurried over to check on him, wincing when I felt how hot his forehead was. I changed into something dry and got him a bottle of water.

"Jackson, can you wake up for a minute? I have

your medicine." He moaned and struggled to open his eyes. I helped him sit up, gave him the pills, and made sure he swallowed them. "The truck got a flat. Cooper gave me a ride back and said he'd take care of the tire."

His eyes opened wide and he sat straight up. "What? Are you okay?"

"I'm fine!" I swallowed hard. "Um. Carter was there. He scared me, but I stayed in the locked truck until Cooper passed by. He hit Carter and told him to leave me alone. He also told him we're getting married."

Jackson ran a hand down his face. "I'm sure he's pissed. You okay, darlin'?"

"I'm fine. Really. Just get some rest and get better." I kissed his forehead. "It's my turn to take care of you."

He gave me a tired smile and lay back down. I had to hope this was the last time Carter would cause any trouble. But I had a really bad feeling... He wasn't the type to back down. If he thought I was happy with Jackson, he'd do whatever he could to ruin our lives. I only hoped he wouldn't do anything to cause either of us physical harm.

Chapter Three

Mia

A few days later, I watched from the stands as Jackson prepared for his event at the rodeo. The anticipation in the air was palpable, and I felt a mixture of pride and worry for him. I knew how much he loved bronc riding, but I couldn't shake the nagging feeling something was wrong. A prickle of unease had washed over me off and on all day. Carter had been quiet since Cooper punched him. Too quiet.

"Jackson!" I suddenly heard someone shout, panic evident in their voice. My heart leapt into my throat as I saw him struggling with his rigging, which looked like it had either broken or been cut.

"Get him down!" another voice bellowed, and several cowboys rushed to his aid, grabbing hold of the rigging and carefully lowering him to the ground. I clutched the railing in front of me, barely able to breathe until I saw him standing safely on solid ground.

"Jackson." My voice quivered as I called out, trying to get through the crowd to reach him. "Are you okay?"

"Shaken up, but I'll be all right," he replied, his eyes filled with concern. "But, Mia, that rigging was cut. Someone did this on purpose. Looked like someone sawed through it, just enough it would have snapped if I'd stayed on any longer."

"Is it Carter?" I asked, my suspicions growing stronger. It all seemed too convenient -- a flat tire one day and now sabotaged rigging. Or could it be someone who felt threatened over his position for nationals?

"Maybe," Jackson admitted, his jaw clenched.

"We need to stay alert, darlin'. He's trying to create chaos in our lives. Either that, or I've pissed off the wrong person."

"Jackson," I whispered, gripping his arm tightly. "Please promise me you'll be careful. I can't lose you."

"I promise, Mia," he said softly, pulling me close. "I'll do everything I can to keep us safe."

As we left the arena, I couldn't help but look over my shoulder, feeling the weight of unseen eyes watching us. My heart raced with fear and determination -- whatever Carter had planned, we would face it together.

The sun dipped low in the sky, casting a golden glow over the dusty rodeo grounds as Jackson and I sat on the tailgate of his truck.

"Jackson, I really think Carter is behind all these incidents," I said quietly. I hoped he could hear me over the distant sounds of bucking bulls and cheering spectators. "I mean, I get that it could be a coincidence, but I don't feel like it is. He was clearly waiting for me when the tire went flat. And then after he finds out we're engaged, your rigging gets cut?"

Jackson's jaw clenched, and I knew he was considering my words carefully. His eyes were filled with a mix of concern and determination as he finally responded. "I've been thinking the same thing, Mia. As much as I don't want to believe Carter could do something like this, I think you're right. The moment I saw him yelling at you, and realized he'd hit you, I knew he wasn't the man I'd thought he was."

"Then what do we do?" I asked, my heart pounding in my chest. "How do we protect ourselves from someone who knows our every move? There are only so many rodeos left. The odds we'll keep running into him are high, especially if he gets a good enough score to make it to the national rodeo."

"We'll need to come up with a plan." Jackson's hand found mine, squeezing it tightly. "We won't let him win, Mia. We're stronger than that."

"Is there anyone we can turn to for help?" I questioned, feeling a sense of desperation growing within me.

"Maybe the Dixie Reapers," Jackson mused, his gaze turning thoughtful. "My dad's club has dealt with threats like this before. They might be able to offer some assistance."

"Would they really help us?" I asked hesitantly, uncertain about involving an outlaw motorcycle club in our lives. He'd mentioned them a few times when I'd been dating Carter. At the time, I hadn't thought much about it since it didn't concern me. Now it was a different story. If they were so great, why hadn't he taken me there to meet them yet? I knew he was from Alabama. Our current rodeo was probably within a day's drive of his hometown. We could have gone there instead of the cabin.

"Trust me, darlin', they'd do anything to keep their own safe," Jackson assured me, his tone confident. "Even if I didn't want to prospect for the club, I'm still family. And now, you and the baby are too. I'll make a call and see what they can do."

As he pulled out his phone and dialed a number, I couldn't help but feel a little bit of relief wash over me. The thought of having the Dixie Reapers on our side was intimidating, but their reputation for loyalty and protection gave me hope that we might stand a chance against Carter.

"Hey, it's Jackson," he said when the call connected. "I need to talk to you about something serious. But first, I need to know you won't share this conversation with anyone, Wire."

I didn't know who Wire was, but I listened as he explained everything we'd been facing. I noticed he'd left out the part where we planned to get married, or the fact I was pregnant. Part of me felt hurt he wanted to keep our relationship a secret, but on the other hand, I understood. I knew he valued his reputation, and getting engaged to a pregnant eighteen-year-old probably hadn't been his greatest idea.

"We think Carter's trying to hurt us, and I don't know what to do."

I listened as Jackson talked a bit more about the different incidents to the person on the other end of the line, his voice steady and determined. My heart swelled with gratitude and love for this man who was willing to face any danger to keep our family safe. My cheeks flushed. Love? No. I liked him and felt grateful. That's all it was. Right?

"All right, thanks," he concluded, hanging up the phone and turning to me with a reassuring smile. "Wire is going to help us figure out how to handle Carter. We're not alone in this, Mia. The man is one of the best hackers in the world, so he'll probably try to find proof of what Carter's done."

"Thank you, Jackson," I whispered, tears prickling at the corners of my eyes. "You have no idea how much this means to me."

"Anything for you, darlin'," he replied, pulling me into his strong arms. As we held each other in the fading light, I knew that together, we would find a way to overcome the darkness threatening to consume us. Carter's attempts at hurting us might seem mild right now, but I knew firsthand it could get much worse. I truly believed he was capable of killing us.

"Maybe we should head home," Jackson

suggested. "We'll be safer there, behind locked doors."

"Are you sure?" I hesitated. "I don't want to ruin your night."

"Hey," he said softly, cupping my face in his rough hands. "Your safety is more important than any rodeo event. Let's get out of here."

As we rode back to the cabin, I wondered if I should learn how to defend myself. Jackson couldn't be with me all the time. What if Carter cornered me when I was alone again? I didn't want to be helpless.

"What's on your mind?" Jackson asked as we pulled up to the cabin.

"Just wondering if I should learn how to protect myself."

He nodded. "Not a bad idea. Since I hadn't planned to leave for a few more days, we can research a few options. We can either lengthen our stay here or find something at our next stop."

"I'm fine with either. I just don't like feeling like I have to rely on other people to keep me safe all the time."

Jackson lifted my hand and kissed the back of it. "Whatever you want."

* * *

I stared at my reflection in the full-length mirror, my hands clenched into fists by my side. The woman looking back at me appeared worn down and vulnerable, but deep within her eyes, I could see a flicker of determination. I refused to be a victim any longer. If Carter thought he could terrorize me and my family, he had another thing coming.

"All right, ladies, let's get started," called out the self-defense instructor. I took a deep breath and focused on her words as she guided us through various techniques designed to fend off attackers. Each move made me feel stronger, more capable, and it fueled my resolve to protect those I loved.

"Hey, Mia, you're doing great," said one of my classmates, a woman named Laura who had become a friendly face during our sessions. "You've come a long way since we started."

"Thanks," I replied with a small smile, appreciating her encouragement. "I just… I need to know I can protect myself and my baby."

"Girl, you've got this," Laura assured me, giving my arm a squeeze. "No one's going to mess with you after this class."

As our session ended, I felt a newfound sense of empowerment coursing through me. I may not have been a skilled fighter like Jackson, but I was no longer helpless. I could stand up for myself.

Jackson met me outside the gym, leaning against his truck with that easy grin that always sent a flutter through me. "How'd it go?"

"Better than I thought," I admitted, allowing myself to sink into his embrace for a moment before pulling away. "I'm starting to feel more confident, like I can actually do something if Carter tries anything."

"Good," he said, his eyes softening. "I'm proud of you, darlin'. I knew you had it in you."

"Thanks," I said, feeling my cheeks warm at his praise. "But we're not out of the woods yet, are we?"

"Unfortunately, no," Jackson admitted, his expression darkening. "Carter's still out there, and he's unpredictable. We need to stay vigilant, but I promise you, Mia, I won't let anything happen to you or our baby. And Wire is doing everything he can to track down the asshole and get proof he tried to hurt the both of us. Although, once he finds it, I doubt he's going to turn the bastard over to the law."

"Is he not still competing?" I asked.

"He is, but he's been sneaky about it. He's signing in the day of the event, staying only long enough for his ride, then he's gone. The times he's won, no one could get to him fast enough. He'd already gotten his prize and taken off by the time Wire got someone over there. Then he goes off the grid again, which means he's using cash and being careful about cameras."

The weight of our situation hung heavy between us, but I found solace in Jackson's presence. He was my rock, my protector. Even though the rodeo at this location had ended a week ago, he'd stuck around so I could keep taking classes.

"Come on," he said, opening the truck door for me. "Let's go home."

I wondered if he'd ever say that phrase and mean an actual house that was ours, one where our baby could grow up and make friends in the neighborhood. Maybe if he became a national champion like his dad things would change.

I'd also begun to think about what our lives would be like as a married couple. Not once had Jackson done more than kiss my cheek, forehead, or hand. He'd never tried to really kiss me. Hadn't made any other move either. Did he find me the least bit attractive? He'd called me beautiful before. What if he hadn't meant it? Or what if he found me pretty but I wasn't the type of woman he was sexually attracted to?

"Are we still getting married?" I asked.

"I was thinking we'd do it in Vegas. I know that's not the most romantic wedding, but..." He rubbed the back of his neck. "There's a not-so-legal way, but our marriage would look legit. But if we do that, it involves the club. I'd rather have a real wedding, even if it's just at a Vegas chapel."

"It's the least amount of fuss," I said. "I'm fine with that, but when are we going to Las Vegas?"

"As soon as your classes are done. We'll drive there, get a nice hotel room for a few days, get married and have a short honeymoon."

My cheeks warmed. "Honeymoon?"

He glanced at me. "We can sightsee or do whatever you want."

So, he didn't mean a *real* honeymoon. He still didn't plan to touch me. Why did I feel so disheartened by it? He'd held my hand easily enough. Even seemed to freely offer hugs. Was that all we'd ever have between us? I wanted a kiss from him, not just one on my cheek or forehead. Part of me worried I was signing myself up for a passionless, loveless marriage. It would still be the best option for me, and for the baby. But was I wrong to want him to desire me? How did he see me? As a friend? Sister? Did I even rate that high? Why couldn't Jackson look at me like I was the most beautiful woman in the world?

As the thoughts bombarded me, I felt guilty. He was giving up so much to marry me. I should be grateful instead of wanting more. I shouldn't be so greedy.

"Sure, sightseeing sounds great. We can see shows and eat at those fancy buffets." I forced a smile.

"Do you know when your last class will be?" he asked.

"I think I have two left. So, we should be able to leave in the next few days. Don't you have another rodeo in order to qualify?"

He shook his head. "I have enough points I'm guaranteed a chance at the championship. Right now, I'm top three. It wouldn't hurt to go to one or two more, but we have more important things to do right now. If it looks like I'll drop out of the top fifteen, then I'll hit a few more."

"But still… The extra points would help, wouldn't they?" I asked.

"Mia, I'd give it all up if that's what it took to keep you and the baby safe. Now, stop worrying about my qualification score, and think about where in Vegas you'd like to get married. They have some themed chapels, but also regular ones."

Why was he willing to give up so much for me? There were times I wondered if he saw me as… more. Then he'd say something that proved he'd drawn a line in the sand, so to speak. I didn't know where I stood with him.

"I think I'd prefer something more traditional. But I don't have a dress."

He kissed my cheek. "Let me worry about that. I'm not exactly broke. My dad still puts money in my account from time to time, even though I've been an adult for a while now. It's not going to hurt me financially to buy you a wedding dress. We can even get pictures taken. Most of the chapels offer packages."

Another cheek kiss. What would happen if I turned my face at the last second and our lips met? Would he be horrified? No. Knowing Jackson, he'd take it in stride. Maybe even apologize. That alone would break my heart. He might be sweet, but part of me wondered if he'd have done this for another woman in the same situation. Was any of it really for me or just because he wanted to be someone's hero?

"How do you know all this?" I asked, suddenly wondering if he'd been married before.

"I know a few people who've gotten married there. Two cowboys I met on the circuit, and one of the barrel racers. They all eloped to Vegas when they decided to get married. Although, I don't think any of the relationships lasted. Doesn't mean ours won't."

Right. Because a marriage based on nothing more than me being in trouble was sure to end with a happily ever after. Now I knew for sure he was a dreamer. Either way, I was going to grab hold of Jackson and never let go. He might be settling by choosing me, but I knew I was getting the better deal out of this. Any woman would be lucky to have a man like him.

"All right. Let's get married in Vegas." It didn't really matter where or how we did it. The important part was the fact we'd be married afterward.

Chapter Four

Jackson

As the Las Vegas sun blazed overhead, I pulled the truck up to the hotel. My heart raced with anticipation for our new beginning together. Mia was becoming my priority. I still felt uncertain over how to act around her. How much intimacy was too much? I'd done my best to treat her as I would a good friend. Sometimes I thought I caught a flash of disappointment in her eyes. If she wanted more, all she had to do was tell me. The way she'd chased after Carter, I didn't think she was shy when it came to things like that. Maybe she just didn't find me attractive. Carter and I didn't look anything alike.

"Can you believe we're here, Jackson?" Mia's eyes sparkled like the neon lights surrounding us.

"Hardly," I replied, a mix of fear and desire coursing through me. Was I doing the right thing? I couldn't think of a better way to protect Mia, but I had to wonder what my family would think about this.

No, my true fear was what would happen after the wedding. I'd planned for us to sleep in the same bed. Now that we were here, I worried I'd want to do more than sleep. What if I reached for her in the middle of the night? The last thing I wanted to do was scare her. I'd be lying if I said Mia wasn't beautiful. I'd thought so from the moment I'd first met her, but it had been clear she was Carter's. She'd only had eyes for him. Now I'd essentially stolen my friend's girl. No, he'd thrown her away and we were no longer friends. I wasn't doing anything wrong. Except that Mia might not appreciate my thoughts, or the way I found myself watching the sway of her hips.

Hell, other people had noticed. I didn't know

how Mia didn't. I had more than one cowboy shoot me a knowing smirk when I'd been walking behind Mia or watching her bend over to pick something up. By some miracle, she hadn't noticed the times she'd made me hard. Mia needed a gentleman, and I was determined to be one. We were getting married so she'd be safe, and I wanted the baby to have my last name. I had to admit the thought of being a dad scared me, but I also looked forward to it.

We checked into the hotel and quickly entered our suite. If I was going to do this, might as well do it right. I only ever planned to have one wedding. Eager to freshen up before finding a chapel for our ceremony, we stepped inside the dimly lit room. Mia turned to me with uncertainty in her gaze.

"Are you ready for this?" she asked softly. I knew she had to be as scared as I was.

"More than anything," I answered without hesitation, embracing her tightly. She needed me to be confident right now. If she knew I had any doubts, it would only send her running. Although, my fears centered around me scaring her, screwing up as a dad, or just failing at this marriage completely.

As I changed into a nice pair of jeans and new boots, I couldn't help but think about the incredible journey that had led me here. Growing up as the son of a Dixie Reaper named Cowboy, I never imagined I'd be lucky enough to find someone like Mia. The only girls I'd been around were buckle bunnies or the ones I'd grown up with at the compound. Neither had really appealed to me. The kids at the Dixie Reapers all felt like family. The mere thought of kissing any of Tank's daughters, or anyone else old enough, made me want to gag.

But Mia... Despite all she'd been through, she

was still so sweet and trusting. It made me want to shelter her from the world, make sure no one could ever hurt her again, and just hold her close. I wasn't sure what to call the way I was feeling, although I knew I was definitely protective over Mia. Without someone standing in her corner, I had no doubt the world would chew her up and spit her out.

I didn't deserve someone like her. A rough cowboy like me shouldn't get to claim a woman who still had an air of innocence about her, even if she was already carrying a baby. She'd put her faith in the wrong person. Nothing less and nothing more. It could have happened to anyone. When she'd told Carter about the baby, I'd seen the fear in her eyes. It should have never happened that way. If she'd been mine and told me we were having a kid, it might have shocked the hell out of me, but I'd have gathered her close, kissed her, and asked her to marry me.

Instead, she'd essentially been kicked by a mule instead, with Carter's dumb ass being the mule. I still wanted to beat him senseless. Not just for being a dick to Mia, but I couldn't believe he'd actually hit her. An angel like her deserved so much better.

"All right, darlin'," I said, holding out my hand to her. "Let's go find us a chapel."

Mia smiled, her eyes shining with excitement, and took my hand. Together, we stepped back out into the sweltering heat. I had no idea if she felt as apprehensive as I did. While I'd have done anything to keep Mia safe, I had to wonder if this was truly what was best for her, or was I just hung up playing the part of her hero?

"Jackson, I've never been happier than I am right now." She smiled up at me. "I never thought I'd meet someone like you. The only men I've ever known were all like Carter. Even my father."

It was the first time she'd mentioned her family, other than telling me her homelife hadn't been a nice one. I'd known she'd run away from home and helped her as best I could. But hearing her mention her dad, made me want to ask questions. I refrained, knowing it would ruin the moment. I hoped one day she'd trust me enough to open up about her past. I had a feeling what she called a bad homelife would make me want to track down the assholes she called parents and teach them a lesson.

"No matter what challenges come our way, I promise to stand by your side and face them head-on," I said, hoping she knew I meant every word.

"Jackson," Mia murmured, squeezing my hand gently. "Thank you for choosing me. I know you aren't in love with me, and that's okay. Although, I do worry that you'll come to regret this one day."

"Never," I vowed. "I may not be a part of my dad's club, but I still uphold a lot of their values. One of those is never giving up on the woman we've chosen. So, once we get married today, there won't be a divorce later. You'll be mine until the day one of us dies."

I could feel Mia's hand trembling in mine as we approached the entrance of the chapel, whether it was from nerves or excitement I wasn't sure. Or perhaps I'd scared her with the no divorce talk before coming here. Probably something we should have talked about before we made it to Vegas. I normally viewed things in a calm and logical manner. When it came to Mia, it felt like someone had scrambled my brains.

"Here we are," I said, giving her hand a reassuring squeeze. "Are you ready?"

"More than ever," Mia replied.

As we stepped through the chapel doors, we were greeted by the warm smile of the officiant. He was an older gentleman, his silver hair contrasting sharply with the deep tan of his weathered face. His eyes held a warmth that attested to how much he loved his job.

"Welcome," he said, extending his hand to us both. "I'm Pastor John. You must be Jackson and Mia."

"Nice to meet you, sir," I replied, shaking his hand firmly.

"Please, call me John," he chuckled, his laughter rich and inviting. "Now, let's get down to business and make sure everything is perfect for your special day."

We followed him to a small office where he had us fill out the necessary paperwork and discuss the finer details of our ceremony. As we spoke, I couldn't help but notice how attentive he was to Mia's desires, making sure she felt heard and valued every step of the way. That alone made me certain I'd booked the right chapel. Nothing mattered more to me than making this day one Mia would look back on fondly.

I just had to keep reminding myself there wouldn't be a conventional wedding night. I'd have to come up with something for us to do. If not, I'd spend the rest of the night and possibly tomorrow thinking about the fact I'd love to do more than hold her hand, give her hugs, or kiss her cheek.

"All right," John said after we'd ironed out the last of the details. "Now that we've got everything set, it's time for the fun part -- finding the perfect dress for the beautiful bride-to-be. We have some you can rent just for the ceremony, or you can also purchase them."

He led us to a room filled with wedding dresses of all shapes and sizes. The sight of them took my breath away, each gown more stunning than the last.

But none compared to the beauty of Mia as she stood among them, her eyes wide with awe.

"Take your time, darlin'," I whispered, giving her a gentle nudge. "I'll be right here."

Mia smiled at me before turning her attention back to the dresses. She tried on several gowns, each one making her look more radiant than the last. But it wasn't until she stepped out in a simple yet elegant dress that I knew we'd found the one. It accentuated her natural beauty, hugging her curves in all the right places and making her eyes sparkle like the stars above us. Even though she didn't have a baby bump yet, she'd been filling out a bit more over the last few weeks.

"Jackson," she said softly, as tears welled in her eyes. "What do you think?"

"Darlin', you look absolutely breathtaking," I replied, speaking nothing but the truth. "There's no doubt in my mind that you're the most beautiful woman in the world."

As Mia hugged me tightly, I couldn't wait to see what the future had in store for us. At least the flush to her cheeks told me she'd been pleased with my words. Had I not told her I thought she was the prettiest woman I'd ever met? I'd need to do better in the future.

I'd intended for ours to be a marriage of convenience, but I had to hope that one day we might have the same kind of marriage as my parents. It's what I'd always wanted. And the more time I spent with Mia, the more certain I became that I wanted so much more from her. I wanted her under me, crying out my name, begging me for more. To be able to kiss her like she was my everything. For everyone who saw us to know exactly what she meant to me just by looking at us.

We followed the pastor back into the chapel, and I watched Mia as she stood at the entrance, ready to walk down the aisle. While this wasn't a traditional wedding exactly, it was the closest we could get with the limited time we had available. I'd arranged to have pictures taken during the ceremony and after, so Mia would have photos or a wedding scrapbook. She might not care now, but one day she might change her mind.

As the notes of the bridal chorus began to play, Mia started her slow walk down the aisle. Her gown shimmered under the lights, and the matching shoes I had bought for her clicked softly against the faux stone path. With every step she took, my heart swelled with admiration for this incredible woman who had accepted me as her partner in life.

"Wow," I breathed out, unable to tear my eyes away from the vision that was Mia. Her radiant beauty seemed to light up the chapel, stealing the breath from my lungs. My heart raced as she drew closer, her eyes locked on mine, brimming with happiness and perhaps a little uncertainty.

"Please face each other and join hands," the officiant instructed us once Mia reached my side. As our fingers intertwined, the world around us seemed to fade away, leaving only the two of us standing there, ready to commit our lives to one another.

"Jackson, please recite your vows," the officiant prompted.

"Uh… right," I stammered, my voice trembling with emotion as I looked into Mia's eyes. I hadn't exactly written any vows, but I did have an idea of what I wanted to say. So, why couldn't I think of a single word all of a sudden? The officiant cleared his throat, and I knew I had to say something.

"Mia, when I first met you, I never imagined that you'd be the one to tame this wild cowboy's heart. But you did. You showed me what it means to have a partnership built on trust and respect, that it's okay to embrace the future. I can't wait to spend the rest of my life with you. Today," I continued, pausing to swallow the lump in my throat, "I vow to honor you, cherish you, and protect you with every fiber of my being. I promise to stand by your side, through thick and thin, for better or for worse. And above all else, I pledge my unwavering love and devotion to you for the rest of our days."

"Beautifully spoken, Jackson," the officiant said softly, nodding his approval before turning to Mia. "Now, Mia, please recite your vows."

"Jackson," she began, her voice steady and full of warmth, "you came into my life at first as a friend, and later as my hero. You showed me that good men really do exist. I'm so grateful to have you in my life. You've been my rock, my confidant, and my best friend through some of the darkest times in my life, and I can't imagine facing this world without you by my side."

The officiant's words echoed through the quaint chapel as he declared us husband and wife. "You may now kiss the bride."

I pulled Mia closer. The moment our lips touched, a surge of desire and passion ignited within me. It felt like a wildfire racing through my veins. Her lips parted under mine and our tongues tangled. Her kiss tasted like innocence and desire mingled together. A gasp slipped from her, and I slowly pulled back. I knew in that instant that our relationship had evolved into something more than friendship. At least for me. With each passing second, I grew more certain that I

wanted more from Mia than just friendship. I
wanted... everything.

When had I fallen for her? Had it been so subtle
that it slipped past me until now? I knew kissing her
hadn't made me fall head over heels, although I did
want to do a lot more of it. As I gazed into her eyes, I
saw forever... having a family, going on trail rides
together, picnics, watching fireworks on the Fourth of
July, growing old together. I wanted all of it, and only
with Mia. I'd often heard my dad's club brothers talk
about how they just knew the moment they met the
woman meant for them. Had some part of me
recognized Mia as mine, and I'd been holding back
because of her relationship with Carter?

I now understood how my dad must have felt.
He'd not only helped Mom escape from my birth
father, but he'd treated me and Danica like his own
from the beginning. It was exactly the same for me and
Mia, although our baby hadn't been born yet. I didn't
care if I didn't share DNA with the kid. They were
mine, and that was all that mattered. I'd do anything to
keep my new family safe.

Someone cleared their throat and I realized I'd
been too lost in my thoughts, and the dazed expression
on Mia's face told me plenty. Even if she wasn't in love
with me, she definitely felt something. It gave me hope
we'd have a very happy life together.

"Congratulations," the officiant said, pulling us
back to reality. As we made our way back down the
aisle, hand in hand, I marveled at how much had
changed in such a short time. I'd walked into this
chapel questioning my decision, and now I knew with
a certainty Mia was meant to be mine. How had I been
so blind to my true feelings for her until now?

"Can you believe it? We're actually married!"

Mia exclaimed as we stepped outside the chapel.

"Believe it, beautiful," I replied, squeezing her waist. "And I wouldn't have it any other way."

We went back to our hotel suite with the idea we'd change clothes before going out to eat and sightseeing. Except, once the door clicked shut behind us, I had to fight to control the urge to kiss her again. When she turned and smiled at me, I knew it was a lost cause.

Pulling her into my arms, I slanted my mouth over hers. Deepening the kiss, I savored every second. My hands explored the small of her back, then I slid one up between her shoulder blades and grabbed a handful of her hair, holding her in place as I ravaged her lips. Her body tensed, then relaxed under my touch, a silent surrender.

"Jackson," she moaned, fanning the already raging flames within me. Navigating the maze of laces and fabric at the back of her dress became my sole focus, each deft stroke causing goose bumps to rise on her skin. I managed to unfasten the dress and slid it off her shoulders. It pooled at her feet, and my breath caught at the sight of her in nothing but tiny scraps of white lace.

Her chest rose and fell heavily under my gaze as I allowed myself a moment to appreciate the incredible woman standing before me. The blush creeping across her cheeks served only to heighten my arousal as I slowly reached for the clasp between her breasts.

"You're sure?" I asked, locking eyes with her for reassurance. She simply nodded, threading her fingers into my hair and pulling me back in for another searing kiss.

I undid the clasp of her bra, unveiling a pair of perky breasts with the prettiest nipples I'd ever seen.

While I wasn't the man whore some of my friends were, it wasn't like I was a virgin. I'd been with a few women, but no one memorable. This was different. Mia was *mine*. My wife.

I cupped her breasts, the heat radiating off her skin making my fingers tingle with anticipation. Her gasp was music to my ears as I gently brushed my thumbs over her nipples, watching them harden in response. Slipping one hand lower, I traced a line down her abdomen toward the last piece of fabric separating us. Feeling her shiver under my touch, I dipped my fingers underneath the lace panties she wore and lightly explored. As my fingers stroked her slit, I felt how wet she was already.

Trailing a path of hungry kisses down her neck and between the valley of her breasts, I paused to swirl my tongue around one hardened nipple, while my fingers slid into her wet heat. Every sweet sound she made left me aching for release.

"Mia," I groaned against her skin, "I need you."

My words seemed to ignite something within her because the next thing I knew, we were stumbling toward the bedroom, where she pulled me down on top of her on the soft mattress. I couldn't help but kiss her again. Each one we shared seemed sweeter than the last.

Drawing back, I stared down at her, taking in the beautiful sight of my new wife spread out beneath me. My cock jerked behind my zipper, begging to be set free. I stood and toed off my boots, yanked off my socks, and started working on the buttons on my shirt. Mia watched with a hungry expression. Once I'd stripped all the way, she leaned forward and traced her finger down my hard cock.

"I never thought this part of a man was pretty,

but in your case, I'll make an exception." She licked her lips and dropped to her knees at my feet. Before I had a chance to process what she was doing, she'd taken me into her mouth, flicking her tongue over the sensitive head.

"Jesus, Mia. You're killing me with that wicked mouth." I sifted my fingers through her hair, guiding her. I lost myself in the sensation as she sucked and licked, driving me mad. I felt my balls draw up, and knew I'd be coming in a minute if we didn't stop. "Up! I want to be inside you."

She stood on shaky legs, slid her panties down her legs, then sprawled on the bed again. I yanked her ass to the edge of the mattress, and she immediately spread her thighs, hooking her legs around me. Positioning my cock at her entrance, I slowly sank into her, holding her gaze because I didn't want to miss a moment of this. She arched her back as I completely filled her.

"Feels so good, Jackson." Her nails dug into my shoulders. I pulled almost all the way out before thrusting back in. I must have hit that sweet spot inside her because she shivered and gave a soft cry, her hold on me tightening. It only took three more strokes before I felt the heat of her release.

Gripping her hips tight, I drove into her, taking what I needed. She shuddered beneath me, screaming my name as she came again. I pounded into her, not slowing until I'd emptied every drop of cum from my balls. Panting, I leaned down to kiss her softly.

"That wasn't quite how I wanted this to go. Our first time together should have been…"

She placed her finger over my lips. "It was perfect. No one's ever made me feel like this before, Jackson, so don't spoil the moment. Besides, it's not like we can't do it again."

I smiled down at her. "Naughty girl. You're right. We have plenty of time."

I eased out of her and flopped onto the bed on my back. Mia squealed as I grabbed her around the waist and hauled her on top of me. Even though I'd just come, my cock was still hard. "Cowgirl up, Mia. Show me how well you ride."

Her cheeks flushed as she sank onto my cock. "I'm definitely staying on for more than eight seconds."

How the fuck had I managed to find the one woman who was perfect for me in every way? As much as I wanted to beat the hell out of Carter, I also felt like I owed him a beer. If he hadn't been such a dumbass, I wouldn't be here like this with Mia right now.

Chapter Five

Jackson

Over the next several days, we explored the vibrant city of Las Vegas, indulging in romantic dinners, and enjoying each other's company. I found myself constantly amazed by the woman I'd married -- her strength, resilience, and unwavering determination to overcome the scars of her past. And yet, there was still a part of me that feared losing her.

Before the wedding, I'd thought of Mia as a friend, someone who needed me. Even though she wasn't a weak woman, I'd known she'd struggle if I'd left her on her own. It's why I'd stepped up and offered to help. She'd seemed so lost that day. Now I knew *I* was the one who needed *her*. She brightened my world, made me feel warm inside, and when I held her my heart raced. I'd fallen for Mia a little more each day, and if something were to happen to make her leave me, my world would seem cold and dark. Every morning, I woke up, reaching for her or I'd just watch her sleep, feeling happy just knowing she was by my side. I'd never experienced anything like it before.

I'd reached out to Wire again, to make sure Carter wasn't anywhere near us. Except, he hadn't seemed to know where the man disappeared to. According to Wire, the day before we left for Vegas, Carter went off the grid. He didn't use his bank card. Hadn't checked into any motels or hotels. If he was still using the same vehicle, Wire hadn't spotted him on any traffic cameras. I hoped he was merely lying low and wasn't planning his next attack on us.

"Jackson, what's wrong? You've been quiet tonight." She looked at me as we strolled down the Strip.

I hesitated, unsure of how to put my fears into words without coming across as a weak-ass man who couldn't protect her. "Carter vanished. It bothers me because I have no idea what he's thinking. While it's possible he's going to leave us alone now, I somehow don't think he's finished. And there's also…"

"What?" she asked.

"I have to wonder if I'm going to be enough for you. I wasn't the one you picked at first. You've seemed happy enough since we got here, but what if you're the one who changes your mind later?" I glanced down at her. "I haven't had a serious relationship before. I'm bound to fuck up sooner or later."

"Hey," she said, stopping in her tracks and turning to face me. Her eyes bore into mine. "You are more than enough for me, Jackson Adler. You've shown me what it means to be cherished, and that's something I'll never take for granted. No one's ever been this kind to me or made me feel special like you do. If anything, I should be warning you that I'm in danger of falling head over heels for you."

I pulled her close, wrapping my arms around her and burying my face in her hair. "Thank you, Mia. I promise to never give you a reason to regret marrying me. Realistically, I know there will be times we're mad at each other. We'll fight, and hopefully we'll make up. And if you do ever fall for me, I hope you tell me. I can't think of a greater honor than having your love."

As we continued our journey through the city, exploring all it had to offer, I couldn't help but feel an overwhelming sense of gratitude. In Mia, I'd found a partner who not only understood me, but embraced the fact I was a cowboy chasing a dream. Together, we'd forge a life we could be proud of, and we'd become stronger both as a couple and individually.

More than that, she'd become an essential part of my life. I'd never experienced romantic love before, but I had to wonder if that might be what I was feeling toward Mia. No matter how much time I spent with her, I always wanted more. And our nights... I'd never met anyone as passionate as Mia. I didn't have to worry about her faking whether or not she enjoyed being with me. Hearing her cry out in pleasure, knowing I was the one who made her beg for more, made me feel ten feet tall. It wasn't that I hadn't cared if the few women in my past had enjoyed themselves, but with Mia everything felt different. Was it because she was mine?

I liked that thought... Mine. I'd never had a woman I could claim as my own until now. Never met one I'd wanted to spend forever with for that matter. I didn't see me ever growing tired of Mia. Even if we lived for one hundred years as husband and wife, it still wouldn't be enough time together.

We rounded a corner and our attention was drawn to a small crowd gathered around a street performer. He moved with grace and skill, juggling flaming batons as if they were mere extensions of his limbs. We stopped to watch, our bodies pressed close together.

"Wow, he's incredible," Mia whispered, her breath warm against my neck.

"Almost as incredible as you," I murmured. Our eyes met, and it was as if the rest of the world faded away. All that mattered was Mia and the life we were starting.

"Watch this," the street performer called out, drawing our attention back to him. With a flourish, he tossed the flaming batons high into the air, catching each one effortlessly as they descended. The crowd erupted in applause, and Mia's eyes sparkled with delight.

"Have you ever seen anything like that?" she asked, her voice filled with wonder.

"Never," I admitted, knowing that this moment was one we would treasure forever. In the midst of the bright lights and cacophony of Las Vegas, we had found a small piece of magic. Although mine was different from Mia's. While she marveled at the performer, it was her that I watched.

I couldn't help but think about how far we'd come since that fateful day at the rodeo. And as we continued down the bustling streets, hand in hand, I knew that our future would be bright. No matter what life threw at us, we'd pull through.

As the street performer took his final bow, Mia and I continued our journey through the vibrant streets of Las Vegas. The neon lights lit up the area as we passed one casino after another. If she were older, I'd have let her try gambling. Hell, I hadn't ever done it myself. But since my new wife was only eighteen, that wasn't going to happen.

"Ready for a surprise?" I asked.

"Surprise?" Mia asked, raising an eyebrow playfully.

"Absolutely." I winked.

"Bring it on, cowboy," she said, smiling up at me.

We strolled down the Strip until we reached an upscale restaurant, its warm glow beckoning us inside. I'd been surprised when Mia hadn't asked why I'd insisted she buy a dress to wear tonight. I'd even worn a nice shirt with the new boots I'd bought for our wedding.

"Jackson, this looks incredible," Mia said, her eyes wide.

"Only the best for my girl," I replied, leading her to our reserved table. The candlelit ambiance cast a soft glow on her face, making her already radiant smile shine even brighter.

Our dinner was perfect -- filet mignon for me and tender seared scallops for Mia, something she'd once mentioned she'd never tried. As we savored each bite, our conversation flowed effortlessly. We talked about everything from my upcoming rodeo, to where we might want to live in the future, and even what we'd name the baby. The minutes ticked by, and all I could do was wish there were more hours in the day… more opportunities to spend time with her.

"Jackson, I never imagined I could be this happy," Mia confessed. "Thank you for showing me that life can be beautiful."

"Darlin', all I did was remind you of the strength you've always had inside," I responded, reaching across the table to clasp her hand. "I gave you a shoulder to lean on, but you're the one who decided to take charge of your destiny by getting your GED and taking self-defense classes. I'm just here for the ride."

As our evening drew to a close, I wondered if Mia felt the same surge of emotion as I did. Even now, my cock was half hard. Since getting my first taste of her, I found it hard to keep my hands to myself. I craved her like a damn drug. Every breath she took made her breasts rise and fall, and I found myself staring at them throughout the day. The way she smiled reminded me how sweet her lips tasted. When she laughed and her cheeks flushed pink, I thought of how she looked lying under me, eyes glazed with passion. It took everything in me not to sling her over my shoulder and take her straight to bed.

We made our way back to our hotel, my hand wrapped protectively around Mia's. The electricity in the air seemed to mirror the growing desire between us, and I could feel her pulse quicken with every step. Yeah, it seemed I wasn't the only one anxious to return to the hotel and tumble into bed.

"Jackson," she whispered, her voice breathy with anticipation. "I want you… now."

Her words sent a jolt of heat straight to my dick, and I couldn't wait to have her under me again. As soon as we entered our suite, I pulled her close, my lips crashing against hers with a hunger I couldn't contain. She responded eagerly, her hands gripping my shoulders as if trying to anchor herself in the storm of our passion.

"Darlin', I need you just as much," I murmured, my mouth tracing a fiery path down her neck.

As we stumbled toward the bedroom, our clothes fell away like the last remnants of my restraint. The intensity of the passion between us was enough to leave me breathless. My heart hammered in my chest, and my cock throbbed in time with every beat.

"Jackson… oh God, Jackson…" Mia moaned, her nails digging into my back as I slid into her wet heat. She fit me like a glove, and I knew I'd be keeping her up all night again.

"Baby, you feel so good," I groaned, my own pleasure building as I sought to bring her to new heights of ecstasy.

With each thrust, I felt her walls squeeze around me tighter, fueling my desire even more. Her moans turned into gasps for air, and her body arched off the bed in bliss.

With a final deep thrust, I let go, my entire being

shuddering as an intense wave of pleasure washed over me. Hot cum filled her up, and she cried out my name over and over again.

She pulled me down for a long, passionate kiss as we came down from our high. Her breathing was heavy, her eyes filled with desire. I kissed my way down her neck, nipping playfully at her skin as I trailed my hands down her body.

"I want to fuck you like you've never been fucked before." The trust she gave me as she completely surrendered was enough to make me fall for her a little more. She'd stolen my heart. The thought hit me like a freight train. I loved Mia. In that moment, I vowed to give her everything she deserved. And right now, that meant more orgasms.

I took her three more times, until I had nothing left to give. At least, not until I'd rested a little. In an hour, I'd probably be reaching for her again. At this rate, she'd probably think I only had sex on my mind. And when it came to Mia, that was pretty damn accurate.

As we lay tangled together in the aftermath, I couldn't help but wonder how I would ever find the courage to tell my parents about Mia and the baby. My father was a Dixie Reaper through and through, and his opinion mattered more than anything else. What if he didn't approve? What if my mother felt that Mia wasn't good enough for me?

"Jackson, what's wrong?" Mia asked softly, her hand running through my hair as she sensed my inner turmoil.

"Nothing, darlin'. Just thinking about the future," I replied, trying to hide my fears from her. But I knew I couldn't keep my worries bottled up forever. The weight of the secret I carried threatened to crush me under its burden. I'd never kept anything from my family before. As I held her close, I vowed to find the strength needed to protect our family -- no matter the cost.

My thoughts were interrupted by the sudden ringing of my phone on the nightstand. I reached over and grabbed it, glancing at the caller ID before answering.

"Hey, Wire. What's up?" I asked, trying to keep the worry out of my voice as I looked over at Mia, who had propped herself up on one elbow, watching me with concern.

"Jackson, I've got news about Carter," Wire said without any prelude. "He's been spotted several states away. It looks like he's attending the rodeo there. Think you may be in the clear."

A wave of relief washed over me, and I could feel my muscles finally start to unclench for the day Carter went after Mia. The distance between us and Carter meant that Mia was safer, at least for now. I glanced over at her, and her eyes held a mixture of hope and gratitude as she registered the news.

"Thanks, Wire. That's really good to hear," I replied, my voice cracking slightly from the weight that had just been lifted off my chest. "I owe you one, man."

"Hey, that's what family's for," Wire said warmly. "You know whatever you're trying to tackle on your own, we're all here for you. Especially your parents. I haven't told anyone I've been in touch with you. Except Lavender. She knows what's going on too but won't say anything. But just the same, you really need to talk to your parents."

"I know. I will," I promised, hanging up the phone and setting it back on the nightstand. As I turned to look at Mia, I saw tears glistening in her eyes, and I pulled her close, wrapping my arms around her protectively.

"Did you hear?" I asked softly, already knowing the answer. She nodded against my chest, her body trembling as the enormity of our situation began to sink in. "We're safe, Mia. He's far away, and we've got two fantastic hackers watching our backs. We can focus on building our life together, and figuring out how to be the best parents we can be for our baby."

"Thank you, Jackson," she whispered, her voice soft and low. "For everything. I don't know what I would have done without you."

"Shh, don't think about that now," I said gently, stroking her hair. "We're together, and that's all that matters. We'll face whatever comes our way, side by side."

My eyes drifted to the nightstand, where the phone still rested. I took a deep breath, trying to gather my thoughts and process everything. Reaching out to Mia, I pulled her into my arms. As we lay together, I whispered soothing words in her ear. I needed her to know she wasn't alone, that I would always protect her. The only thing I really wanted was for her and the baby to be safe and feel loved, even when danger was breathing down our necks.

I hadn't told her much about the Dixie Reapers. The truth was that if we did decide to live close to my parents, there would be times our lives would be in jeopardy. It was like every man in the club was a magnet for women on the run from horrendous situations. Although, it looked like I'd fallen into the same trap since I'd rescued Mia. Maybe we all really did have hero complexes. I might not be an official Reaper, but I was still part of their family.

"I'm here for you, Mia. Always will be." I kissed her brow and held her close. It wasn't long before her breathing evened out and sleep claimed her. I hoped she had the sweetest of dreams.

Chapter Six

Jackson

I stood there, gripping the rough rope tightly as I stared down at the horse shifting restlessly under me. I tightened my grip, then pounded on my closed fist, making sure I could hang on. My heart pounded in my chest, and I could feel the adrenaline coursing through my veins. I took a deep breath, trying to steady myself. This rodeo was no different than the others I'd competed in, but somehow, it felt like there was more on the line this time.

Making sure my hat wouldn't fly off with the first buck, I gave a nod to the men keeping the chute closed. The moment it opened, the horse shot out into the arena, bucking and twisting. His hooves barely touched the ground before he was airborne again. Mid-buck, he rotated, doing his best to throw me off. The asshole got close to the rails on the arena, slamming my leg into the post. I winced, but clung to him, refusing to let go.

The buzzer went off, and I prepared to dismount. The crowd erupted into deafening applause and whistles as I managed to beat the clock.

"Eight seconds! And he's done it, folks!" the announcer bellowed, his voice crackling with excitement as I hung on for dear life to the bucking bronc beneath me.

I exhaled sharply, my heart pounding in my chest, sweat dripping down my face. The arena seemed to vibrate with their energy, and I couldn't help but feel a surge of pride at having given them the show they'd come to see.

On the next buck, I released the rigging. I flew through the air and landed in a crouch on the arena floor. The demented horse ran for me, charging with his head down as if he were a bull. I ran for the rails, and barely launched myself to the top before he rammed his side into them.

Rodeo clowns came and managed to get him into the exit chute. Another grabbed my rigging and returned it to me. I dusted myself off and waved my hat to the crowd, letting them know I was fine. I put pressure on my leg and nearly bit my tongue off trying not to let out a slew of cuss words. Wouldn't do me any good to let people know I'd actually been injured. I needed to discreetly get to the med tent and see if they could ice and wrap my knee. Thankfully, it didn't seem to be broken.

"Damn, Jackson! You killed it out there!" Anna called out, her grin wide. Beside her, Lily nodded in agreement, her eyes sparkling with admiration.

"Thanks, ladies. Good luck to both of you," I replied, smiling back at them. Their eyes lingered on me, making it clear that their interest extended beyond my performance in the arena. Barrel racing would be next, so I knew they were getting ready to perform. Both women were young and while they weren't the type I'd go for, I knew plenty of cowboys found them attractive. They each had a fierce determination that matched my own when it came to competing. I couldn't help but admire them, even though I knew their presence directly in my path only signaled trouble. And I needed to get by them without anyone realizing I'd been injured.

"Hey, y'all," I said, giving them a nod as they approached. "Ready to put on a show?"

Come on. Move along. You know damn well I'm not going to agree to a date or anything else with either of you. I ground my teeth together and focused on remaining upright.

"Always," Anna replied with a confident grin. She was a tall, slender woman with long, wavy blonde hair that cascaded down her back when she didn't have it braided, like she did now. Her bright blue eyes sparkled with excitement, and I could tell she was itching to get started. Even before Mia, I'd never been tempted. But I'd heard plenty of my friends talking about much they liked holding onto all that hair.

"Wouldn't miss it for the world," added Lily, flashing a dimpled smile. She was shorter than Anna, but just as fit, her lithe body exuding power and grace. Her dark brown hair was pulled back into a tight ponytail, and her hazel eyes held a mischievous glint. While the other cowboys didn't rave about her looks, I knew plenty had let her take a ride on their cocks. I hadn't been one of them, and never would be.

"Good luck at the national championship, Jackson," Anna said, her tone flirtatious. "I think you'll definitely be the winner this year."

My mom had taught me to always be polite, especially with women and the elderly. So, I did my best to adhere to what she'd drilled into my head. Even now, when I really wanted to tell these two to go the fuck away.

"Thanks," I replied, trying to keep my voice steady. I didn't want to give them any mixed signals. Being polite was one thing, but if I gave these two an inch, they'd be all over me. And had in the past, no matter how much I'd pushed them off. I'd wanted to be friends with them, but they made it really damn hard. I had a pregnant wife waiting for me, and I needed to stay focused on my career -- and I was getting damn tired of sidestepping these two. Besides, if I even thought of cheating on Mia, my dad would castrate me. Assuming the Dixie Reapers didn't rip me to shreds first. Not that I would ever do such a thing.

As they rode away to prepare for their event, I tried to make my way to the medical tent without anyone noticing. Except people were constantly stopping me to talk. After the fifth one, I gave up and used the arena fence to hold myself up.

Even though I knew I needed to distance myself from them, I enjoyed being part of all aspects of the rodeo, which included watching the other events and mingling with the crowd. I wasn't going to let two troublesome women keep me from it. Maybe I could get to my truck before they started looking for me. Heading to medical wasn't going to happen. I'd have to get through too many people to reach it.

The electric hum of the crowd intensified as the announcer's voice boomed over the loudspeakers. "Ladies and gentlemen, it's time for the barrel racing competition! Let's hear it for our contestants, Anna Miles, Sadie Parker, Gina Masters, Rebecca Pierce, and Lily Rhodes!"

The cheers and applause swelled like a tidal wave, surging through the arena and making the very ground beneath my boots vibrate.

Despite the noise, I found myself drawn to the sight of women entering the arena on their powerful horses, their smiles bright as they did a lap while waving to the crowd. I spotted Anna and Lily in the group, and I couldn't help but feel captivated by the way they moved so easily with their horses. Not everyone could ride and look so natural.

"All these talented riders are known for their impressive records, folks," the announcer continued. "This is sure to be an exhilarating event!"

"Damn right, it will be," I muttered under my

breath, my eyes glued to the action unfolding before me.

As the women cleared the arena and the first one lined up, I could see the fire in her eyes, the unwavering focus that drove Anna to push herself to her limit. She leaned low, her body a blur of motion as she guided her horse Thunder around the first barrel. The powerful animal responded instantly, their movements synchronized in a breathtaking display of agility and speed. I couldn't help but marvel at Anna's ability to ride -- it was as if she and the horse shared one mind, each anticipating the other's moves with uncanny precision.

"Anna's really going for it today, huh?" a fellow cowboy remarked from beside me.

"Yep," I replied. My admiration for her skill was strong, but my mind couldn't help but wander to thoughts of my wife. The desire to see Mia made it difficult to fully immerse myself in the excitement of the rodeo.

Anna cleared the last barrel and urged Thunder to move faster as they raced out of the arena. I glanced at her time on the clock and knew it was good enough to at least put her in the top three.

"Nice job, Anna!" I yelled, clapping along with the crowd as she raced toward the second barrel. But my thoughts were already shifting to Lily, who'd just entered the arena atop her black gelding named Midnight.

"Looks like she's got some serious competition, though," the cowboy added, nodding at Lily as she entered the arena for her run. She navigated the course with smooth control.

"Absolutely," I agreed, unable to tear my gaze away from the spectacle. Her body and mind seemed to be perfectly in tune with the powerful animal she rode. My sister Danica used to compete in this event, and she'd been damn good at it.

"Go, Lily!" I called out, watching as she picked up speed, guiding Midnight effortlessly around the first barrel. Their style contrasted sharply with Anna's -- where Anna seemed to attack each turn with ferocity, Lily glided smoothly through the course, her movements fluid and precise. It was like watching a dancer execute a series of intricate steps, each one carefully choreographed to align perfectly with the music.

"Wow," I muttered under my breath, genuinely impressed. As much as I tried to remain impartial, I couldn't deny that both women had managed to capture my attention. Sadly, they knew it too. The difference was that I admired them as athletes, and they only wanted in my pants.

"Hey, Jackson," a nearby cowboy said, leaning over the railing to get a better look at the action. "Your friends Anna and Lily are pretty good, huh?"

"Yep," I replied. I wouldn't exactly call them *friends*, but... close enough.

As the competition neared its end, I knew I needed to make my escape before Anna and Lily found me again. I had made sure everyone heard about my recent marriage and the fact we had a baby on the way, but cheating was a common thing around the circuit. Those two women wouldn't care if I was married or not.

I watched the rest of the event, and as the last barrel racer crossed the finish line, my heart pounded with anticipation. I watched the scoreboard and let out a *whoop* when I saw Anna in first and Lily right behind her in second. They might cause more trouble than they were worth, but I had to admit they excelled in their event.

I tried to make my escape before Anna and Lily found me, but with my knee hurting, I wasn't fast enough. Both of them rode over on their horses. Even if I'd left sooner, I wasn't sure I'd have made it out of here without running into them. Sometimes it felt like they knew exactly where I was at all times.

"Hey, cowboy! Do you want to grab a drink later? There's a bar not too far from here that has the best margaritas," Anna suggested, her tone flirtatious. "Or beer for you. I know how you hate those girly drinks."

"Yeah, we could celebrate your win together," Lily chimed in, her smile equally inviting. "Should have known you'd come in first for the bronc riding."

My mind raced as I weighed my options. A part of me longed for the carefree camaraderie of going out with my fellow rodeo cowboys and cowgirls, but I knew that succumbing to temptation would only lead to regret. These two wanted far more from me, and I knew the easy-going time I'd have enjoyed would never happen. Besides, my family was my priority, and I couldn't afford to let anything distract me from that commitment. Not to mention, I'd much rather be with Mia.

"Thank you for the invitation, but I've got to get back to my wife," I explained, trying to keep my tone light and friendly while still making it clear I would not be joining them.

"Come on, Jackson," Anna persisted, her blue eyes narrowing as she shot a challenging glance at Lily. "One drink won't hurt."

"Exactly," Lily agreed, her hazel eyes twinkling with determination. "Besides, what's life without a little fun?"

Their idea of fun and mine were different. I wanted a few cold beers with my fellow competitors. These two wanted in my pants. No matter how many times I turned them down, they didn't seem to get the hint. But at the same time, I couldn't bring myself to be rude or cruel. It just wasn't the type of man I'd been raised to be. Even my dad had a harsh side, but that was the one way I hadn't really followed in his footsteps. Maybe part of me worried if I ever let that side loose, I'd end up like my birth father, a complete monster.

"Sorry, can't do it," I said, my voice strained. "I've got to stay focused on what's important: my family and my career. And you and I both know the two of you want more than a drink. It's not going to happen."

"Suit yourself," Anna replied with a shrug, though I could see the disappointment in her eyes. She glanced at Lily, as if silently daring her to keep trying.

"All right, Jackson," Lily conceded, her smile tight. "We'll respect your decision. But if you ever change your mind, you know where to find us."

I had this niggling feeling they were saying one thing but meant another. I hoped they weren't going to cause problems. Mia was such a sweet girl, and while we hadn't come together by conventional means, I knew I was lucky to have her in my life. She'd completely stolen my heart, captivated me every second of the day, and I woke each morning thanking God she was my wife. I only wished I'd tried to steal her from Carter earlier, then we could have been together as a couple a lot sooner. Mia meant everything to me, and if these two tried to hurt her, I'd do whatever I could to make their lives hell. For now, I'd play nice on the off chance they were only being a little catty.

"Good luck making it to the national championship, ladies," I said, offering them a warm smile before turning to head to my truck in the parking lot. I'd promised Mia after I got back and showered, we'd go out to eat somewhere. But first, I either needed to find a medic, or stop by a pharmacy on the way to the motel. I could tell I needed to wrap my knee.

I managed to get in my truck without anyone else stopping me. After I started the engine, I headed for the nearest pharmacy. Despite the late hour, they were still open. I parked and went inside, feeling the weight of the day's events. It didn't take long to find the items I needed, but as I approached the counter, I froze. Carter Bales stood in front of the cashier, flashing her his charming smile. The same smile that got Mia into so much trouble.

What the fuck was he doing here? According to Wire, this asshole should have been hundreds of miles away. He finally moved on, and I quickly checked out. Rushing to the parking lot, I scanned the area to see if he was still nearby. Was it possible I was wrong? No. It had definitely been Carter.

I shot off a text to Wire to let him know, hoping he'd be able to track him somehow. My hands shook a little as I drove to the motel. I kept an eye on my rearview mirror, on the off chance the jackass pulled up behind me. Even when I parked and still didn't see him, I couldn't seem to shake the feeling something bad could happen.

"Get it together," I muttered. I didn't need to freak out Mia. Blowing out a breath to steady myself, I grabbed my sack from the pharmacy and headed into the motel room.

Mia threw her arms around me and kissed me softly. "Did you win?"

I nodded. "Yeah. But…"

I lifted the sack for her to see it. The moment she saw the bandages inside, she started to strip my clothes off one piece at a time. By the time my jeans were around my ankles, I could see my right knee was twice the size it should be.

"What happened?" she asked.

"Bronc slammed me into an arena post. I'll be fine. Aleve, a little ice, and the wrap. That's all I need. I don't need to do any more events until the national championship. Plenty of time to rest and recuperate. As long as I don't run a race, or get another bronc right away, then it will heal just fine. Feels like it's probably a sprain and some bruising."

"Let me get some ice. You need to get the swelling down before you shower or do anything else. Then I'll help you wrap it when you're clean. I think you brought half the arena home with you."

I grinned at her. "Well, it wasn't like I tried to."

Seeing her like this made my heart skip a beat. Other than my family, no one had cared about me like this. Being with Mia always brought unexpected joy to my life. When I'd said I would marry her, I'd never thought we could settle into a somewhat normal relationship so quickly. But with her, everything just felt… right.

She used a plastic bag to make an ice pack, then held it over my knee. As filthy as I was, there was no way I'd get into the bed. I sat in the chair with my leg extended. If I weren't hurting, and didn't still have on my underwear, I might have been tempted to do more than just sit here. But there was always later.

"I think I may quit after the championship," I

said. "I've always wanted the national champion title, and I've worked my ass off to get it. It's been my dream since I was a kid."

"Because of your dad?" she asked.

"Yeah. Now I have a new dream, though. I still want the title, but there's no need for me to keep chasing rodeos after that. No reason I can't get a job that lets me come home to you and our kid every night."

"I'd really like that." She gave me a soft smile. "Any idea where we should live? I know we tossed around some ideas."

I cleared my throat. "After I tell my parents about us, I thought maybe we could live there. I have a house on their land. It's not huge by any means, but big enough. Might be nice for you to have my mom nearby when I'm not home, and our baby would grow up with their grandparents close enough to visit every day."

"All right." She looked away. "I'm not sure they're going to like me, though, Jackson. It's not like I'm anything special. If you hadn't helped me get my GED, I would have just been a high school dropout. At least I have options now, or I did before I got pregnant."

I leaned down and tapped her nose with my finger. "You still do, darlin'. Having a baby doesn't mean you give up on everything else. If you want to go to college, or get a job, then I'm not going to stop you."

"One thing at a time. We have enough on our plates right now."

She wasn't wrong. "Fine, but when you're ready to talk about it, or have an idea as to what you'd like to do, just let me know."

Chapter Seven
Mia

We'd only been seated a few minutes when I noticed two women come in and request a table near us. Had they not pointed to Jackson, I wouldn't have thought much of it. Except, now they were talking about me, low enough they could pretend it was a private conversation, but loud enough I could hear every word.

"Do you know them?" I asked him.

"Hmm?" He glanced their way before focusing on me again. "Yeah. They're barrel racers. Anna and Lily. The blonde is Anna. I'm sure you've seen them around before."

Had I? It was hard to remember. I'd never paid attention to that particular event. It was the bronc and bull riders who held my attention. Even team roping wasn't bad. All right. Maybe what I'd really paid attention to were all the men in jeans and boots.

"Guess I don't remember them," I said. He glanced over the menu and I tried to do the same.

"Can you believe her?" Anna muttered, the bitterness evident in her voice. "She just waltzes in here and suddenly she's the center of his world."

Lily scoffed, folding her arms across her chest. "I know, right? It's like he's forgotten we even exist."

Jackson froze and looked over at them. The look in his eyes made my stomach twist into knots. Exactly how well did he know them? Had he dated them? Or… No. He wouldn't cheat on me, right?

"Something needs to change," Anna said. Lily nodded in agreement, her gaze boring into us.

Jackson leaned down to murmur in my ear. "Ignore them. They're being jealous and petty. You're my wife and the only woman I want. You know that, right?"

I forced a smile and nodded, even though I felt a little inferior to the other women. They weren't going to cause trouble, were they? Jackson didn't seem the least bit interested in them. Surely they'd give up?

* * *

"Hey, Mia!" Anna called out to me the next morning. Her smile seemed forced. What rotten luck! Why did we have to be in the same motel? "You *are* Mia, right? Jackson's wife?"

"Yes, I'm Mia. Just getting some fresh air."

"Great, great," Anna said. "You know, I was just thinking… It's such a shame that Jackson doesn't spend as much time with us anymore. You guys are always together."

I shifted uncomfortably. "Well, we're married. That's kind of how it works."

"Of course," Anna agreed, nodding knowingly. "But it's just… he used to be so close with Lily and me, you know? We were practically inseparable. And now we barely see him at all. And it's not like being married means he has to be chained to you all the time, right?"

"Wait. Are you saying it's my fault he doesn't hang out with you anymore?" I asked.

"Hey, I didn't say that," Anna replied, holding up her hands in a gesture of innocence. "But it does make me wonder if he feels like he has to choose between us and you. I mean, rodeo life is difficult enough without feeling torn between friends and a wife, right?"

I frowned, wondering if she could be right. Did Jackson feel like he had to pick between being with his friends or spending time with me? Was I holding onto him too tight?

Glancing toward the motel office, where Jackson was extending our stay a few days, I saw Lily strut her way over to Jackson with a sweet smile plastered on her face. I couldn't help but feel a pang of jealousy as she approached him, chatting away like they were old friends. They probably were, before I came into the picture. My heart ached at the thought of somehow ruining their friendship. But was that really all they had between them? They seemed… cozy.

I inched closer without even realizing it. It wasn't that I didn't trust him, but… I wasn't sure I trusted *her*.

"Jackson," Lily drawled, her southern accent thick and syrupy. "You know I've always cared for you, right?"

"You care for me? Seriously? Lily, you make it sound like we've dated or something, and last time I checked, we haven't. We're acquaintances and nothing more. I wouldn't even consider us friends, even though you've certainly made it clear you want to be friends with benefits, so… what do you want? Just spit it out already."

"Well, it's just…" She hesitated, biting her lip in a practiced display of concern. "I can't help but worry about you, darlin'. This whole thing with Mia… Are you sure she's really the one for you?"

My pulse quickened, my ears straining to hear every word as I pretended to be looking elsewhere. The way Jackson had just spoken to her gave me hope, but her words… I had to admit that made me feel lower than low.

"What do you mean by that?" Jackson asked. "And make sure you're real clear or we might have a misunderstanding."

"Y'all are just so different," Lily continued, her voice soft and caring. "The age difference, for one. And with a baby on the way… I hate to say it, but it might just be too much for someone your age to handle. I mean, is it even your kid? Everyone knows she was all over Carter."

"Are you serious right now?" Jackson's tone was incredulous. "How the hell could you say something like that? What did Mia ever do to you? You say you're only concerned, but it doesn't come across that way, Lily."

"Look, I'm just saying what everyone else is thinking," Lily insisted, giving his arm a comforting squeeze. "I want you to be happy, Jackson. But maybe happiness doesn't have to look like this."

As the conversation unfolded, my insecurities began to fester like an untreated wound. I couldn't help but wonder if there was some truth to what Lily was saying. Was I really what Jackson needed? Was it possible I was making him miserable?

My heart felt heavy with doubt and fear. I hurried back to our room, and when he returned, I wasn't sure how to act around him. I'd heard something I shouldn't have. Now I wasn't sure what to do. My emotional withdrawal did not go unnoticed by Jackson. His usually bright eyes clouded with confusion as I averted my gaze when he entered the room.

"Hey, is everything okay?" he asked softly, reaching out to touch my arm.

"Fine," I muttered, barely able to look him in the eye. "Just tired."

"Are you sure?" he pressed, concern etched into his handsome features.

"I'm fine," I repeated, more forcefully this time. We both knew it was a lie, but I hoped he'd ignore it and leave things as they were. I didn't deserve to be happy by his side. And I was too much of a coward to tell him I'd just heard everything said between him and Lily.

Jackson reached out and cupped my cheek with his rough palm. "I don't believe you. Mia, we can't have a happy future if we aren't honest with each other. I genuinely care for you, and I hope you know that."

I swallowed hard. He really was such an amazing guy. "I care about you too."

It was the closest I could get to admitting my true feelings. I hoped one day, if I was still by his side, I'd be able to tell him I'd fallen for him. Although, there were times I couldn't even admit it to myself.

He leaned down and pressed his forehead to mine. "Don't let them get to you, darlin'. Their opinions don't matter. Only mine and yours do."

I smiled at him, feeling warm inside.

* * *

Four days later, we were still at the motel, and thankfully, so was my friend Bella. We'd quickly become friends after meeting at two different rodeos. Now we hung out whenever we ran into each other. I was so glad she'd ended up going to this particular rodeo. Even though she was closer to Jackson's age, we got along pretty well. She didn't treat me like a child, which I appreciated.

"Jackson's amazing, but I can't help but feel like I'm holding him back," I admitted, tears pricking at the corners of my eyes. "He deserves so much better than me, Bella. You should see the women who flirt with him. I'm nothing compared to them. And if it weren't for me and the baby, he'd probably not have even thought about quitting the rodeo. I can't help but feel like it's all because of me."

I hadn't told anyone about my past. Not Jackson. Not Bella. They had no idea what sort of trash I came from. I worried how they'd see me if they knew. Although, there were times I thought Jackson might suspect. Maybe not everything, but enough to know I came from a very poor family.

"Hey now," she said, taking my hand in hers and giving it a reassuring squeeze. "You are more than enough for him. Don't let anyone else's opinions or insecurities make you question what the two of you have together. He married you, didn't he? And I've seen the way he watches you, how he can't keep his hands off you."

I wanted to believe her words, but the seeds of doubt had already taken root. And as they grew, our relationship began to crack under the weight of my silent uncertainty. I'd felt a coldness between the two of us the last few days.

"What do I do?" I asked. "I told you about my relationship with Carter. That's all the experience I really have. It wasn't like I had boyfriends before him. I'm not sure it counts."

"Well, I have to agree that what you had with Carter couldn't be considered an actual relationship. You were aware he was sleeping with other women, right?"

I nodded. Once Jackson had found out, he'd taken me to a clinic to get tested. Thankfully, I hadn't caught anything from Carter -- except a baby. He'd even asked them to confirm the pregnancy.

"I wasn't at the time, though. I found out later." I put my head in my hands and sighed. "What should I do, Bella?"

"Be honest with him?" She patted my shoulder. "Look, you're both adults. You're married and have a baby on the way. If you can't talk about this now, it's only going to get worse. The number one thing that can make a marriage, or any relationship work, is communication."

"But it's so hard," I muttered.

"I say this with love, Mia, but if you're grown up enough to have sex, get married, and have a baby, then you're enough of an adult to talk about your problems and fears with your husband."

I knew she was right, but it didn't make it any easier. Right now, Jackson was over at the fairgrounds helping out with the horses they'd brought in for the kids to ride. It wasn't far from the diner where I'd met Bella, so I decided to head over and see if I could find my courage.

I saw him standing near a corral, three horses trotting around inside. The smile on his face made my knees weak. He really was a beautiful man, and he looked genuinely happy right now. Before I could convince myself to wait, or put it off indefinitely, I called out to him.

"Jackson!" He turned toward me, and I waved at him, moving closer.

"Hey, what's wrong?" he asked softly, his hand reaching out to touch mine. "You look stressed."

"Can we talk?" The words came out more strained than I intended, but there was no turning back now.

"Of course," he replied, guiding me to a quieter spot near the picnic tables. "What's on your mind?"

I took a deep breath, steeling myself for what I needed to say. "I've been hearing some things, Jackson. From Anna and Lily. They're saying you don't really want to be with me... that I'm holding you back."

His face darkened, anger flashing momentarily

Harley Wylde   Prophet/Cowboy Up Duet

before he collected himself. "Mia, listen to me, I'm committed to you and this baby. None of those rumors are true. I don't know why they're doing this, but don't let their lies come between us."

"So, there's nothing going on?" I asked.

"No. Even before we got married, I'd never slept with either of them. Easy women like them don't really do it for me."

I felt the blood drain from my face. Right. I really didn't need to tell him anything about my past. Carter hadn't been my first. Not by a long shot. The first time I'd had sex was when I was fifteen. I'd been the class whore, sleeping my way through all the boys who'd look my way. Would he be disgusted if he found out? I hadn't dated them. Never had a boyfriend before Carter, and looking back, I wasn't sure I could even call him that.

I forced a smile. "Okay, I trust you."

"Good," he murmured, pulling me into a tight embrace. "Just ignore them, and they'll give up. I promise I haven't encouraged them."

I left him to his work and went back to the motel, but the whispers along the way made me want to run as far away as I could get.

"Did you hear?" a male voice whispered as I walked by. "Apparently, Jackson's only with her because he feels obligated. Poor guy."

"Such a shame," another chimed in. "He had so much potential, before her."

Their words stung like salt in an open wound, and my heart ached with each vicious remark I heard. From the corner of my eye, I caught a glimpse of Anna and Lily. The smirks on their faces told me they were proud of the chaos they'd caused. I didn't understand why they were doing this to me. What had I ever done

- 225 -

to them?

Jackson said he'd stop going to rodeos. It didn't seem right. Maybe those women were on to something. Would he have given it up if it weren't for me? I doubted it. He clearly loved it.

As if suspended in a nightmare, I watched Jackson walk toward Anna and Lily with a determined stride. Had he heard what everyone was saying? Was he going to confront them? My heart pounded in my chest, fearing what might happen next.

"Anna, Lily," Jackson said, his voice firm but calm. "We need to talk."

I could see the surprise on their faces, but they quickly masked their emotions and feigned innocence.

"Talk about what, Jackson?" Anna asked sweetly. Did she really think he was going to believe her little act? The look in his eyes clearly said he was done with her antics.

"About the rumors you've been spreading about me and Mia," he replied.

"Us? Spreading rumors?" Lily gasped dramatically, placing a hand on her chest. "Why would we ever do that? We care about you so much, Jackson. You know that, right?"

My fists clenched at my sides, wanting nothing more than to storm over there and call them out on their lies. But I held back, watching as Jackson tried to mediate the situation without escalating it further.

"Look, I don't know what your problem is with Mia, but whatever it is, it needs to stop. Now." Jackson's expression hardened, frustration clear in his eyes. "She's my wife, and you *will* show her the respect she deserves."

"Jackson, we were just looking out for you," Anna insisted, reaching out to touch his arm. "We're your friends. We care about you."

"Friends don't sabotage each other's relationships," he countered, shaking off her touch. "Now, I'm asking you both, to stop this. I'd tried to be friends with you, but it was clear that wasn't enough. I need you to leave me, and my wife, alone."

"Fine. If it means that much to you, we'll stop," Lily agreed reluctantly, though I knew better than to trust her words.

With a final warning glance, Jackson turned away from them and headed toward me. I couldn't shake the feeling that his efforts had only added fuel to the fire, stirring up more trouble than he'd resolved. They didn't seem like the type of women to back down when they wanted something… and it was clear they wanted Jackson.

"Why did you do that?" I asked quietly as Jackson approached me, my eyes never leaving Anna and Lily's retreating forms.

"I think they got the message," he replied, trying to sound reassuring. "I couldn't let them do that to you, Mia. You're my wife, and it's my job to protect you."

The sincerity in his words was comforting, but I couldn't shake the nagging feeling that their interference was far from over. Were we destined to keep trading one problem for another? First Carter, now those women. Would someone else try to ruin the life we were trying to build together?

Or worse, would our pasts come back to haunt us? There was still so much I hadn't told him. Things I hoped he never discovered.

What would he think if he learned about my dirty past? Or about my parents? If he no longer looked at me with such a warm look in his eyes, or touched me gently, it would probably break me. Being with Jackson was unlike anything I'd felt before. Kissing him made my toes curl, and the feel of his hand in mine always made me remember the way those rough palms felt running over my skin. Even now my pulse quickened at the memories of being with him. I had to wonder if I'd met him before Carter, would I have chased after him instead? Everything about him turned me on, and he had the best smile ever. I couldn't think of a single thing I didn't like about Jackson.

With these thoughts swirling in my head, I held on tighter to Jackson. I'd already started falling for him. If anything happened to tear us apart, I wasn't sure I'd survive it. He was the best thing that had ever happened to me.

Chapter Eight

Jackson
Six Months Later

The sun dipped low in the sky, casting a warm golden glow over the small backyard where Mia and I sat together on the porch swing. The scent of fresh-cut grass filled the air as children nearby played in their yards. I placed my hand over Mia's baby bump, and smiled as our daughter kicked me. She'd already chosen a name -- Poppy.

"Jackson, I sometimes wonder what would have happened to me if you hadn't been around when Carter hurt me. I don't know if he'd done worse, or just left me in the dirt. Either way, I'd have had nowhere to go."

I put my arm around her shoulder, knowing it was time to draw out more about her past. She never gave me much, and I hadn't asked outright. I'd been worried it might be stressful for her to relive whatever she'd been through. But at the same time, I felt like I needed to know.

"Couldn't you have gone home?" I asked. "I don't know where you're from."

She pressed her lips together, and I felt a tremor run through her. I almost told her she didn't have to tell me, but I couldn't do it. Something told me finding out about Mia's past would help me understand her more. There were times she seemed confident, but mostly, she came across as timid and scared. I'd thought it was only the issue with Carter, and later with Anna and Lily, that had filled her with fear. What if it went back further?

"Why do you need to know?" she asked softly.

"Because it's part of who you are, darlin'. We're

married, about to have a baby, and there are times I feel like I don't know you very well. Is it really so awful I want to know everything about my wife?"

"No. I just…" She sighed and looked down at the porch boards. "I guess I've worried if I told you about my past, you wouldn't want me anymore."

"I've told you about my mom and dad, right?" I asked.

"Yeah. They sound amazing." She gave me a wistful smile. "I wish mine were as good as yours."

"Hmm. Well, technically, Ty Adler is my stepfather. He legally adopted me and my sister once he married our mom." She stared at me with wide eyes and her jaw dropped. "My sperm donor was a real bastard. He did awful things to my mother. Nearly beat her to death several times. And… he whored her out. Please don't ever tell her you know that. It's a part of her past she'd rather forget. So, my past isn't all roses and sunshine either, darlin'. I think everyone has a bit of darkness in their lives."

"I never would have guessed," she whispered. "You're just so amazing. I thought you'd always had a perfect life."

"Far from it. My mom met Ty at the stable where she boarded her horse. He says he fell in love with her at first sight, and he treated me and my sister like we were his very own. We all loved him, but Mom was too scared to leave her husband. I've never thought of him as my dad and I refuse to call him that. Anyway, Ty convinced Mom to leave. He helped us pack the essentials and got us the hell out of there."

She leaned into me. "My mom split when I was about nine years old. She'd been a prostitute. I think it's how she paid for her drugs. I can't remember a time I didn't see her downing pills or shooting up. As for my dad…"

"An asshole?" I asked.

"That's putting it mildly. Anyway, what's that saying? The apple doesn't fall far from the tree?" She looked away, refusing to meet my gaze. "I was fifteen when I started sleeping with different boys. I was working my way through my class and then the upper classes at school. Everyone knew I was easy."

I saw a tear slide down her cheek and I wiped it away, then turned her face toward mine. Seeing her like this broke my heart. She had to have felt so alone. I only wished she'd told me sooner than now. Even though we'd grown incredibly close, there had been times I felt like I was looking at a stranger. She'd get this far-off look in her eyes, and I'd wondered what she'd been thinking about. I should have just cowboyed up and asked her. Instead, I'd told myself it was better to wait for her to unburden herself when she was ready. Now I just felt like an asshole for not pushing the matter sooner.

"Baby, I think it's pretty clear you were seeking affection. I'm sorry they all used you and threw you away. You deserved better than that."

"They called me a whore," she said softly. "And they weren't wrong. I didn't get money for what I did, but they'd often give me gifts. A new shirt, a necklace, take me out for dinner. Sometimes those meals were the only ones I had, except for the free lunch at school."

"What you are is a sweet, adorable woman… and my wife. The things you did before, or that happened to you, are just a part of who you are. They aren't the *only* part, but you survived all that to become the amazing person you are now. I know you have your doubts, and you've been struggling. I wish you could see you the way I do." I leaned in closer and kissed her cheek. "You're my one and only, Mia. You know that, right?"

What if she didn't? What if I hadn't made it clear to her exactly how much she meant to me? I hadn't ever been all that good with words. My dad always said actions spoke louder, so I'd done my best to show her how I felt. Now I had to think I'd fucked that up too.

"You're leaving soon, aren't you?"

"Yeah. Thought you might want to come and cheer me on. This is my last shot at being a national champion. I'm still in the top fifteen, which means I still have a chance. If the others had done any better, I'd have needed to win a few more events. Thankfully, I was able to stick it out. It either happens or it doesn't. Either way, I'm hanging up my spurs after this one."

"I feel like I'm forcing you to give up your dream," she said.

I placed my hand on her belly again. "No, just trading it for a different one. Chasing the rodeo was my boyhood dream. Now I'm a man with a family, and the two of you are far more important. We'll head to Alabama once this one is done, and I'll introduce you to my family."

I should have done it long before now, but I'd had a few reasons for holding back. One was Mia's fear over meeting my family. The second was the fact I didn't want to chance Carter chasing us all the way there. The club dealt with enough already. And third... I knew my parents were going to rip me a new one for jumping into things with Mia, and then not saying anything to them. I wanted to delay the ass chewing from them as long as possible.

"Promise?" she asked. "I know up until now I've been scared to face them, but now... I feel like a dirty secret."

"You have my word. Win or lose, we'll go home."

She looked around. "I'll miss this place. Thank you for renting it. This is the first time I've felt like I had a real home like everyone else. The trailer I grew up in was rusted through in spots, had broken windows, the roof leaked, and you had to be careful where you walked. Some parts of the floor were so soft, you could fall through."

"I told you I have a house on my dad's ranch. It's a three-bedroom two-bath. About eleven hundred square feet, so on the smaller side, but I think you'll like it. There's a porch like this one, and it has a swing. You can thank my mom for that."

"Sounds pretty," she murmured.

"It looks like a log cabin on the outside. Inside it has hardwood floors and tile in the kitchen and bathrooms. Anything you want to change, feel free to make it your own. I want you to feel at home when you're there."

She leaned up to kiss me softly. "You're such a sweet man, Jackson. I don't feel like I deserve you, but I'm selfish and don't want to let you go."

"You'll never have to. Come on. Let's get packed and then spend the rest of the day relaxing. Tomorrow is going to be busy."

I helped her stand and led her into the house. I'd miss this place. It was the first house I'd shared with Mia, and for that reason alone, it was special. Just like Mia…

We'd had picnics on the front yard. Swung on the porch swing while holding hands and talking about whatever popped into our heads. I'd made love to her in the bedroom countless times. Cooked dinner together in the kitchen, when she didn't run me off and tell me to go relax. They all might seem like mundane things, but it was in those everyday moments we'd created some of my most favorite memories, at least the ones pertaining to Mia.

Big obstacles brought people together, but the quiet moments counted too. I honestly felt they were worth more. Stolen kisses, hugs, nights snuggled on the couch watching TV. Every single minute spent with Mia was precious to me.

* * *

Las Vegas hadn't changed since we'd last been here. As the days passed, today's upcoming rodeo event loomed large in my mind. I spent most of this week worrying about my performances, and hoping I'd draw good bucking horses. There were a few who'd hardly buck or not at all, which meant getting a shitty score.

We'd rented a suite that included a kitchenette. Mia had taken advantage and practiced her cooking. She'd done quite a bit of it in the house we'd rented. I'd bought her some cookbooks, and she'd enjoyed trying different things.

"Jackson?" Mia's voice broke through my thoughts, and she pointed to my dinner, now cold and untouched. "You haven't eaten a single bite. I'm going to think it's awful. Is everything okay?"

"Yeah, I'm fine," I assured her, though I knew she could see right through my lie. I'd never been so stressed in my life. This was it. My last shot. The finals were starting tomorrow.

"Please talk to me," she pleaded, taking a seat beside me. "I know you're struggling with balancing everything but shutting me out won't help."

I sighed, realizing she was right. I'd pushed her

to talk to me when she wanted to keep quiet. It was only fair I opened up with her now. "It's just... this rodeo is a big deal, Mia. And I want to make sure I do well, not just for me, but for all of us. I always had great pride in the fact my dad was a national champion, and I want our kids to feel the same way about me."

"Jackson, you're going to be amazing out there," she said. "But we need you here with us too. We can't have a future if we don't have a present, and part of that is making sure you eat."

Her words struck me deep. "I'm sorry, darlin'. I promise I won't let this consume me."

"You've done so well. I have no doubt you're going to win, Jackson. Just look at your scores! You're already in the top spot, and while I know it's close with two other cowboys, I just know you're going to win."

* * *

The smell of livestock and dust filled my nose as I walked through the rodeo grounds, preparing for another day of fighting for the top spot. I couldn't help but feel a sense of pride in what I was doing. This was the dream I'd clung to most of my life, and this week, it might actually become a reality.

"Hey, Jackson," Anna called out to me with a sly smile that didn't quite reach her eyes. "I heard a few interesting things recently. About your wife. She's got quite the past, doesn't she?"

"Excuse me?" I asked, tensing up at her words. What Mia went through wasn't anyone else's business. The fact Anna was here running her mouth pissed me off.

"Jackson, don't listen to her," Lily chimed in with a smirk. "But you know, people are talking. They're saying she's only with you because you're her meal ticket now that she's got a baby on the way."

"Y'all need to mind your own damn business," I snapped, feeling anger boil inside me. How dare they talk about her like that? "You think I'm with Mia because she's pregnant? Do the two of you not have fucking eyes in your heads?"

"We're just looking out for you," Anna said dismissively, though her expression told me otherwise.

"Thanks, but I don't need your 'concern,'" I retorted before walking away from them. Looking out for me? More like trying to drive a wedge between me and Mia. I wouldn't let them succeed. All they wanted was the bragging rights to having slept with me, now that I was making a name for myself. They'd cling to me as long as I was in the spotlight, then they'd wander off to the next big rodeo star. At first, I'd thought we could be friends, but it hadn't taken long to realize they were just as bad as every buckle bunny I'd ever run across.

Later that day, as I retrieved my gear from my truck, I overheard Anna and Lily gossiping nearby. What the fuck was wrong with those two?

"See? I told you he'd get defensive," Anna whispered. "He won't be able to resist the doubt we're planting in his head."

"Exactly," Lily agreed. "Soon, he'll realize he can do so much better than some whore who just wants someone to take care of her. Without him, she'd have nothing."

My hands clenched into fists as I listened to their bullshit. I couldn't believe they would stoop so low just because they were jealous of my relationship with Mia. Not to mention, if I could hear them, then other people in the area could too. I needed to put a stop to it once and for all.

"Anna, Lily," I growled, stepping out from behind my truck and staring them down. "I heard everything you just said."

"Jackson, we didn't mean --" Lily started, her voice faltering.

"Save it," I cut her off. "I don't know what your problem is, but you need to stay away from me and Mia. Understood? You don't come talk to us, and you sure the fuck don't talk *about* us. You think I married her because what? I'm just some dumb cowboy who'd do whatever a woman wants? I'm with her because I want to be. I will *never* be with the two of you."

"Fine," Anna muttered, her face flushed with embarrassment. "You don't have to be such an asshole."

"Y'all brought this on yourselves," I shot back, my voice cold and hard. It took every ounce of self-control not to allow my anger to consume me. They were no better than the damn club whores who used to hang out at the Dixie Reapers' clubhouse. "Stay away from us."

As I walked away, I let out a deep breath, trying to shake off the negativity they'd brought into my life. I knew that people like Anna and Lily wouldn't understand what Mia and I had, but their opinions didn't matter. What mattered was that I would fight for our relationship -- no matter what. If they kept talking shit about my wife, I'd have to handle things a different way.

I did my best to shove my anger down deep. Right now, I needed to focus on having the best eight-second ride of my life. Because once this week was over, I would walk away from the rodeo and never look back.

Maybe if I'd known that my wife would find out

about the things people were saying about her, I might have shut up Anna and Lily in a different way… It wasn't until I saw the look on Mia's face that I realized I'd fucked up.

"Can we talk?" Mia asked.

"Of course," I replied, my heart aching at the sight of her distress. I sat down beside her, gently brushing a stray strand of hair from her face. We'd only been back at the hotel for an hour. Long enough for me to clean up and unwind a bit. "What's on your mind?"

She hesitated, her fingers nervously playing with the edge of her shirt. "I've been hearing things. People talking about us. About me, actually."

It seemed like Anna and Lily had continued to run their mouths even after I'd told them not to. I was starting to think I needed to handle them the way the Dixie Reapers would handle mouthy club whores. Clearly, being nice wasn't going to cut it.

"Mia, those people don't know anything about us," I reassured her, my voice firm but gentle. "They're just jealous and trying to cause trouble."

"I know, but…" She bit her lip. "It still hurts. And it makes me wonder if maybe they're right. If I'm not good enough for you."

"Hey, look at me," I urged, cupping her face in my hands so she had no choice but to meet my gaze. "You are more than good enough for me. You're strong, beautiful, and you're going to be an amazing mother to our daughter. Don't let anyone make you doubt that."

"Really?" she asked.

"Really," I confirmed, pressing a soft kiss to her forehead. "You're my wife, Mia. My friend, and the woman I cherish above all others. I'm committed to making this work -- no matter what other people say or do. Our marriage has nothing to do with anyone other than you and me."

Mia smiled, and it seemed as if some of the weight lifted from her shoulders. In that moment, I knew I had to do something to prove just how much she and our daughter meant to me. Some grand gesture so everyone would realize how important my family was to me, that I wasn't with Mia because of some bullshit reason.

"Listen," I began, taking a deep breath. "I want you in the stands until this is over. Since we're down to the last day, this is my final ride in the rodeo. Not just this rodeo, but the last one ever. If it's not too much to ask, I'd love to see your beautiful face right before I come out of the chute."

"Are you sure? I was worried I'd distract you if I was there."

"I'm sure. And thank you," I whispered, leaning down to kiss her. "You're my everything, Mia. I might be closing this chapter of my life, but the one I'm going to forge with you is just beginning."

Mia leaned into me and kissed me. It was one of the few times she'd started anything, and my heart warmed at how far we'd come. I slid my fingers into her hair, holding her still as I took control of the kiss. With her due any day, I'd been hesitant about being intimate. We'd been assured it was fine as long as I was careful, but I couldn't help but worry I might hurt our daughter.

"Please, Jackson. I need you." She took my hand and slid it between her legs. "I'm hurting for you right here."

"Are you sure, Mia?"

"Positive. I've missed our nights together.

Sleeping beside you or in your arms has been torture when you won't give me the one thing I really want." She kissed me again, deeper this time. "Make love to me, Jackson."

With her begging me so sweetly, there was no way I could deny her. My cock throbbed behind my zipper. It wasn't that I hadn't desired Mia these last few weeks. I'd just been too worried about her and the baby.

"If it hurts, you'll tell me?" I asked. "Or maybe…"

She bit her lip and straddled my lap. The light scent of her perfume teased my nose as her hand slid up my chest and around the back of my neck. My heart hammered so hard I worried she might be able to hear it.

She leaned in and captured my lips with hers. Her tongue danced against mine, teasing and seductive. My cock twitched in anticipation. I couldn't believe how much I'd missed this feeling. The warmth of her body against mine felt like fucking heaven.

She broke the kiss and trailed her lips down my neck, nipping lightly at my skin. "I want you so bad. I need you, Jackson."

Her words sent a jolt of electricity through me. I couldn't resist her any longer. Reaching for her, I slid her shirt over her head, tossing it aside. I placed my hand over the swell of her belly, smiling when our baby gave me a little kick. "I think you're more beautiful than ever."

Mia reached down and grabbed my hand, then placed it over her breast. "Wrong spot."

I undid the clasp of her bra, letting it fall to the floor. Her full breasts spilled out, topped with rosy nipples that were already hard. I groaned, unable to resist the urge to taste her. Leaning in, I took one into my mouth, sucking gently as I traced circles around her other nipple with my fingers.

She arched her back, moaning softly. "God, Jackson. That feels so good."

I pulled back, my eyes locked on hers as I reached down and tugged at her skirt. She lifted her hips, helping me slide the material up her thighs. Her panties came into view, already damp from her excitement.

I reversed our position, placing her under me. I placed a kiss on her belly, then spread her thighs, easing between them. Wanting to tease her a little, I ran my tongue along the edge of her panties before finally pulling them aside and exposing her to my hungry gaze.

"Fuck," I groaned, unable to resist the urge any longer. With one swift movement, I lifted her up and carried her toward the bedroom.

Once inside, I set her down on the bed and followed her down, my body pinning hers to the soft mattress. She squirmed underneath me, her eyes filled with desire. I couldn't help but think how lucky I was to have her like this.

I stripped down, then gently removed her skirt and panties. She lifted her hips, making it easier for me. I knelt beside the bed and spread her legs wide. Parting the lips of her pussy, I leaned in and gave her a slow lick. Mia moaned and I felt her thighs tense. I took my time, savoring her. I eased a finger inside her, then a second one. She gasped, her body trembling. I lifted my head and held her gaze.

"Tell me you want this."

"More! I need more," she said.

"What do you want? Tell me, Mia."

"Inside me! Now, Jackson. Please."

I stood and slid my cock up and down her slick pussy before easing inside her. She gave a little cry, and I felt her contract around me. It took every ounce of control I possessed to take my time with her. reaching between us, I rubbed her clit with small circles. She shivered, and after only three more strokes, she came.

I could have fucked her all day and night, but I didn't want to exhaust her. Gripping her hips, I took her faster, fighting not to be too rough with her. My balls drew up, and then I was coming. I didn't stop thrusting until every drop of cum had been wrung from me.

Reaching down I smoothed her hair back from her face. "You all right?"

"Perfect." She smiled up at me. "I've missed you. Missed *this*."

"Me too." Pulling out, I stretched out beside her on the bed. "Sorry I've been pushing you away. I've just been worried I'd end up hurting you."

"I'm pregnant, Jackson. Not made of glass. Besides, the baby will be here soon. Once that happens, the doctor said we can't have sex for at least six weeks while I recover."

I kissed her, soft and slow. "Then I guess we'd better make good use of the time we have."

She gasped and sat up quickly. "Crap! Jackson, the rodeo… Aren't you making your final ride?"

I looked at the clock and winced. "Yeah. In an hour. Guess we better hurry and get over to the arena."

"Go! Shower and get your stuff together while I rinse off. I'll move as quickly as I can."

With one last kiss, I got up and did as she said. This was it. The very last time I'd get on a bronc. I only hoped I never came to regret my decision, but when I thought about my dad and how happy he seemed, I knew this was the right thing to do.

Chapter Nine

Jackson

I arrived at the arena, thankful this one was indoors. The sun blazed outside, and even this late in the year, Las Vegas still felt too hot for my taste. My heart pounded in my chest, adrenaline coursing through my veins, as I made sure everything was prepared for my final ride. This was it -- my last chance to prove myself in the rodeo ring.

"Hey, Jackson," a fellow competitor greeted me with a slap on the back. "Ready for your big moment?"

"Damn straight," I replied with a grin, trying to hide the nerves gnawing at my insides. I knew I had to give it my all tonight, not just for myself but for my family too -- especially my father, the legendary Ty Adler, who had been a national champion back in his day.

As I entered the chute and settled over the bronc, the crowd's cheers washed over me. I could feel their excitement. It was intoxicating, and I couldn't help but be swept up in it. The bronc I'd drawn was magnificent. I felt a pang of sadness at the thought of leaving this life behind. The rodeo had been such a huge part of my identity, and now it was coming to an end. I'd have to figure out who I was if I wasn't a rodeo cowboy anymore.

"All right, big fella," I murmured. "Let's make this one count, huh?"

With a deep breath, I settled my hat more firmly on my head.

"Jackson!" I heard someone call out from the sidelines. Glancing over, I saw my sister Danica waving frantically, her husband Ranger standing beside her with a proud smile. I raised a hand in acknowledgment, a surge of warmth filling me at the sight of my family cheering me on. Then I realized... Looking out at the audience, I saw Mia. Shit. It looked like time was up. She'd be meeting part of my family today.

I gave myself a mental slap, focusing on the task at hand. *Don't screw this up. It's your last chance*!

I gave the men a nod and the gate swung open. The horse burst out of the chute. I spurred him on as he twisted and bucked beneath me. Time seemed to slow down as I focused all my energy on staying on the back of the horse, feeling the burning desire to do my father proud and prove that I was worthy of the Adler name. The crowd roared around me, their cheers blending together into a cacophony of sound that only spurred me on.

As I held on for dear life, I couldn't help but think about how much I owed to the people who had supported me over the years -- my mother, who had always been there to soothe my wounds after a tough ride; my dad, who had been my idol since I was a small boy; my sister Danica, who had never once doubted my abilities; and most importantly, my wife, who had stood by me and brought so much joy to my life.

I'm doing this for you. For all of you. The bronc continued to buck beneath me, our bodies moving in sync like a finely tuned machine. I steeled my resolve and prepared to see this final ride through to the very end.

My heart pounded in my chest like a wild stallion as the bronc beneath me strained to get me off his back. I gripped the rigging tight, taking a deep breath of that familiar scent of dirt and livestock that filled the arena. This was it -- my final ride, the culmination of years spent chasing glory in the rodeo circuit.

"Come on, Jackson! You got this!" someone shouted from the crowd, even over the roar of cheers and pounding hooves I could hear her voice. I could feel the eyes of the spectators upon me, but rather than let it rattle me, I channeled their energy into my own performance.

Eight seconds, just hold on for eight seconds. Gritting my teeth, I expertly leaned into each buck and twist. With every movement, I felt more and more in tune with the animal beneath me, our bodies working together to provide the audience with an amazing show.

"Eight seconds, folks! This cowboy has given us one hell of a ride! Wait… What's this? He's still going?" The announcer's voice boomed through the arena as the buzzer sounded. In that moment, I knew I had done it. I had shown everyone what I was made of and proven to myself that I still had what it took to compete at the highest level. But I wasn't done. I was going out with a bang.

"I've never seen anything like it," the announcer said. "Not since Lane Frost, and as you know, he was a bull rider. Folks, this is one hell of a cowboy!"

"Whoo! That's how you do it, Adler!" one of my fellow competitors called out as I let go and flew off the bronc, adrenaline still coursing through my body. "Hell of a ride, man!"

"Thanks," I replied, climbing the rails of the arena. A grin spread across my face as I took in the sea of applause that washed over me. It was like a wave of pure joy, and I couldn't help but feel humbled by the outpouring of support.

"Eleven seconds, folks! This cowboy held on for

an eleven-second ride. Amazing!"

I scanned the crowd and spotted Mia. I waved to her and gave her a wink.

"Jackson! You were amazing!" Danica gushed as she made her way through the crowd toward me, her eyes shining with pride. "I wish Dad could have seen this."

"I'm sure he watched it on TV," Ranger said.

"Thanks, sis," I said, pulling her into a tight hug. "There's something I need to tell you. Or rather someone I need you to meet, but Mom and Dad don't know yet."

Her eyes went wide. "Are you seeing someone?"

Mia pushed her way through the crowd and threw her arms around me. "I can't believe you rode for eleven seconds! I've never seen anyone do that before."

My sister eyed Mia, then me, and I saw the moment she realized this was the person I wanted her to meet. "Mia, this is my sister, Danica, and her husband, Ranger."

Mia gasped and glanced at them. "Oh. Um…"

"You have a pregnant girlfriend?" Danica asked. "And you didn't tell any of us? Are you insane?"

I held up my left hand. "Actually, she's my wife."

Ranger let out a low whistle. "Man, I do *not* want to be you. Your parents are going to kill you when they find out."

"Don't say anything. Please. I want to tell them in person. In fact, we're heading to Alabama when we leave Vegas."

"Fine." Danica shook her head. "But it's your funeral. And don't you dare tell them I knew about this!"

My sister turned to Mia and gave her a soft smile. Ranger reached out to take Mia's hand. "It's nice to meet you."

"Why don't we take your wife and find a quiet place to sit? Maybe a nearby restaurant?" Danica asked.

"You don't want to stick around and see if I won?"

Ranger snorted. "Yeah, like anyone is going to beat that score? Have you seen your stats? You've won. Congratulations, man."

Mia hugged me once more and reluctantly left with my sister and Ranger. And just as he'd said, I'd won. As of today, I was the national champion bronc rider, and it felt fucking fantastic.

"Thank you, Mia," I murmured. "For everything."

It wasn't until now I'd finally realized I didn't just like her. I loved her. As soon as we got away from the rodeo crowd, and my family, I'd tell her. It was time for me to confess how I felt.

"Jackson!" a voice called out, pulling me from my thoughts. A man in a black cowboy hat approached, extending his hand with a business card. "Impressive ride out there. I represent a major sponsor, and we'd love to have you on board."

I glanced at the card before looking back at him, weighing the implications of what he was offering. The temptation tugged at me, but I knew deep down that it wasn't the life I wanted anymore. Not now that I had something -- someone -- even more important to me.

"Thank you," I said, handing the card back. "But I'm done with the rodeo circuit after tonight. I appreciate the offer, though."

"Are you sure?" he asked, eyebrows raised in

surprise. "There are some great opportunities for you here."

"I'm sure. My wife and I have other plans. We're expecting our first baby, and I'm not going to miss out on all my daughter's firsts."

"All right, then," the man said, tipping his hat. "Best of luck to you both."

I waited with the others for the announcements of the winners for each event, each of us anxiously shifting, our boots kicking up dust. As each winner's name came over the loudspeaker, the crowd went wild. The moment I saw my event was next, every muscle in my body tensed up. Had I scored high enough? Sure, I'd held on longer than anyone else, but that wasn't going to count. However, there were other factors aside from holding on for eight seconds. No matter how long I'd hung on, if any other aspect of my performance had been lackluster, I could still fall short of coming in first place.

"Let's hear it for this year's bareback bronc champion... Jackson Adler!" the announcer boomed over the loudspeakers. "Now folks, this is what we call a legacy. His daddy, Ty Adler, was also a national champion. Let's give it up for Jackson Adler!"

The rest of the awards passed in a blur. Once it was all done, I knew it was time to go share the news with my family. I checked my phone and located the restaurant Danica had selected. The moment I walked into the place, I received congratulations from multiple people.

Danica stood up from her table and waved at me. I hurried in her direction, leaning down to hug Mia and kiss her cheek.

"You did it, Jackson!" Mia smiled up at me. "I'm so proud of you."

"Dad and Mom were watching," Danica said. "Thankfully, the cameras didn't catch our little family reunion, and the broadcast didn't say anything about your wife. But seriously, Jackson, you need to tell them. Mia said you've been married for six months, and clearly she's far more pregnant than that. What the hell were you thinking?"

Ranger grabbed her hand and made her sit down. "Let it go, Dani. He's a grown-ass man. You have to let him live his own life."

"Yeah, sis. Loosen up the apron strings. Save that shit for Langston. Or better yet, your own kid." I winked at Mia before facing Danica. "Where's Tucker? Did you leave my nephew behind?"

"Not exactly. We dropped him off with Mom and Dad," Danica said. "Then we flew to Vegas. Since you drive to all your rodeo events, I guess you'll be going back to Alabama the hard way. Although…"

"What?" I asked.

"How pregnant is Mia, exactly?" she asked.

"I'm due within the next week," Mia said. "Why?"

"Didn't your doctor caution you about traveling this late in your pregnancy?" Danica asked. "You really shouldn't have come all the way to Vegas either, unless the two of you have been living here."

I reached over to take Mia's hand. "We've had to move around so much she doesn't have a regular doctor. She's gone to clinics when we've been able to work an appointment into the rodeo schedule. There's one here she's seen three times, but without insurance…"

As a rodeo cowboy, it wasn't like I had an easy way to add her to an insurance plan. The one I had was through the Dixie Reapers. Although, since Wire knew what was going on, I should have asked if he could discreetly add her. I wasn't sure how it was set up, though. There was a chance the officers would have seen the information, and then my dad would have found out.

Danica narrowed her eyes. "Seriously, Jackson? That sounds like some fucked-up shit Foster would pull, you know, if he rode horses and not a motorcycle."

I winced, not appreciating the comparison. "I'm not a fuckup like him."

"Can't prove it from where I'm sitting," she muttered.

Once Ranger calmed my sister down, the rest of dinner went smoothly. We parted ways and I took Mia back to our hotel. After hearing what my sister said about traveling this close to her due date, I was more than a little worried. What if we'd hurt the baby by driving all over the place?

"Jackson?" Mia asked, breaking the silence that had enveloped us. "Are you okay?"

"Ah, just thinking about how to tell my folks about us," I admitted. "I'm not sure how they'll take it."

"Your family loves you, Jackson. They'll understand," she reassured me, her hand resting gently on my thigh.

"Maybe," I muttered, unconvinced. My mind raced with what-ifs, each more terrifying than the last. What if they judged Mia for her past? What if their disappointment severed our already fragile relationship? I'd finally felt like Mia and I were in a good place, but it wouldn't take much for her to start doubting herself again.

"Jackson, we can't control how they'll react," Mia

said softly. "We just have to be honest and hope for the best."

"Right," I agreed, though my heart still weighed heavy in my chest.

"Besides," she continued, a mischievous smile playing at the corners of her lips, "once they meet Poppy, they'll be too busy falling in love with her to worry about anything else. Do you really think they'll be able to act cold toward us once they see our precious baby?"

Just as I began to relax, imagining my family's adoration for our baby girl, Mia gasped, clutching her belly.

"Hey, what's wrong?" I asked, my heart hammering in my chest.

"Jackson… I think… I think my water just broke," she stammered, panic lacing her voice.

I glanced down at the floor and realized she was now standing in a puddle. Shit! What the hell was I supposed to do? She didn't have a bag ready or anything. I grabbed a duffle and threw in a change of clothes for her, a onesie she'd bought the baby, and a handful of diapers out of the package she'd insisted on getting last week. Maybe deep down she'd known it was time.

Once I had everything I thought she'd need, I helped her out to the truck. I broke every speed limit on the way to the hospital.

"Almost there, babe," I reassured Mia as we pulled into the driveway. "Just hold on."

A few minutes later, I pulled up to the ER. Helping Mia from the truck, I saw an orderly come out with a wheelchair. While he took her inside, I parked and then rushed back to Mia's side. A nurse was asking her questions, but her contractions were causing her so much pain she couldn't seem to focus.

"She's my wife. Can I fill out the paperwork while someone helps her?" I asked.

"Jackson…" Mia groaned, her breathing labored as her contractions grew more intense. She held out her hand to me, and I grasped it.

"Let me fill out these forms and I'll come find you."

The triage nurse finished entering the basics, gave her a wristband, then sent her to the maternity ward. When I got to the part about insurance, I knew we were going to have an issue. I called Wire, not knowing what else to do.

"Hello," Wire said, answering on the second ring.

"It's Jackson. Listen, Mia just went into labor, and we're at the hospital in Las Vegas. She doesn't have insurance. I don't know what the hell to put for all this financial shit."

"Well, I didn't see that one coming," Wire said. "I mean, I found your marriage certificate, and her medical records. I thought she still had a little time before the baby got here. And you still haven't told your family?"

I cleared my throat. "Technically, Danica and Ranger know. They came here for the national rodeo. Fuck. I need to call Danica and let her know we're at the hospital."

"I'm transferring ten grand into your account. Tell them you'll pay that for a deposit and ask them to bill you for the rest. They'll probably want a credit card on file." Wire sighed. "You really need to tell your parents."

"I will, just… not right now. And thanks, Wire."

I hung up and quickly shot off a text to Danica,

then filled out the rest of the papers. Once I'd made the ten-thousand-dollar payment, I went to the maternity floor where a nurse had me scrub up and put some weird gown thing over my clothes, something to cover my hair, and even little paper booties to go over my shoes. By the time I got to Mia's side, she looked exhausted.

"You're doing such a good job, Mia," I said, doing my best to remain calm. "Ready to see our daughter?"

She nodded and gave me a tight smile right before another contraction hit. Hours later, as the first light of dawn filtered through the curtains, Little Poppy made her way into the world. She was tiny, healthy, and beautiful -- everything I'd hoped she'd be. As I cradled her in my arms, I fell head over heels in love.

"Welcome to the world, Poppy Adler," I whispered, tears misting my eyes. "You're going to be one hell of a ride."

Chapter Ten

Mia

The sun dipped below the horizon, casting a warm glow over the desert landscape as we settled into our new life. Our rental home, a charming bungalow nestled on the outskirts of Las Vegas, offered a sense of security and stability I hadn't felt in a long time.

Honestly, the *only* time I'd felt it was the last time Jackson rented a house for us. We'd decided to stay here in Las Vegas until Poppy was at least six months old before making the long journey back to Alabama. The doctor had cleared her to travel that far, but we'd wanted to be certain she could handle being in the truck for so long.

I didn't know how he'd found a furnished home in our price range in such a short amount of time. It seemed almost like a miracle. Not that the hotel had been bad, but I knew it was too costly to stay there for long. Now that Jackson wasn't going to be hitting the rodeo circuit, we'd need to conserve money. Although, I'd refused to look at his bank account. He'd insisted on getting a debit card in my name and adding me to the account, but I still didn't feel right spending the money.

"All right, little lady," I cooed, cradling Poppy in my arms as I stepped through the front door. "Welcome to your new home."

"Let me help you with the bags, darlin'," Jackson said, his voice laced with the comforting drawl I'd come to love. He took the weight of the bags from my shoulder and tenderly kissed the top of Poppy's head. Despite the rough exterior of the rodeo cowboy, he was gentle and kind -- especially when it came to us.

As we made our way inside, I marveled at how

quickly my life had changed. Becoming a mother had been an adjustment, but I already loved Poppy more than I could have ever imagined. Each day brought new challenges, yet the bond between us only grew stronger. Little Poppy was now two weeks old. My body still ached, but not as much as it had right after giving birth. Jackson had found a doctor for both me and our daughter, and he'd declared we were both in good health.

"Her nursery's all set up," Jackson announced, guiding me toward the pastel-painted room. We'd spent days preparing it, filling it with soft toys and colorful mobiles that would twirl above her crib. It was perfect, just like our little girl. I hadn't been in here since Jackson put the finishing touches on it, but I should have known he'd do an amazing job. This had been the only empty room when we'd rented the place. Now it had everything Poppy would need.

"Thank you, Jackson," I whispered, suddenly overcome with emotion. Tears welled in my eyes as I looked around the room, knowing that without him, none of this would have been possible. I hated the fact I kept crying over every little thing. The doctor said it was just my hormones and would taper off as the weeks passed. I hoped he was right.

"Hey now," he murmured, wrapping his arm around me and pulling me close. "We're a family, Mia. We take care of each other."

I eased Poppy down into her new crib and went to our bedroom to unpack our things. There was still quite a bit to do, but Jackson had taken care of most of it. He'd already stocked the fridge and pantry, made sure we had things like laundry detergent and dish soap, so all I had to do was make a quick run through the house to see if we'd missed anything.

This would be the second longest I'd ever stayed in a nice house. It felt a little surreal. Not once in the times I'd dreamed about a better life had I ever thought I'd actually have a home like this one. I liked it even more than our other rental. I knew it was only temporary, but the way Jackson talked about his house in Alabama, I knew it would probably be even better than this one.

My life kept changing in the most amazing ways, all because of the cowboy who'd decided to save me when I needed help the most.

I put the last of our clothes away and realized how very little we actually owned. Even Poppy... We'd bought her a handful of outfits, but I'd had to constantly wash them. She was always spitting up on them, having accidents that leaked from her diapers, or messing them up in some other way.

"What's wrong?" Jackson asked, coming up behind me and placing his hands on my shoulders.

"Just thinking we all need more clothes than this if we're going to be here for six months. But..."

"You're worried about the cost," he said. "We're fine, Mia. I didn't want to tell you, but the club helped us get this house. Not only did Wire locate it for us, but he shuffled some funds into my account to help pay for it. Or maybe instead of saying the club helped, I should say Wire and Lavender did."

"Why would they do that? It couldn't have been cheap," I said.

"Remember when I said they were hackers? They have a tendency to drain the bank accounts of bad people, like human traffickers, murderers, rapists, corrupt officials... He just funneled some of that money to me. I'm sure most people wouldn't want to touch it, thinking it was dirty money, but if we didn't use it for something good, then what's the point of taking it away from assholes like that?" he asked.

I wasn't sure how to respond. He made sense, but at the same time, I was a little concerned his friends knew how to even find people like that to take money from them. What if they went looking for those funds and tracked them to us? My anxiety must have shown because he gave my shoulders a squeeze, then wrapped his arms around me.

"Everything will be fine, Mia. It's not the first, or even twentieth time Wire has done something like this. The Dixie Reapers aren't like a lot of other motorcycle clubs. At one time, they were complete outlaws. Over the years, the club had tried to ditch the law-breaking stuff. With one exception... They'll still take out the trash, if you get what I mean."

I nodded. Yeah, I thought I understood perfectly. Which meant it was possible if my parents caused us any trouble, then the club would handle them. I had to admit, that made me feel a little more at ease. Maybe going to Alabama and meeting all of Jackson's family wouldn't be so bad after all.

* * *

As the days turned into weeks, we settled into a routine. Jackson took on his new role as a father with gusto, changing diapers and soothing Poppy when she cried. I'd catch him rocking her to sleep in the moonlight, humming soft lullabies that seemed to come straight from his heart.

"Y'know," he said one night, as we lay in bed with Poppy nestled between us, "I never thought I could love someone as much as I love you two."

"Me neither," I confessed, my heart swelling with affection for this man who had saved me from a dark path and given me a future worth living for. It was the first time either of us had mentioned loving the other. The way he'd casually said it was so very like him.

As I gazed at our family -- our beautiful, loving, imperfect family -- I knew that I would do anything to protect them. There was nothing more important than the love that bound us together against all odds.

My phone rang and I grabbed it, checking the display. *Danica.* "It's your sister."

"You should answer it. I'll stay here with Poppy," he said. "I'm glad you and Danica are getting close."

I was too. Smiling, I answered the call and went to the front porch. A cool desert breeze ruffled my hair. It really was pretty here. It wasn't the type of beauty you found in the east or even along the southern coast, or so I'd been told, but it was still peaceful and a bit breathtaking.

"Hey, Danica," I said, feeling a mix of excitement and nervousness at the prospect of talking to Jackson's sister. As Jackson had said, we'd been growing closer over these past few weeks through our phone conversations. But there was still so much I didn't know about her or her family.

"Hey, Mia!" she replied brightly. "How's my favorite sister-in-law?"

"Favorite by default," I teased, a small smile tugging at my lips. She always said things like that. It warmed my heart, even when I knew I was her *only* sister-in-law. "But I'm good, thank you. How are things in Tennessee?"

"Can't complain," she said, and I could hear the warmth in her voice. "Ranger sends his love. Wish we could be there to help with little Poppy."

"Tell him I said hi," I replied. "And I'd be more

than happy to get some help with my daughter. Not that your brother isn't awesome. He's doing an amazing job. It's me who…"

She sighed. "So, you've already fallen down that rabbit hole, huh? The *I suck at being a mom* train of thought. I think most of us go through it. I promise when Poppy starts sleeping more, and you can too, then things will get better."

"Jackson said we're staying here until Poppy is six months, then we'll go to your parents' place." I hesitated a moment before voicing the fear that had been gnawing at me. "Danica… do you think your parents will like me?"

As far as I was concerned, it was a legitimate worry. If they hated me, would Jackson eventually regret choosing to marry me? He'd already said it would be forever, that he didn't believe in divorce.

"Of course, they will, Mia," she reassured me gently. "You're sweet, kind, and you've made my brother happier than I've ever seen him. Besides, they're going to fall head over heels for Poppy. That girl is going to be your trump card. The second my dad sees her, he's going to do his best to give her the entire world. I should know. He used to spoil me and Jackson rotten when we were kids."

"Thanks," I murmured, touched by her encouragement. "I just… I don't want to mess this up, you know? They're his family -- *your* family -- and I want them to accept me."

"Trust me," Danica said firmly, "you're already a part of this family, even if you haven't met them yet. And they're going to love you, just like Jackson and I do. Besides, I have a feeling if they tried to give you a hard time, Jackson would walk away without even looking back. That's how much he cares about you,

Mia."

Her words brought a sense of relief, but the internal turmoil that plagued me as a new mother surfaced once more as I ended the call and retreated indoors. It was more challenging than I'd ever imagined, and I couldn't shake the feeling that I was constantly on the verge of making some terrible mistake.

Every bath, I worried I'd somehow drown Poppy. When she cried, I felt anxious as I tried to figure out what she needed. And every time she woke me in the middle of the night, I thought I might burst into tears. I grappled with self-doubt and inadequacy as I navigated the uncharted waters of motherhood. There were days I felt like a complete failure as a mother.

I slid back into bed, marveling at how perfect Jackson looked with our daughter resting on his chest. I used my phone to snap a picture, then sent it to Danica. Setting it aside, I watched my two favorite people in the world. How did he make that look so easy?

"Jackson, what if I'm not good enough for her? What if I can't take care of her like she needs?"

"Hey," he murmured, pulling me against his side. "You're doing an amazing job, Mia. You love her with all your heart, and that's what she needs most. We'll figure everything else out together. It's not like I have any idea how to be a father. I mean, I did have an amazing example, but it's different when you have to put everything into practice."

"Promise?" I asked.

"Promise," he replied, sealing his vow with a tender kiss. "Would it make you feel better if you found a group of mothers to join? Like one of those…

what are they called? Mommy and Me classes? Is that a thing or did I get that off a movie?"

"You're asking me? I'm just as clueless as you are," I said. "But a group of mothers... I'm not opposed to it exactly, I'm just..."

"I know it's not easy for you to meet new people or make friends. And I understand why you feel that way. Still, it wouldn't hurt to give it a try. I'll look around online tomorrow and see what I can find. I think you need a support system here, other than me. And what better group of people than mothers who have been where you are, or are currently going through the same thing? I'm sure there would be a mix of new moms and women who are on their second or even fourth child."

I nodded. "All right. I'll give it a try."

I gathered Poppy in my arms and carried her back to her room. I knew if I didn't, Jackson would let her sleep on top of him all night, then he'd wake up with stiff joints. Even though he was only twenty-five, being a rodeo cowboy had been hard on his body.

"I love you, my little angel," I whispered as I covered Poppy with her blanket. Tiptoeing from the room, I went back to bed and curled up against Jackson.

"How many more weeks did the doctor say?" he asked.

I knew exactly what he meant. "They said I needed six weeks to heal, but it could be a little longer since I tore when Poppy was born."

He winced. "Thanks for that reminder. I think that part freaked me out more than the rest."

I kissed his cheek. "The time will fly by. But if it's any consolation, I miss getting to be with you in that way too. You're not the only one looking forward to me being all better."

"Love you, Mia. More than anything."

I snuggled against him, smiling. "Love you too."

Chapter Eleven
Mia

Poppy had only been awake for an hour when I heard the front door creak open, my heart lurching in my chest. Jackson had gone out to run errands, leaving me and Poppy alone in the house. He never entered so quietly. A chill ran down my spine as I held our sleeping daughter close, my mind racing with fear.

"Who's there?" I called out, my voice trembling. The silence following my inquiry hung heavy with unspoken threats. Each passing moment felt like an eternity. The tension thickened to the point of being suffocating. The floor in the hallway creaked, letting me know I definitely wasn't alone.

I clutched Poppy to my chest, praying I was wrong and it was only my husband returning. If it wasn't…

"Who's there?" I called out once more. I could hear the fear lacing my voice, and trembled as I held my small daughter. The silence mocked my unease with cruel stillness.

Footsteps drew nearer, slow and deliberate. Whoever was out there *wanted* to scare me. I knew whoever it was, they would most likely try to hurt us. My heart hammered in my chest, the sound thundering in my ears. My mouth went dry, and I scanned the room, wishing for a way to escape. Even if I did manage to get out the window, they'd catch up to me before I could get very far.

The door to the bedroom burst open, revealing two shadowy figures. They lunged toward me, one of them grabbing Poppy from my arms while the other restrained me.

"Let go of her!" I screamed, desperate to protect

my precious girl. But nothing could prepare me for the shock of recognizing my parents' faces, twisted with malice, as they held us captive. Why were they here? No, why were they together? I couldn't remember the last time I'd seen my mom. What was going on right now?

"Keep your mouth shut," my father snarled. "You're coming with us."

"Please, don't hurt her," I begged through gritted teeth, tears streaming down my cheeks. Their grip tightened on me and Poppy, and I knew we were in grave danger. I had no way of alerting Jackson to what was happening, nothing I could drop to leave a hint as to who had taken us.

I fought every step of the way, kicking over an end table. The lamp shattered as it hit the floor, and I knew Jackson would see it and realize we'd been abducted. But would he get back in time to find us? How far would my parents travel with us before he even discovered we were missing?

"Stop it!" My father released me long enough to smack me across the face. Heat bloomed across my cheek and made my eyes water. "Look here, you little bitch. Keep it up, and I'll make sure you suffer twice as much."

As they dragged us out of the house, I overheard their hushed conversation, their words searing into my memory.

"That woman Lily said she'd be here, all vulnerable and alone. She was right. We'll take her back home and make sure this little family never sees each other again," my mom said. "The baby should fetch a high price."

Oh, God! They were going to sell my child? What did that mean for me? I could only imagine... Had my mother already promised me to one of the pimps she'd worked with? Was that the entire reason they were both here? She wouldn't have been able to do this on her own, which meant she'd most likely offered to cut my father in on the deal. But why? No, I knew exactly why… she hadn't kept in touch with me in all these years, so she'd needed my father in order to find me. At least, I had to assume that's how they'd come together again. Or maybe my father had been the one they approached? It would make sense. Actually, none of this did. Why couldn't they just leave us alone? Jackson had made it clear he didn't want them. Why did they have to try and ruin our happiness?

My heart broke at the thought of never seeing Jackson again, never watching our daughter grow up together. And the knowledge that Lily had betrayed us added another layer of pain. I couldn't understand why she would do such a thing. Why had she been so jealous? Jackson said he'd never been hers. I didn't know how someone could be so cruel.

They forced me out to a waiting car, I swore to myself that I would do everything in my power to protect Poppy and reunite us with Jackson. He was our only hope, and I prayed he would find us before it was too late.

My parents shoved a cloth into my mouth, then put tape over it before binding my hands. They shoved me into the trunk and slammed it shut. Since my mother still had Poppy, I couldn't do anything. If I made them angry again, or tried to escape, my daughter could be in even more danger.

And here I'd thought the only person I had to be leery of was Carter. Instead, he'd disappeared after he'd caused all that trouble before. Once Cooper laid him out, he'd caused trouble once more, then given us a wide berth. In fact, I'd often thought it was odd how quiet he'd been. He couldn't be part of this too, could he? Wait. What if he'd been around and Jackson hadn't told me? Would he have kept something like that from me?

The darkness felt suffocating. I felt every bump in the road, and every turn slammed me into one side or another. I had no sense of time and wondered if we'd only been on the road a few minutes or longer. I could hear Poppy crying in the car, and my mother's angry voice as she yelled at her to shut up. Tears pricked my eyes, and I hated being so helpless. All those self-defense classes, and my junkie parents had gotten the best of me. I felt worse than useless.

"Where are you, Jackson?" I whispered to myself. "Please find us."

Every second that passed took us farther away from him. I didn't know how Lily had found my parents, or why. *Think, Mia!*

I couldn't remember if any neighbors had been out when my parents snatched us. Had anyone been watching from a window? Maybe sitting on their porch, unnoticed by my parents? If they had been, maybe the police had already been called.

I hadn't seen Lily or Anna in Las Vegas at nationals. They must have been there, but how had they known about Poppy? I doubted Jackson had told them. They'd made him so angry he'd avoided them. Somehow, my parents had been prepared for Poppy.

I closed my eyes and took a deep breath, trying to calm my racing thoughts. I knew I had to be strong, and I had to trust in myself. I had to find a way to survive and save my daughter. As the car sped down the road, I clung to the hope that we would be reunited with Jackson soon. I knew that the future was uncertain, but I was willing to fight for it -- for us.

I prayed for strength, knowing I couldn't fall apart right now. Poppy needed me to be calm. We had to survive this. If we did, we'd be stronger for all we'd suffered. One way or another, I'd escape this nightmare and take Poppy with me.

* * *

By the time we stopped, I felt like my bladder would burst. I also ached from head to toe. My dad opened the trunk and hauled me out. I blinked to adjust my vision and saw we were at a rundown motel. The kind where people wouldn't ask questions. My parents probably felt right at home here. Thanks to Jackson, this place made my skin crawl now. I'd been living a life so different from what I'd known before meeting him. He'd spoiled me.

Dad dragged me into a room and shoved me inside. Once he took the gag off, I cried at the pain from the tape being torn off.

"Shut up!" He punched me and I saw stars. Not only did pain spread through my face, but I staggered and fell into the wall. He untied my hands and pointed to the bathroom. "Go piss if you need to. Then sit your ass in the corner and don't fucking move."

I did as he said. When I went to wash my hands, the water came out brown and I cringed. I caught sight of my reflection in the cracked mirror and noticed I already had a bruise blooming across my cheek and down into my jaw. My dad pointed to the corner again and I wedged myself between the wall and dresser.

"Why won't this kid shut up?" Mom demanded as she glared at Poppy.

"She's probably hungry." My voice came out as a croak. "Her formula was at the house, as well as her diapers. She'll need both."

- 268 -

The motel room door opened and both Lily and Anna walked in. My eyes went wide as I stared at them. Lily smirked at me, and I knew she'd been the mastermind behind my kidnapping. How could they be so evil? Why did they want to destroy our lives? Did they not care about Jackson at all? I didn't understand how they could think he'd be happy with his wife and daughter missing. He had to be going out of his mind, assuming he'd already found the mess I'd made in the living room and realized we weren't home.

"Are you sure this is going to work?" Anna asked, sounding uncertain as she glanced at me.

"Of course, it will," Lily snapped back. "We just need to keep them apart long enough for Jackson to see what a mistake he made by choosing Mia over us."

"Besides," my mother chimed in, her words dripping with disdain, "once we get that little brat away from her, she'll be as good as useless to him. Didn't you say they only got married because she was pregnant? No baby, no reason to keep her."

My blood boiled at their callous disregard for my daughter's safety, but all I could do was watch her, and hope she'd make it through his. I'd failed to protect her from the evil in the world. How sad was it that my parents were the type of scum who'd sell their own flesh and blood?

"Remember, ladies," my father warned them, "if anything goes wrong, we're all in this together. There's no turning back now."

Yeah, sounded about right. My dad wouldn't go down alone. No way in hell. He'd drag them all down with him. I didn't know how he'd found the courage to pull off something like this. Now that I'd been apart from him for so long, I realized he was rather spineless.

If Jackson were here, my dad would have run instead of trying to stay and fight. It was just the type of person he was. How had I been afraid of him for so long?

"Fine," Anna muttered, before adding defiantly, "but if this doesn't work, it's on your heads. You'll have to pay back every penny."

Wait. What? Did they seriously give my parents money to kidnap us? How had they even known how to find them? I had a feeling someone smarter, and possibly wealthier, was behind all this. I just couldn't figure out who, or why. I narrowed my eyes at Anna, and hoped she'd rot in hell. With any luck, someone would send her there soon.

A shiver ran down my spine as the weight of their conspiracy pressed down on me. *Jackson, I need you more than ever*.

As the hours ticked by and the darkness seemed to grow even thicker, I couldn't help but fear that our time was running out. And so, with each beat of my racing heart, I prayed that Jackson would find us before it was too late -- not just for me, but for our precious daughter who deserved so much more than the horror she'd been born into. If she'd had a better mother, none of this would have happened.

* * *

Jackson

Hours had passed since Mia and Poppy were taken, and rage bubbled within me. Staring at the barren crib and rumpled sheets, determination surged -- I would bring them home. Even if it meant calling my parents. I'd tried to let the law handle it, but so far they hadn't done a fucking thing.

A neighbor had thankfully seen a man and

woman taking Mia and Poppy from the house, and she'd taken note of the color and make of the car, and even had caught part of the license plate number. Despite having that much information, the idiots hadn't made any headway. I'd finally asked them to leave, in the hopes they'd actually do their fucking jobs if they weren't in my house. Clearly whoever had taken them didn't plan to ask for a ransom. Which meant this was most likely personal.

I took a breath and called Wire. Before he even had a chance to say hello, I blurted out, "Mia and Poppy were kidnapped. I need help."

"Shit," Wire muttered. "Give me everything you've got."

I passed along the information the neighbor collected, as well as the time of the abduction. I heard Wire's fingers flying across the keys of his computer. It didn't take long before he grunted and gave me at least something.

"Caught them on a traffic cam on their way out of town. Looks like they're heading southeast."

"Any way to follow them farther?" I asked.

"I think they got on the interstate. After that last clip of them turning, there's nothing. I checked every camera in the area, including some of the shops."

"Fuck!" I wanted to throw my phone and barely managed to stop myself.

"You still haven't told your parents, have you?" he asked.

"No, I fucking haven't. Is this really the time, Wire? My wife and daughter are gone. I have no idea who took them or why. They could be out of my reach by now."

"I've got an image of the man behind the wheel. I'll run it through a facial recognition program and see what I get. Might take a while, though. If they haven't left the state, then I can reach out to the Savage Knights. They're in your area. I'd already clued them in to your presence, even though you aren't technically part of the club. It wasn't like you needed permission to be in their territory, but I wanted a connection there in case I needed help fast. Like now."

"I appreciate it. Even if I don't sound like it."

Wire sighed. "This is going to take me a while. I'll get Lavender to help. We'll locate cameras near all exits in both directions and see if we can get lucky. But don't expect a call back anytime soon. Probably not even tonight."

I didn't know what the hell to do in the meantime. The cops didn't seem to have a clue where to even start, or else they were just keeping me in the dark. Hell, if they figured out I had a connection to a motorcycle club, they'd likely put me at the top of the suspect list. Then again, if the movies and shows were even slightly accurate, the husband was usually the first person of interest.

In all honesty, I knew I wasn't being fair. I'd met my share of good officers and deputies. But the club had also taken down some rotten, corrupt bastards. Like any job, there were bad mixed in with the good. I just felt impatient because I had no idea if my girls were hurt, scared, or even still alive. What the hell did those people want with them?

"Just do what you can. Please. I have to get them back, Wire." I swallowed hard. "I love them, and I don't think I can live without them."

"Hey! Knock that shit off right fucking now. If your dad heard that bullshit come out of your mouth, he'd knock you on your ass."

I snorted. "Really? You think Cowboy would lay

a hand on any of his kids, regardless of our ages?"

"You're right. He wouldn't," Wire admitted.

Chapter Twelve

Jackson

It took another two days for Wire to finally locate my family and help me gather reinforcements. Even though Mia and Poppy were no longer near Las Vegas, the Savage Knights still sent Seeker, Knuckles, and Doc with me. We hauled ass to Oklahoma, where the Savage Raptors met up with us. Lynx was technically family since his sister was part of the Dixie Reapers. I was happy to see him, as well as Rebel and Ravager. With seven of us, I hoped we'd be able to extract Mia and Poppy without any issues.

"What intel do we have?" Lynx asked, as we gathered in the Savage Raptors clubhouse.

"Wire said it looked like Mia's parents had taken them, but he found two other people. Anna and Lily, two barrel racers on the rodeo circuit. I shot them down and they weren't happy about it." I cleared my throat. "Fidelity in the rodeo is a bit rare. Guess the excitement goes to everyone's head, and there are a ton of buckle bunnies who want a good time. Not much different than dealing with club whores, except the cowboy version. Anna and Lily were competitors, but the way they chased after the cowboys… well, you get the picture."

Lynx nodded. "All right. Anyone else? Or is it just the two women and Mia's parents?"

"As far as I know, that's it. But… there's one other person who caused a lot of trouble for us, then sort of vanished. Carter Bales. He's a rodeo cowboy who slapped Mia around before we were married." I bit my lip. "What I'm about to say doesn't leave this room. Understood?"

Lynx crossed his arms. "Of course."

The others nodded their agreement, so I told them how Mia had been dating Carter and what had happened when she told him she was pregnant. It was the first time I'd admitted Poppy wasn't my biological child. I also told them Mia had only been seventeen at the time, which infuriated every last man standing with me.

"When we're done, if this Carter person isn't there or a part of this, I'm still going to find his ass and teach him a lesson," Knuckles said. "I can't let that shit fly. Doesn't matter if it happened in my territory or not."

"Where are they right now?" Seeker asked.

"As long as they haven't moved since the last update I received from Wire, they're at a motel outside of town. Rundown place. You know the type. Owned by people who prefer cash, and never see or hear anything."

"Do you know the layout or which room they're in?" Rebel asked.

"It's the Shady Pines Motel. Room 6. Not on the highway or near it. They picked a really remote place. No idea how they even found the damn place," I said.

"I know it," Ravager said. His eyes darkened and his jaw tensed. Shit. Whatever happened at the place must have been bad. "Only way in is through the door. Even the window in the bathroom isn't big enough for an adult to fit through."

"Think we'll have any issues with interruptions or cops being called by other people renting rooms?" Doc asked.

"No." Knuckles cracked his neck. "Only criminal types and prostitutes stay there. You'll find just as much blood as semen soaked into those mattresses."

I tried not to think about my wife and kid being

in such a nasty place. I'd get them back no matter the cost!

"It would be better to go before nightfall," Ravager said. "Quieter. Most people there aren't up and moving during daylight hours. Or rather, not as many will be."

"So if this place is as bad as you say, then he could slaughter the kidnappers and no one would care?" Lynx asked.

Ravager shrugged. "He could probably give the guy at the desk a hundred-dollar bill and he'd handle the cleanup. So, yeah… he can do whatever the hell he wants without repercussions."

Seeker let out a low whistle. "Damn. On the upside, that makes things easier on us."

"So we're going in today?" I asked. "Everyone on board with that?"

"Let's make sure we're properly armed, maybe get some eyes on that place just in case someone is helping them. I don't want any surprises," Lynx said.

Technically this was my mission since it was my family who was kidnapped, but Lynx had way more experience with this sort of thing. They all did. I was happy to let someone else lead the way. All that mattered was getting Mia and Poppy back safe and sound. Didn't care how I did it.

"Do you have anyone we can use?" Seeker asked.

"I may." Ravager pulled out his phone. "Never thought I'd use this number again. Shit."

I winced, wanting to tell him to forget about it, but I couldn't. Not when it might mean the difference in my family getting back safe and sound. Ravager walked off, speaking low enough we couldn't hear him. I glanced at Lynx, wondering if he knew the story behind Ravager's statement.

"How's my sister?" Lynx asked. "She doesn't call very often."

I smiled. "And do you call her often?"

He shrugged. "Guess not. Still, she doing okay?"

"You know Venom adores her. Ridley is fine, and so is Dawson. Although, I think he's about to move out. Not sure if he's told Ridley. The club life really isn't right for him. Unlike Foster and Owen, he doesn't want to be a Prospect."

"I can see that," Lynx said. "He always seemed a little too soft. Not saying there's anything wrong with how he is. I just know he wouldn't last long if he was trying to patch in."

I nodded. It was something we'd discussed before. He'd struggled to figure out his place. He had more than one secret he was keeping from Venom and Ridley. When he finally opened Pandora's box, I hoped I was far the fuck away. No way I wanted to be around for that shit.

Ravager came back, a grim look on his face. "I got us eyes on the place. They'll let me know how many people come and go. Let's give it a few hours before we make a move."

It was hard to agree since I wanted my girls back in my arms, but I understood why it was better to sit still for the moment. The minutes dragged by slowly, and I started to feel a little stir crazy. When my phone rang, I jolted. *Wire.*

"What's up, Wire?" I asked as the call connected.

"Got more info for you. Remember how you had me looking for a Carter Bales?" he asked.

"Yeah. What of it? Wait. That fucker was in Vegas. Did he do something to Mia and Poppy?"

"I'm getting there. Apparently his family is rather well-off. Found information on an engagement between him and some debutante… from over two years ago. He was engaged when he was with Mia."

"Wait, what?" I wasn't sure how to process what he'd said.

"I don't think he's been lying low. I didn't find a paper trail, but maybe I didn't look hard enough. I think he could be behind Mia and Poppy getting kidnapped. It wouldn't look good for him if Mia showed up with Poppy and tried to get child support or something." I heard the keys clicking and knew Wire was still working at his computer. "I think this engagement is more than just a merging of families. Her parents have all kinds of ties that would benefit Mr. Bales' businesses. The Bales family wouldn't want anything to possibly throw a wrench in their plans."

"So is Carter at fault or his family?" I asked. "And how would they even know about Mia?"

"Maybe he told them? Or he could be acting independently. I'm still not sure he has anything to do with it. I'm going through every text and call between Anna and Lily, and cross-checking any common numbers between the two."

"Anything?" I asked.

"Yeah, I found a number that's popped up repeatedly the last six months. Seems to be a burner. I'm not sure those girls came up with this idea on their own."

"Is there a way to see if he's in the area?" I asked.

"I'm not finding him. The phone he'd been using is still pinging at his last known location. That boy never stays put this long. I think he ditched it, which means I have no way of finding him unless I get lucky and spot him using cameras around the country in his usual spots."

I swallowed hard. "Can you look at the all the

footage you can access around this area? If he's here, I want to know."

And if that bastard was trying to take my family from me, I'd fucking kill him. I'd never felt like that was something I could do before. Then again, I hadn't had a reason to fight so hard for anyone. For Mia and Poppy there wasn't anything I wouldn't do.

"It's going to take time, Jackson. The kind you may not have. Just be cautious. If anything happens to you, your dad is going to have my ass."

He wasn't wrong. If things went sideways and I didn't make it out, my dad would lose his shit. Especially since I'd told Wire to keep this from him. It wasn't that I didn't want him to know about Mia and Poppy... I just worried he'd be disappointed in me, and that was one thing I couldn't handle.

Ravager's phone rang. I couldn't hear what was being said, but when he ended the call, he looked pissed as fuck. "We need to go. Now."

"What's going on?" I asked.

"More cars pulled up. A rich man and woman just strolled into the motel room, with a young man in tow. My contact said they looked like they were all related." Ravager held my gaze. "Any ideas?"

"Yeah. I think it's Carter Bales and his family." Motherfucker! I had to get to Mia, and I needed to be there ten minutes ago. "I'm going. I don't care if there's a plan or not. I can't sit back and do nothing."

"We're with you," Ravager said.

"Let's roll out." Lynx headed for the door and we all followed.

* * *

My heart hammered against my ribcage, each beat echoing the urgency that consumed me. One thought pulsed through my veins: I had to rescue Mia and Poppy.

"Stay sharp," Seeker murmured "The slightest mistake could cost us everything. And I do mean *us* and not just you, Jackson. All our lives are on the line."

I nodded, the weight of my responsibility threatened to crush me, but I couldn't afford to falter now. *Mia and Poppy are counting on me.*

As we watched the motel, I realized it looked like a place where hope went to die. Every last person in this place must have given up long ago. Dread coiled in my stomach, tightening with each passing second. *Please let them be okay.*

"Ready?" Lynx asked.

"Let's do it," I whispered, swallowing the fear that clawed at my throat. If things ended badly, Mia and Poppy could get hurt. Just the thought of losing them was enough to make me feel more than a little crazy. I couldn't live without them. Wouldn't want to even try.

We crept toward the motel, our footsteps seeming loud against the pavement, but no one paid us any attention. Knuckles and Doc took the lead, expertly avoiding any potential traps. I followed close behind, clutching my weapon, praying I wouldn't have to use it. While I knew how to use a gun, I'd never particularly liked them.

"Jackson," Doc whispered, his eyes scanning the perimeter. "I know you're anxious to burst into the room and get your family back, but we need to be cautious. Wait for my signal."

I nodded, crouching low as we moved into position. Sweat trickled down my back, but I ignored it, focusing on the task at hand. When Doc gave the signal, I lunged forward, swiftly moving across the parking lot and placing myself near the door of the motel room.

Knuckles came up beside me, patting me on the shoulder. "Let's get inside."

Knuckles kicked open the door and trained his gun on one of the men. Lynx entered behind him, incapacitating another. The other men filed in and left me for last. By the time I entered the room, Carter and the people I assumed to be his parents were on the floor with guns trained on them. Same for Mia's parents. Lily and Anna stood with their hands up.

"Jackson," Mia sobbed, relief and terror warring in her eyes. She clung to Poppy protectively, shielding her from harm.

"Stay back!" Anna snarled, trying to sound brave even though fear flickered in her gaze. "You don't know what you're getting into."

"It's over, Anna. Be glad you didn't hurt Poppy or Mia. I'd have killed you with my bare hands if you had."

"Save your threats," Lily spat, her eyes narrowing. "You won't do anything to us. You're too weak."

I'd never been the type to be violent with women. But this little bitch... I stomped over to her, grabbed a handful of hair and yanked her head back. "Listen up, you fucking psycho. When it comes to my wife and kid, there's not a damn thing I wouldn't do to keep them safe. If that means I end your miserable life, then so be it. I won't lose any fucking sleep over it."

Her lips parted and her eyes went wide. "What?"

"Who's weak now?"

"Fine," Anna sneered. "Take your precious family and leave."

"Are you fucking stupid?" Carter demanded. "We had a deal! You have to pay back every cent my family put into this."

"Thanks for confirming you're a piece of shit," I said. "I'm sorry I ever considered you a friend."

He snarled at me. "Is that why you married my little whore? Were you acting on my behalf?"

"No. I did that because I wanted to. I love Mia and Poppy. You just used her, Carter. Did you even tell her you had a fiancée?" He glared at me. "Yeah, I know about her. What were you going to do? Kill them to hide the evidence of your infidelity?"

"No. I'm going to sell them," he said, staring at me with pure hatred. "I could have gotten rid of the brat in her belly if you hadn't interfered. You fucked everything up. I knew once you married her, I'd have to plan more carefully. If you'd just stayed out of it, then I could have taken care of all this so much easier."

"No, Carter. This is your fault and yours alone," I said.

"What about us?" Lily asked. "He tricked us into helping him, saying you'd get over Mia and give us a chance."

"You two really are stupid," I said. "I will never want you. Even if something happened to Mia, the two of you still wouldn't have a chance. But just so you know, I'll never marry anyone else ever again. Mia is my one and only."

"Oh, Jackson," Mia murmured.

"Why don't you get your girls to safety?" Lynx suggested.

"But I…"

Lynx shook his head. "You may be Cowboy's son, but this isn't your way of doing things, Jackson. Don't lose who you are. I have no doubt you'd do whatever you needed to in order to keep your family safe. Right now, that's not necessary. You have us here, and we're more than capable of taking out the trash."

I held out my hand to Mia and she hurried over to me. I pulled her and Poppy into my arms. "You sure about this?"

"Positive. We'll call Wire and find out the best way to handle this. He's already done his homework on these people. Just do me one favor... take them home. And I mean *your* home in Alabama. Deal?"

I looked down at Mia and Poppy, knowing it was time to face my parents. "Deal. Come on, Mia. Let's get out of here."

She leaned into me. "Can we get a nice hotel somewhere so Poppy and I can get cleaned up? We smell and need clean clothes."

"Yeah, darlin'. We can do that." I looked back into the room one final time before taking my girls outside. I helped them into my truck and drove away without a moment's hesitation.

Chapter Thirteen

Jackson

I stood there, arms crossed as I leaned against the bar in the Savage Raptors' clubhouse, the weight of my decision bearing down on me. Mia stood beside me, Poppy cradled in her arms, their presence a reminder of what I'd found and what was now at stake. Returning home to Alabama meant facing my family, especially my father, Cowboy. It wasn't going to be easy, but I had to do it for Mia and Poppy -- my wife and daughter. They deserved a stable home, and I was determined to provide that for them, no matter what it took.

Deep down, I knew my parents would accept Mia. What worried me was the fact they might be disappointed in me. I'd kept silent for so long, and pretty much ghosted them. I knew it had to have hurt them. I didn't think they'd be upset over me stepping up to claim Mia. But I also didn't want to admit to them Poppy wasn't mine biologically. However, the moment they did the math and realized Mia had gotten pregnant at seventeen, my life would be over because they'd both murder me.

"Are you sure about this, Jackson?" Mia asked, her eyes mirroring my own uncertainty.

"Yeah, babe," I replied, forcing a smile. "We need to be with family, and the Dixie Reapers are our family too. Besides, Poppy deserves to know her grandparents. They're going to love the two of you."

"Okay," she said, nodding. Her trust in me both humbled and terrified me. I couldn't let them down. No matter how pissed-off my dad might be, I'd have to face it. I knew Danica had been right back at nationals. I should have told my family long ago.

Taking a deep breath, I pulled out my phone and dialed Wire's number. The line rang twice before he answered.

"Hey, Wire," I said when the call connected.

"How's my favorite cowboy?" Wire replied, his lively tone bringing a slight grin to my face.

"I need your help. Again. Mia, Poppy, and I are moving back to Alabama, and I want to make sure everything goes smoothly. Can you handle the logistics? No one knows about them except you and Lavender. I know a lot of people are going to feel hurt and even angry, but I don't want them taking it out on my wife and kid."

"Of course," Wire assured me. "You just focus on getting your family settled in, and I'll take care of the rest. Head straight to your place. I'll get Lavender to drop off some groceries."

"Thanks, Wire," I said, my gratitude evident in my tone. "I appreciate it more than you know."

"Hey, we're family," he replied. "That's what we do."

Hanging up, I turned to Mia and Poppy, determination settling in my chest. It was time to face the challenges that lay ahead, but with them by my side, I knew we could handle anything. And as long as we had the support of our Dixie Reapers' family, we'd find our place in this new chapter of our lives.

I hoped I'd be able to give Mia and Poppy the home they deserved. They both needed stability, and people who cared. I knew I was the only one who'd ever loved Mia, and it broke my heart when I thought about it. Her parents should have been there for her, not used and abused her.

"Ready to go home?" I asked. "This time will the last… Unless we outgrow the house."

She nodded. "As I'll ever be. Let me just change Poppy once more."

Thankfully, Meredith, Lynx's wife, had found some clothes for Mia, as well as the basics Poppy would need until we made it back to my parents' ranch. I'd driven here, so I had my truck, which meant I was out of reasons to delay the trip any longer. I helped Mia get Poppy settled in her infant seat, then buckled Mia into the passenger seat. Leaning in, I brushed my lips against hers.

"Everything's going to be fine. I love you," I said.

"I love you too." She kissed me again.

"Give me just a minute to ask Lynx something, then we'll head out." I backed away and shut the door.

Lynx watched me with a raised eyebrow, and I shoved my hands into my pockets, suddenly feeling like a kid approaching the principal's office. "Something on your mind?"

"Mia's parents, Carter and his… I know your club is handling them, but I need proof they won't come after my family again. Otherwise, I'll be sleeping with one eye open for a while," I said.

Lynx pulled out his phone and sent a text to someone. Not long after, he got a reply and the images he showed me nearly made me throw up. I knew the club would be brutal, just like the Dixie Reapers, but I hadn't expected them to dismember the bodies.

"What the fuck?" I asked.

"The girls had it easier. At least they were dead when they were cut up. Looks like they had their teeth knocked out, and I see some bruising along what's left of their necks. Want me to find out all the details and give you a definitive answer as to what happened?" he asked.

I lifted my hands. "Hell no. I'm good. Although,

I may not eat for a while."

"Get your family home, Jackson. Don't think about those people ever again and do your best to forget those images I just showed you. You may be a Reaper's kid, but that's not your lifestyle and you know it. Let the rest of us handle the gory details."

I thanked him again and got into the truck. It was going to be a long-ass drive, and I wasn't looking forward to it.

We drove for several hours before pausing to stretch our legs, and I could tell my girls needed a break. After a bite to eat, we'd gotten back on the road. After roughly twelve hours since we'd left the Savage Raptors' clubhouse, I could see the fence line for my parents' place.

The stars shone brightly overhead as we pulled down the long drive of my parents' ranch. The familiar sight of the white wooden fence and weathered red barn filled me with a mixture of nostalgia and trepidation. I could see the house in the distance, its wraparound porch a warm and comforting embrace that held memories of laughter and family gatherings.

Mia's hand gripped mine tightly, her knuckles turning white with tension. I knew she was just as anxious as I was, if not more so. We'd talked about this moment countless times, but the reality of it weighed heavy on our hearts.

"Time to get this over with," I said.

Mia glanced at Poppy in her car seat, gently brushing a wisp of hair from the baby's forehead. Together, we stepped out of the truck, my boots crunching on the gravel as the sounds of the ranch enveloped us -- the distant whinny of horses and the soft rustle of leaves in the wind. It felt like both an eternity and a heartbeat ago since I'd last stood here.

Mia got Poppy out of the truck and held her close.

As we approached the house, I couldn't help but recall all the times I'd run up those steps, eager to share stories of my rodeo triumphs with my family. This time, however, I wasn't bringing home trophies or tales of victory -- I was bringing a wife and a child they'd never met, born from less-than-ideal circumstances.

My heart pounded in my chest, my lungs constricting with each breath. I felt the weight of their potential judgment bearing down upon me, threatening to suffocate me. I wanted nothing more than for my family to accept Mia and Poppy, to welcome them with open arms and understanding. But the fear of disappointment gnawed at the edges of my mind, threatening to consume me whole.

"Jackson," Mia whispered, her eyes searching mine. "No matter what happens, we're in this together. Remember that."

I nodded, taking a deep breath to steady my nerves. I knew she was right -- our love and commitment to each other was what mattered most, and together we could face anything.

"Let's do this," I murmured, my resolve strengthened by her unwavering support.

With one last look at the home that held so many memories, I squeezed Mia's hand and led her up the porch steps, my heart racing with anticipation and anxiety. My hand hovered over the doorbell, hesitating for only a moment before pressing it firmly.

As the chime echoed through the house, I braced myself for the unknown, praying that my family would find it within themselves to accept the new life I'd built with Mia and Poppy.

The door swung open, revealing my father's

imposing figure. His icy blue eyes narrowed as they took in the sight of me, Mia, and Poppy nestled in her arms. I could feel the tension radiating off him like heat from a bonfire.

"Jackson," he said gruffly, his voice laced with both surprise and disappointment. "You've got some explaining to do."

My throat tightened, and for a moment, I struggled to find the words. Mia's fingers dug into my hand, a silent reminder of our strength together.

"Dad, this is Mia, my wife," I began, fighting to keep my voice steady. "And this little one is our daughter, Poppy."

His gaze shifted to Mia, then to Poppy, before settling back on me. The silence hung heavy between us, each passing second stoking the fire of his disapproval.

"Inside," Cowboy ordered, stepping aside to let us enter. As we crossed the threshold, I could sense the storm brewing within him.

Once we were all gathered in the living room, Cowboy finally spoke, his voice dangerously calm. "You think just because you went out there, playing cowboy and starting a family without so much as a word, that you can waltz back in here and everything will be fine?"

"Poppy is your granddaughter, Dad," I replied, trying to keep my emotions in check. "Isn't that enough?"

"Enough?" He scoffed, shaking his head. "You left us, Jackson. You abandoned your family, your responsibilities. And you know damn well I don't mean because you were gone. You've done the rodeo thing for a long-ass time, but you were always in constant contact with us, and you came home between events if you were close enough. But now you come back with a wife and a child, expecting us to pick up the pieces?"

I flinched at his words, feeling the sting of truth behind them. My own doubts and fears echoed in my mind, mocking me. Was I really worthy of their forgiveness, of their acceptance?

"Maybe it'd be better if we just left," I choked out, the weight of my father's disappointment crushing me. "We can find our own place, make our own way."

"Jackson, don't," Mia whispered, her eyes pleading with me to reconsider.

But as I searched my father's face for any sign of acceptance or understanding, all I found was a cold, hard wall of resistance. Maybe it was better this way, I thought. Maybe I didn't deserve their love after all.

"Fine," Cowboy said, his voice tight with barely restrained anger. "If that's what you think is best, then go. But know that you're walking away from more than just your family, Jackson. You're walking away from everything we've built together, from the life you could have had here."

As his words sank in, I felt my heart shatter into a million pieces. The weight of my choices, my responsibilities, pressed down on me, threatening to crush me beneath their burden. And for a moment, I almost let them.

Just as the last word left my father's lips, my mother appeared in the doorway, her eyes soft and kind. She took one look at the scene before her and instantly understood the gravity of the situation. With a grace that only she possessed, she stepped forward and placed a gentle hand on Cowboy's arm.

"Enough," she said firmly, her voice steady but soothing. "This isn't helping anyone, least of all

Jackson. I understand why you're angry. I'm upset too, but it looks like we have more important things to consider right now. Our boy may not have kept in touch, and lied his ass off by omission, but we have a new daughter-in-law and grandbaby to focus on."

Cowboy clenched his jaw and looked away, his anger simmering just beneath the surface. But even he knew better than to argue with my mother when she took that tone. It was the voice of a woman who'd spent years nurturing and guiding our family, a voice that demanded respect and obedience.

"Jackson," my mother continued, turning her gaze to me. "Your father is worried, as any parent would be. But we are your family, and we will always be here for you, no matter what. You don't have to face this alone."

Her words were like a balm to my wounded heart, easing some of the pain and doubt that had taken root there. I wanted so badly to believe her, to trust that my family would stand by me despite everything.

But before I could respond, Poppy's cries pierced the tense silence, her tiny voice a desperate plea for comfort. The sound seemed to jolt Mia into action.

"Shh, it's okay, baby girl," Mia whispered, her voice a soothing lullaby as she rocked Poppy gently in her arms. "Mommy's here."

I watched as Mia's love for our daughter shone through every movement, every touch. Despite everything she'd been through, she was strong, resilient, and fiercely protective of our little girl. And in that moment, I knew I would do whatever it took to give them the life they deserved, even if it meant standing up to my own father.

"Thank you, Mom," I murmured, feeling a

newfound resolve settle in my chest. "I know this isn't easy for anyone, but I'm not walking away from my family. Mia and Poppy deserve better than that."

My mother smiled at me, her eyes warm and proud. She reached out and squeezed my hand, a silent promise of support and understanding. And as I stared into her loving gaze, I felt a spark of hope ignite within me, a fragile flame that refused to be extinguished.

Poppy's cries echoed through the room, drawing everyone's attention to Mia and the tiny baby cradled in her arms. My mother was the first to move, stepping forward with a soft smile and guiding hand. "Here, let me help," she murmured, gently adjusting Poppy's position in Mia's arms.

"Thank you," Mia whispered, her eyes filled with gratitude as she looked up at my mother. I could see the relief in her expression, and it warmed my heart to know that she was beginning to feel welcome here.

"Would you like a bottle for her?" my mother asked, already heading toward the kitchen. "I can heat one up."

I started to ask why they had stuff like that already but decided to keep my mouth shut. Either Mom had been helping out single mothers in the area again, or someone had tipped her off I'd be bringing a baby home, and she'd just put on the best act of her entire life.

"Please," Mia replied, returning her attention to our daughter as she continued to rock and soothe her.

"Jacey, why don't you show Mia where the nursery is?" my father suggested, his voice softer than before. It seemed that Poppy's arrival had shifted the atmosphere in the room, reminding everyone of what truly mattered.

"Of course," my mother agreed, leading Mia and Poppy down the hall.

As they disappeared from sight, my father turned to me, his expression unreadable. "Jackson, I'm sorry if I came across too harsh earlier. It's just... hard to see you like this, with so much responsibility on your shoulders. This is different from helping out around here. You have two people who will be relying on you from now. And that girl..."

"Thank you, Dad," I said, swallowing the lump in my throat. The weight of his words hung heavy in the air, but I couldn't deny the truth in them. I had changed, and so had my life. But I wouldn't let that hold me back -- I would do whatever it took to make things right for Mia and Poppy. "I'll tell you more about them later. Just know, I married Mia because of your influence in my life."

"Your mom wants the three of you to stay in the house the next few days. Your place needs to be aired out and properly prepared for a family. She saw Lavender heading over there and stopped her. Guess that means you asked her or Wire for help in setting your place up before you got here."

"I did, and I don't want to be an inconvenience. I know I should have told the two of you about Mia sooner, but... I was scared. I didn't want to disappoint the two of you."

"Your mother and I are here for you, son," he continued, placing a comforting hand on my shoulder. "We may not always agree on everything, but we want what's best for you and your family."

"Thank you, Dad," I replied, my voice thick with emotion. "That means more to me than you know."

As we stood in the living room, our differences momentarily put aside, I felt a strange sense of belonging wash over me. It was as if, for the first time in a long while, I truly understood where I fit within this family. I'd spent so much time doubting myself and my parents. Not that I had ever worried I'd never be able to achieve my dream, but there had been times I'd worried I wouldn't be enough for Mia and Poppy. Even though I had a great example of what being a father was all about, it didn't mean I'd be any good at it. And though the road ahead would be filled with challenges and uncertainty, I knew that, together, we could face it all.

My mother's laughter drifted down the hall, accompanied by Mia's responding giggle, and my heart swelled with love and gratitude. This was the beginning of a new chapter in my life -- one filled with hope, healing, and the promise of a brighter future for Mia, Poppy, and me.

Epilogue

Mia
One Week Later

The warm glow of the setting sun bathed the Dixie Reapers' compound in golden light as everyone busied themselves preparing for the welcome party. Colorful streamers danced in the gentle breeze, while balloons bobbed at every corner. The scent of mouthwatering barbecue wafted through the air, mixing with the sweet aroma of fresh-baked pies and spicy chili. Lively country music blared from the speakers, setting a festive tone that seemed to sweep everyone up in its contagious energy.

On the sidelines, I stood watching the whirlwind of activity, feeling like an outsider intruding on a private family gathering. My heart thudded against my chest, and I rubbed my clammy palms on the worn fabric of my jeans. A part of me longed to join in the camaraderie, but the fear of rejection held me back.

"Are you all right, honey?" a voice asked, pulling me from my thoughts.

I glanced over to see a woman with kind eyes and a warm smile. "Yeah, I'm just… nervous."

"Understandable," she said, nodding sympathetically. "New places can be overwhelming, especially when it feels like everyone already knows each other."

"Exactly," I agreed, relieved that someone understood. Though the Dixie Reapers had been nothing but welcoming, I couldn't shake the feeling of inadequacy that gnawed at my insides. What did I have to offer these people? And would they still accept me if they knew the whole truth about my past?

The woman patted my arm reassuringly. "Give it

some time, sweetheart. You'll find your place here soon enough."

"Thanks," I murmured, hoping she was right.

As the party got underway, I hovered near the edges, observing the interactions between the Dixie Reapers and their families. Laughter rang out, punctuating the air with a sense of joy that I hadn't experienced in far too long. My heart ached to be a part of it, but fear kept me rooted to my spot. I scanned the area and saw Jackson with his dad. Their relationship had been good the last few days, and I didn't want to intrude on whatever they were discussing right now.

"Hey there," a voice called out, drawing my attention. "You look like you could use some company."

"Maybe," I replied hesitantly, studying the man who had approached me. He seemed friendly enough, but I couldn't help but wonder what he wanted from me. Wasn't that always the way?

"Listen, I know it's tough being the new girl, but I promise we don't bite. Well, most of us don't anyway," he joked, attempting to put me at ease.

"Thanks," I said, managing a small smile. "I appreciate it."

And I did, more than he could possibly know. Everyone seemed friendly, which only made me feel worse. All the doubts I had were my own issue not theirs. No one here had made me feel unwelcome at any point. Not even when Jackson's father had been upset with him.

"Anytime. My name is Slayer. I'm happy to help whenever I can," he assured me, before sauntering off to join the others. As the sun disappeared behind the horizon and the party carried on into the night, I allowed myself to take small steps toward joining in. I chatted with a few people, shared a few laughs, and even dared to hope that maybe, just maybe, these people could become my family.

But deep down, a shadow of doubt still lingered, whispering that I didn't belong here. That they would never truly accept someone like me. And as much as I wanted to silence it, part of me feared that it might be right.

"Hey there," a voice called out, breaking through my reverie. My gaze landed on a tall man with fiery red hair, his green eyes warm and inviting. He strode toward me, his confident gait somehow reassuring. "I'm Wire."

"Hi," I said hesitantly, my fingers fidgeting with the hem of my shirt. "I'm Mia."

"Nice to meet you, Mia," he replied, offering me a genuine smile that immediately put me at ease. "You look like you could use a friendly face."

"Is it that obvious?" I asked, half-joking, half-serious.

"Only if you've been around as long as I have." Wire chuckled. "Don't worry, though. We're not as scary as we might seem."

"Thanks," I murmured, grateful for his kind words. "I appreciate that. And I'm grateful for everything you've done for us. Jackson said you were the reason he was able to find me and Poppy."

"Of course," he said warmly. "Helping is what I do around here. Unless someone makes me mad, then I mess with them a bit. So, how are you finding life with the Reapers so far?"

"Overwhelming," I admitted, surprised by my own honesty. "But I think I'm starting to get used to it. And I really enjoy being on the ranch. We just moved into Jackson's house this morning, and it already feels like home."

"Good." Wire nodded. "You know, when I first joined the club, I felt the same way. But these people, they'll become your family if you let them."

"Really?" I asked, daring to hope that such a thing could be possible.

"Absolutely," he assured me. "You just have to be willing to trust them."

"Trust is… hard for me," I confessed, my voice barely a whisper.

"Understandable," Wire said gently. "But let me tell you something, Mia. I've seen what you've been through, what you've survived. And I think you're one of the strongest people I've ever met."

"Me?" I asked incredulously, feeling tears prick at the corners of my eyes.

"Definitely," he said with conviction. "You've got a fire in you that not even the worst of your past could extinguish. That's something special."

"Thank you," I whispered, touched by his words. "I'm just… so afraid of messing this up."

"Hey," Wire said softly, placing a hand on my shoulder. "We all make mistakes. But the love and support you'll find here, it won't just disappear because you stumble. And if you're worried you're unworthy of Jackson, or some other nonsense like that, you should know most of the women here all had their share of issues when we found them. Those are their stories to tell, but just know you aren't alone."

As we spoke, surrounded by the laughter and warmth of the Dixie Reapers, something inside me shifted. While the fear still lingered in the shadows of my heart, I began to see the glimmer of hope that had been missing for so long.

"Thank you, Wire," I said, my voice strong and

clear. "For everything."

"Anytime, Mia," he replied, his green eyes crinkling as he smiled. "Welcome to the family."

As Wire's encouraging words washed over me, I felt an unfamiliar warmth growing in my chest. He was right. I had survived so much. Maybe, I could find a place within this family. With that thought fresh in my mind, I noticed three girls approaching us with friendly smiles, their eyes sparkling with curiosity.

"Hey there, you must be Mia," one of them said, her hair swishing behind her with every step. "I'm Harlow, and these are my sisters, Kasen and Westlyn."

Kasen nodded at me with a warm smile. Meanwhile, Westlyn looked at me with eager fascination.

"Nice to meet y'all," I replied hesitantly, my nerves beginning to bubble back up.

"Wire has told us so much about you," Harlow continued, her tone inviting and gentle. "We're really happy to finally meet you. And in case you couldn't tell, we're triplets. Our dad is Tank."

I remembered meeting him. He had to have been one of the most imposing men I'd ever met. But he had three daughters? Maybe he wasn't so bad after all.

"Y-yeah? You wanted to meet me?" I stammered, feeling a mixture of surprise and relief.

"Absolutely," Kasen chimed in, her eyes sincere. "We've been looking forward to getting to know you better."

"Tell us about yourself, Mia," Westlyn urged, her voice full of youthful excitement. "What's your favorite thing to do? What kind of music do you like?"

I couldn't help but smile at their genuine interest in my life. Maybe it was time to let go of some of my fears and open up to these people who were offering me acceptance and friendship.

"Well, I love country music," I began, feeling my confidence grow as I spoke. "And I always wanted to learn how to ride horses. I've been fascinated by the rodeo for as long as I can remember. Never thought I'd end up marrying a rodeo cowboy."

"We already have something in common!" Westlyn exclaimed, her eyes wide with awe. "I've always wanted to learn how to ride a horse too. I've just been too scared to ask Cowboy or Jacey."

"Maybe we can all go riding sometime?" Harlow asked. "Since your family has a lot of them. Might be fun."

"Really?" I couldn't help the hopeful note in my voice.

"Definitely," Kasen confirmed, her smile warm and genuine. "We're family now, Mia. And that means doing things together. Besides, you look close to our age."

As I stood there, surrounded by these kind-hearted young women who seemed so eager to include me in their lives, I felt a long-forgotten sensation of belonging swell within me. The fear and uncertainty that had weighed me down for years began to lift, replaced by a newfound sense of hope and acceptance. And in that moment, I knew -- whatever challenges lay ahead, I wouldn't have to face them alone. Because with my daughter Poppy and the Dixie Reapers by my side, I had finally found a place where I belonged.

Surrounded by the warm embrace of laughter and conversation, I couldn't help but marvel at the transformation taking place within me. What had begun as a hesitant interaction with Tank's daughters had blossomed into a lively exchange of stories and experiences, each word spoken serving to strengthen the bonds that were forming between us. As Harlow, Kasen, and Westlyn continued to draw me out of my shell, I found myself opening up in ways I hadn't thought possible. It was as though a long dormant flower had finally found the sunlight it so desperately craved.

"Hey, Mia, have you ever tried bull riding?" Cowboy's wide grin was infectious.

"Uh, no," I admitted, feeling my cheeks flush as several sets of eyes turned toward me. "I was too young to go into the bars with the mechanical ones, and the live ones scare me."

"Aw, come on!" he teased, laughter dancing in his eyes. "Where's your sense of adventure?"

"Maybe someday," I replied with a smile, appreciating the light-hearted banter for what it was -- an invitation to be part of something greater than myself. It also made me feel as if he'd truly accepted me as his daughter-in-law.

"Fair enough," he conceded, raising his beer in a mock toast before turning back to his own conversation.

As I listened to the hum of voices around me, I felt a tidal wave of gratitude wash over me. Here, amidst the Dixie Reapers, I was finding something I'd spent a lifetime searching for -- a sense of belonging, a place where I could let down my guard and simply be myself without fear of judgment or rejection.

"Can I ask you something, Mia?" Westlyn asked hesitantly, her gaze meeting mine with genuine curiosity. "How did you end up with Jackson? Don't get me wrong. He's a sweetheart, but... He's never shown much interest in women."

The question hung in the air like a delicate thread, one that could either draw me closer or unravel the fragile connections I'd been weaving. And yet, as I looked into Westlyn's eyes and saw the warmth and understanding that lay within them, I knew in my heart that it was time to trust -- to share a piece of myself with these remarkable young women who were so willing to accept me for who I was.

"Life hasn't always been kind to me," I began softly, my voice barely audible above the din of the party. "But when I met Jackson, he was so nice to me. He always looked out for me and tried to include me in things. And when the guy I'd been seeing got rough, he stepped in and saved me. I owe him... everything."

As I spoke, I could feel Harlow, Kasen, and Westlyn listening intently, their faces open and empathetic. And in that moment, I understood that I'd found something truly precious -- not just a place to call home, but a group of people who would stand by me, no matter what life might throw my way.

The laughter and chatter of the party swirled around me, creating a lively atmosphere that was both comforting and overwhelming. I took a deep breath, feeling my nerves slowly starting to settle as I continued to mingle with the Dixie Reapers who had welcomed me into their fold. My gaze fell upon Cowboy and his wife standing near a table laden with food and drinks.

"Hey there, Mia," Cowboy called out with a warm smile, his blue eyes twinkling beneath the brim of his well-worn hat. "Come on over and join us."

"Thank you," I replied softly, making my way toward them, noting Cowboy's strong yet gentle presence. He was tall and broad-shouldered, his blond hair streaked with silver -- an image of a seasoned rodeo cowboy.

"Sweetheart, are your arms getting tired? Why

don't you let me hold Poppy for a bit?" Jacey asked, holding out her hands.

"Thank you," I stammered, handing her over to her grandmother. "Until we came here, only Jackson held Poppy, other than me. He's been so wonderful through everything."

"Jackson's always had a big heart, just like his daddy." Jacey smiled, giving Cowboy a playful nudge.

Cowboy chuckled, his arm wrapping around Jacey's shoulder. "He's a good boy, our Jackson. We're glad he found you, Mia. And we're happy to have you and your little one here with us."

My eyes filled with tears at their genuine interest in me and my daughter Poppy. It warmed my heart to know that they were more than willing to embrace us, even with our troubled past.

"Speaking of little ones," Jacey said, her gaze shifting down to Poppy. "Your daughter is just precious, Mia."

"Thank you," I murmured, my heart swelling with pride. As the evening wore on, I couldn't help but steal glances at Poppy, watching with awe and gratitude as she interacted with her newfound family. We had both been through so much, and for the first time in a long time, I knew that we were exactly where we were meant to be.

With the Dixie Reapers by our side, we could face anything life threw our way -- together.

"Can't believe we're really here, huh?" I whispered to Poppy, who was nestled comfortably in my arms once more.

I glanced around at the smiling faces of the Dixie Reapers, each one of them offering me a warm nod or a welcoming embrace. It was surreal to think that a year ago, I had been lost, alone, and terrified. But now, here

I was, standing amongst people who truly cared about me and my daughter. And I had the most amazing husband.

"Hey, Mia," Wire called out from across the room, holding up a plate piled high with mouthwatering barbecue. "You hungry?"

"Starving," I admitted with a grin, making my way over to him.

As Wire handed me the plate, his green eyes sparkled with genuine warmth. "You know, with your strength and determination, you're going to fit in here just fine. Our women range from outspoken like Ridley to reserved like Mara. So, don't feel like you have to tiptoe around everyone. Just be yourself."

"Thanks, Wire," I murmured, touched by his words. "Honestly, I don't know where I'd be without you and the rest of the Dixie Reapers."

"Right where you belong, darlin'," he replied, giving my shoulder a gentle squeeze before rejoining the party.

As I nibbled on a juicy rib, my gaze drifted across the sea of happy faces, taking in Cowboy's playful teasing, Jackson's laughter as he spoke with some friends, and Tank's daughters animatedly chatting with some of the other girls. In this moment, surrounded by love and laughter, I knew that I had finally found a place where Poppy and I could call home. The Dixie Reapers weren't just a motorcycle club -- they were our family, and I couldn't be more grateful for the connections and friendships we had forged.

"Here's to new beginnings," I whispered, raising my sweet tea in a silent toast before taking a sip of the ice-cold drink. "And to the family I've always dreamed of."

Harley Wylde

Harley Wylde is an accomplished author known for her captivating MC Romances. With an unwavering commitment to sensual storytelling, Wylde immerses her readers in an exciting world of fierce men and irresistible women. Her works exude passion, danger, and gritty realism, while still managing to end on a satisfying note each time.

When not crafting her tales, Wylde spends her time brainstorming new plotlines, indulging in a hot cup of Starbucks, or delving into a good book. She has a particular affinity for supernatural horror literature and movies. Visit Wylde's website to learn more about her works and upcoming events, and don't forget to sign up for her newsletter to receive exclusive discounts and other exciting perks.

Harley at Changeling: changelingpress.com/harley-wylde-a-196

Bad Boys Multiverse

A Bad Boy Romance
Dixie Reapers MC
Devil's Boneyard MC
Hades Abyss MC
Devil's Fury MC
Reckless Kings MC
Savage Raptors MC
Underland MC
Devoted Guardians MC
Balor's Saints MC
Owned by the Mob
Bryson Corners
Dixie Reapers MC Print
Dixie Reapers MC Audio
Devil's Boneyard MC Audio
Hades Abyss MC Audio
Devil's Fury MC Audio

Changeling Press LLC

Contemporary Action Adventure, Sci-Fi, Steampunk, Dark Fantasy, Urban Fantasy, Paranormal, and BDSM Romance available in e-book, audio, and print format at ChangelingPress.com – MC Romance, Werewolves, Vampires, Dragons, Shapeshifters and Horror -- Tales from the edge of your imagination.

Where can I get Changeling Press Books?

Changeling Press e-books are available at ChangelingPress.com, Amazon, Apple Books, Barnes & Noble, Kobo, Smashwords, and other online retailers, including Everand Subscription and Kobo Subscription Services. Print books are available at Amazon, Barnes and Noble, and by ISBN special order through your local bookstores.

ChangelingPress.com